"I didn't want

Rachel admitted, "because I wanted you even then. I knew that if we were alone together, this would happen. And I knew that making love with you, getting that close to you, could endanger Bonnie, and so I promised myself I wouldn't let it happen."

"And now?" Mitch asked.

"And now..." She trembled, swallowing hard. "Now the worst has already happened. You know who Bonnie is and that as far as the law is concerned she doesn't belong here with me. And I understand that you're going to have to turn me in."

But that was tomorrow. Tonight was a sliver of time stolen from the space between her past and her future. Tonight there didn't have to be any lies... or pretense... or holding back. Even though she'd finally been caught, Rachel felt suddenly free.

"I want you, Mitch."

Dear Reader,

Well, it's that loving time of year again! Yes, it's February—and St. Valentine's Day is just around the corner. But every day is for lovers at Silhouette **Special Edition,** and we hope you enjoy this month's six novels dedicated to romance.

The February selection of our THAT SPECIAL WOMAN! promotion is *Sally Jane Got Married* by Celeste Hamilton. You met Sally Jane in Celeste's last Silhouette Special Edition novel, *Child of Dreams.* Well, Sally Jane is back, and a wedding is on her mind! Don't miss this warm, tender tale.

This month also brings more of your favorite authors: Lisa Jackson presents us with *He's My Soldier Boy,* the fourth tale in her MAVERICKS series, Tracy Sinclair has a sparkling tale of love in *Marry Me Kate,* and February also offers *When Stars Collide* by Patricia Coughlin, *Denver's Lady* by Jennifer Mikels and *With Baby in Mind* by Arlene James. A February bevy of beautiful stories!

At Silhouette **Special Edition,** we're dedicated to publishing the types of romances that you dream about—stories that delight as well as bring a tear to the eye. That's what Silhouette **Special Edition** is all about—special books by special authors for special readers.

I hope you enjoy this book, and all of the stories to come.

Sincerely,

Tara Gavin
Senior Editor

Please address questions and book requests to:
Reader Service
U.S.: P.O. Box 1325, Buffalo, NY 14269
Canadian: P.O. Box 1050, Niagara Falls, Ont. L2E 7G7

PATRICIA COUGHLIN

WHEN STARS COLLIDE

Silhouette™

SPECIAL ▼ EDITION®

Published by Silhouette Books

America's Publisher of Contemporary Romance

For Vin and Margaret

 SILHOUETTE BOOKS

ISBN 0-373-09867-7

WHEN STARS COLLIDE

Copyright © 1994 by Patricia Madden Coughlin

This edition published by arrangement with Harlequin Enterprises B. V.

® and TM are trademarks of Harlequin Enterprises B. V., used under
license. Trademarks indicated with ® are registered in the United States
Patent and Trademark Office, the Canadian Trade Marks Office and in
other countries.

Printed in U.S.A.

Books by Patricia Coughlin

PATRICIA COUGHLIN

is also known to romance fans as Liz Grady and lives in Rhode Island with her husband and two sons. A former schoolteacher, she says she started writing to fill her hours at home after her second son was born. Having always read romances, she decided to try penning her own. Though she was duly astounded by the difficulty of her new hobby, her hard work paid off, and she accomplished the rare feat of having her very first manuscript published. For now, writing has replaced quilting, embroidery and other pastimes, and with more than a dozen published novels under her belt, the author hopes to be happily writing romances for a long time to come.

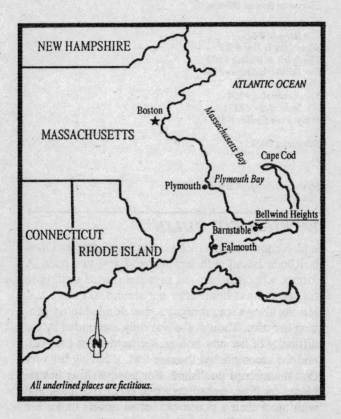

NEW HAMPSHIRE

MASSACHUSETTS

ATLANTIC OCEAN

Boston ★

Massachusetts Bay

Cape Cod

Plymouth • *Plymouth Bay*

<u>Bellwind Heights</u>

Barnstable •

CONNECTICUT

RHODE ISLAND

• Falmouth

N

All underlined places are fictitious.

Prologue

Rachel Curtis was accustomed to fear.

She was on intimate terms with it, in fact, in all its varied facets. She was accustomed to being vigilant, to looking over her shoulder and scanning strangers' faces for any hint of the recognition that could mean disaster. She was accustomed to waking from a sound sleep with her heart pounding and no idea of where she was or what she was running from. Gradually she would come fully awake and she would remember everything, and though her heartbeat would eventually slow to normal, the fear remained, a constant iciness at her core.

What was much less familiar to Rachel was the absence of fear, the lighthearted, carefree feeling that sometimes caught up with her at unexpected moments like this one. It was a feeling that she knew was commonplace for most ordinary twenty-nine-year-old women. She knew because, until a couple of years ago, she had been one of those lucky women. Not that she hadn't had problems back then; she had, and from time to time they had seemed earth-shattering to her. That seemed another lifetime now, one Rachel couldn't help recalling with a sense of irony... and wistfulness.

During the long, desperate months since then, she had learned the hard way the true meaning of earth-shattering, and of precisely what it took to shatter a life, a home, a family. No matter how momentous they had seemed to her at the time, the pressures and problems she'd encountered as a single woman trying to make a name for herself as a television newscaster in the St. Augustine, Florida, market were nothing compared to the nightmare that had forced her to leave all that behind forever.

"Hurry, Mommy."

Five-year-old Bonnie stopped on the sidewalk about ten feet ahead of Rachel and turned to face her. Her small hands were planted on her hips, her green eyes bright with anticipation. The silky chestnut hair that had once reached her waist was now cut in a chin-length bob that framed her pretty face. Rachel hadn't had the heart to cut it any shorter.

She had been much more ruthless with her own hair, lightening it to reddish gold and chopping it into a short, tousled style. It had been an act motivated by desperation, not fashion, and she had been surprised to see how the new style enhanced her delicate features and wide-spaced eyes, which were the same clear green as Bonnie's. She and Bonnie also shared the same pale, lightly freckled complexion that turned a golden brown in summer if they were careful and a bright sunburned red if they weren't. It was a family resemblance that made it easy for them to pass as mother and daughter.

"Mommy," said Bonnie again, more impatiently this time.

Mommy.

How easily she called Rachel by that name. It had been much harder for Rachel to get used to hearing it from her, and harder still for her to feel and act like a mommy. Some days it was still a struggle. Not surprising, Rachel thought wryly, since being anyone's mommy had never been high on her list of aspirations. Besides, unlike Bonnie, she knew the truth.

If Bonnie even remembered a time when she had called another woman Mommy, she never mentioned it. Any confusion she had suffered over Rachel slipping into that most important role in her young life had faded months ago, and no matter how much Rachel sometimes longed to remind the little girl of that other woman, and the other life to which she had belonged, she didn't dare.

"I am hurrying," she told Bonnie, smiling as the little girl did an impatient dance in the center of the sidewalk.

"Hurry faster. Please."

"Relax, Bonnie, Hanson's isn't going anywhere."

"But I want to get there. I want to hurry up fast."

Bonnie whirled around and took a few more steps in the direction of Hanson's Store, still more than a block away, glancing back over her shoulder to make sure that Rachel was following. Rachel grinned and quickened her pace a bit. Though the short trek from their apartment to Hanson's had become something of an afternoon ritual, she understood what a milestone this particular trip was for Bonnie.

Today had been Bonnie's first day of kindergarten and to commemorate that momentous occasion, Rachel was letting her go alone into Hanson's to make her twenty-five-cent purchase of penny candy. Bonnie had wanted to get underway the instant the school minivan dropped her off at home, but Rachel had persuaded her to eat half a grilled cheese sandwich first. Now she was skipping along in front, her head no doubt filled with visions of peanut but-

ter cups and red-hots, Rachel thought with an affection-
ate chuckle.

Up ahead, the blue-and-white striped awning above
Hanson's front door came into view. Hanson's was a
family establishment and for over fifty years it had been
located on Main Street, in the resort town of Plymouth,
Massachusetts. During the summer, it was common to see
a line snaked along the sidewalk out front as tourists and
natives alike waited for a cone of their famous homemade
ice cream. With the busy summer season over, Plymouth
had taken on its quieter winter persona. So far, she and
Bonnie hadn't encountered anyone else on the sidewalk
along the way.

The store was also a favorite haunt of local children, not
only because of the bushel baskets of penny candy lining
one wall, but because of the player piano and the ani-
mated dolls the Hansons had collected through the years,
which the friendly, elderly couple were never too busy to
take a few minutes to show off. Rachel was sure that either Mr. or Mrs. Hanson, whoever's turn it was to mind
the store this afternoon, would be happy to provide any
help Bonnie might need.

She'd made sure of that earlier when she had taken the
precaution of phoning the store from work to explain that
Bonnie would be coming in alone later. Mr. Hanson's
friendly assurance that they would keep an eye out for her
made Rachel think he was accustomed to overseeing this
rite of passage for the town's children. His welcoming attitude had also left her with no excuse not to go ahead with
the outing. After all, she knew that sooner or later she was
going to have to stop hovering over Bonnie's every move.
Hanson's seemed like a safe, painless place to start.

"Stop," Bonnie ordered, lifting her hand in traffic cop
fashion as they reached the front door of the store. "I get
to go in all by myself today, remember?"

As if Bonnie would let her forget, thought Rachel.

"Of course, I remember," she replied, taking care to treat the situation with the solemnity it deserved. "Do you have the quarter I gave you?"

With a wide smile, Bonnie produced it from the pocket of the new yellow-and-white striped dress bought especially for her first day of school.

"Good girl," Rachel told her. "And you know what you want to buy?"

"Kinda. I still need to look a little."

"Of course," Rachel agreed. Though Bonnie had to have the store's entire stock of candy memorized by now, peering into each basket in turn was a part of the ritual. "You take your time and I'll wait for you right over there on that bench, okay?"

"Okay, Mommy."

"And, Bonnie," she said as the little girl turned toward the door, "remember not to touch anything except the candy...not even the piano or the dolls, okay?"

"I won't touch anything, Mommy, just the candy. I cross my heart," she said, making a haphazard cross on the white lace bodice of her new dress.

Rachel had to smile at her earnest expression.

"Okay then, sweetie, go on in. I'll be waiting right outside here," she reminded her again.

In her heart she knew that Bonnie didn't need the reminder, or the last-minute warnings, half as much as she needed to hear herself say them. Bonnie was a careful, cooperative child and the chance of her breaking something or causing a problem that might attract any attention to her was one in a million. With the stakes so high, however, that was more of a chance than Rachel could afford to take.

Ignoring the small, instinctive flutter of apprehension that assaulted her tummy whenever Bonnie was out of sight, Rachel watched until she had disappeared inside the store before strolling over to the nearby bench. She'd brought along a magazine to occupy her mind while she waited and she tried to lose herself in an article that promised ten easy steps to a spotless, well-organized household. She was on step four and thinking that she'd rather keep her pleasantly unorganized home than invest the time and energy the ten easy steps required, when she heard it.

Though she'd never before heard an actual gunshot, Rachel knew without a doubt that's what this was. It was that sharp, that unmistakable. The sound ripped through the quiet September afternoon, ugly and jarring enough to make her leap from the bench. As she glanced around frantically to see where the sound had come from, a second shot followed and this time Rachel was certain it had come from inside Hanson's Store.

"Bonnie," she cried, lurching toward the door.

Just as she reached the door, it was shoved open from within and Bonnie stumbled out.

Rachel gasped at the sight of the glistening red stain covering the front of her dress.

Blood.

"Oh, no, oh, no." She cried, crumbling to her knees on the sidewalk and instinctively yanking Bonnie tightly against her.

As she knelt, her shoulder blocked the door from closing and she quickly jerked it out of the way, wanting to put whatever barrier she could between Bonnie and danger. As the door slowly slid shut, Rachel had time for only a single terrified glance inside. Her panic, coupled with the fact that she was staring from the bright sunlight into the darker interior, made it hard to discern anything more than a blur of motion near the candy counter, almost like shadows flying.

The sound of glass shattering made her jump a second time. Instinctively she clenched Bonnie even more tightly. The sound of footsteps followed. Lots of footsteps, it seemed to Rachel, just as the door closed fully, blocking off the sounds and sights within. It had all happened so quickly, Rachel had no idea what was going on in there, and at that moment she didn't much care. She didn't care about anything except Bonnie.

"Bonnie, Bonnie, what happened to you, sweetie? Where are you hurt?"

Rachel tried to draw back to look at her, but Bonnie clung tightly to her neck. She was trembling and what Rachel could see of her complexion was ghostly white. She wasn't crying, though. Probably too shocked to cry, thought Rachel.

"Where are you hurt, baby?" she asked again, running her hands over Bonnie's small body. Her stomach lurched at the warm slipperiness of the blood that coated her fingers. Fear was like something hard and sharp lodged in her throat.

"Not hurt." Bonnie whimpered. "That man... that man..."

She shuddered, as if she couldn't breath, and Rachel released a sigh of relief as she realized that Bonnie really wasn't hurt, that the blood covering her was not her own. For the first time she thought about the Hansons.

"Wait right here," she ordered Bonnie, pushing her up against the brick wall a safe distance from the door. "And don't move an inch."

"No, no, Mommy, don't go in there!" Bonnie screamed. She grabbed Rachel's arm and hung on. "That man will—"

"Shh, baby. I won't go in. I just have to see if the Hansons are all right." As she was speaking, Rachel eased the door open a crack and leaned forward as much as possible with Bonnie clutching her.

After blinking several times, her eyes adjusted enough for her to make out the shape of someone crouching beside the front counter. Her heart pounded fiercely.

"Holy—" she heard someone mutter.

It was followed by the unmistakable sound of a telephone crashing to the floor. Another muttered expletive, and then a very nervous sounding voice pleaded, "Hang on, Mr. Hanson, I'm gonna get help. I'm calling 911 and...hello? Hello? This is Danny Gates over at Hanson's on Main Street.... There's been a shooting.... That's right, I said a shooting and..."

Rachel let the door close again. Mr. Hanson was the one who had been shot. How badly? she wondered. Danny, the Hanson's stockboy, had talked to him, telling him to hang on. That had to mean that he was still alive, didn't it? Rachel whispered a small desperate prayer.

Bending to keep one arm wrapped protectively around Bonnie, she tried to think of what she should do. As long as Danny had already called for help, there really was nothing more she could do for Mr. Hanson. Already she could hear sirens in the distance. Any minute now the police and the rescue workers would arrive on the scene to help. And to ask questions. They would definitely want to question Bonnie.

Rachel found she wasn't able to think clearly beyond that one terrifying fact. All she could do was react. And as they had been for the past eighteen months, her reactions were funneled though a single narrow porthole, her concern for Bonnie.

There was no way she could let them question Bonnie. No way she could risk the publicity that was bound to follow when the media discovered that a five-year-old had been witness to such violence. Reaching frantically for Bonnie's small hand, Rachel enclosed it tightly in her own.

"Come on, sweetie," she said, and for the second time in the little girl's life, she took Bonnie and ran as fast as she could.

Chapter One

On the best of days, Mitch Dalton didn't like surprises, and today was far from the best of days.

He was tired, his back hurt like hell and his head felt like something he wished he could screw off and toss overboard. Too much sun and too little sleep had left him feeling ornery and inhospitable. If his old pal Ollie hadn't already figured that out, then his powers of deduction had slipped badly. In an attempt to clue him in, Mitch sullenly ignored him as he went about securing the *My Way* to the private dock behind his house.

He'd been surprised to find Ollie waiting here. He hadn't expected a welcome home and he didn't want one. What he wanted was a hot shower and a cold beer. And to be left alone.

Actually being left alone was number one on his wish list. For the past six months he'd made sure to stay far enough away from Massachusetts so that others had no choice but to comply with that wish. An extreme measure, perhaps, but he could see now that it had been a smart move. He hadn't even set foot back on solid ground yet and already Ollie was here, waiting, standing by smiling that infuriatingly smug smile and wanting to talk shop, Mitch could tell. That's what ticked him off the most. The very last thing he wanted to talk about, now or ever again, was the D.A.'s office or any of the cases Ollie and he had worked on together before his self-induced retirement six months ago.

A question occurred to Mitch, and he looked up from the winch he was checking to peer suspiciously at the man who had once been his number-one assistant. Sundance to his Butch Cassidy, Mitch thought contemptuously, recalling what a reporter writing about their phenomenal conviction rate had once dubbed them. There had been a lot of laudatory articles written about Mitch as he'd burned an upward path through the D.A.'s department. The media had loved to tell the tale of the tough young prosecutor from the wrong side of the tracks, a former delinquent himself, who rounded up and put away bad guys with the ease and swagger of an Old West sheriff. That his hand-picked sidekick was as blue-blooded as he was rough around the edges only added to the mystique.

"How'd you know I was getting back today?" he demanded of Ollie.

"A hunch."

"Bull."

"Hey," countered Ollie, trying to look offended, "you used to appreciate my brilliant hunches."

"Yeah, that's when I wasn't downwind of them."

Ollie chuckled softly at his friend's obvious irritation. "Okay, you want the truth?"

"That's what you're sworn to uphold, isn't it?"

"As I recall it, that's what we were both sworn to uphold."

"Fine." Mitch gave the rope he was securing a final tug and straightened, crossing deeply tanned arms across his chest as he faced Ollie. "You tell me how you knew when I'd be coming in and I'll tell you the truth about how happy I am to see you."

Ollie laughed. "Not necessary, pal ... the look on your face when you spotted me waiting here said it all. As for how I knew you'd be getting back today, Howie told me."

"Howie?" Mitch echoed. A scowl deepened lines that the months of sailing and self-recriminations had carved into a face that looked as if it had seen more hard living than even a headstrong man ought to be able to cram into thirty-five years. "Howie from the boat yard?"

Ollie nodded. "The very one."

"Howie called you and told you I was coming back?" he demanded, disbelief on the verge of giving way to anger. He'd trusted Howie.

"Actually," Ollie explained, "I called him. Several times. Knowing how you baby that damn boat, I was sure you wouldn't trust anyone but the man who built her to work on her. So it was only a matter of time until you had to be in touch with Howie."

"Brilliant deduction," Mitch muttered.

"Thanks. I learned from the best."

Mitch responded with a grunt.

Man, he wished he was back in Florida, hiding out in the Keys, spending his days drinking and fishing and forgetting. Or trying to forget, at least. That's exactly where he would be, if not for the major problem with the electrical system that had forced him to bring the *My Way* home for repairs.

Home.

Instinctively Mitch lifted his head to gaze over the rail of his boat, a twenty-two-foot, one-of-a-kind beauty. He looked past the private beach and the wide stretch of overgrown lawn to the house beyond.

Like his boat, his house was also one of a kind, a unique blend of modern ingenuity and traditional substance, according to the fashionable Boston architect who had overseen the renovations on what had once been a deserted, run-down beach house. With the newly built addition, it had four bedrooms, two fireplaces, a three-car garage and forty-two windows, many of which had to be specially manufactured to form the new glass wall overlooking the Atlantic. The house also had a professionally built play tower in the backyard and a light-filled sewing room tucked into the southwest corner. And no one around to make use of either.

A truly magnificent house. But a home? Mitch had thought so once, back when he'd stretched himself to the financial limit to buy it and prove to the world, and himself, that he'd made it. Obviously he'd been wrong. About a lot of things.

What it was, he thought grimly, was a comfortable place to hang out while he waited for his boat to be fixed. At least he would be able to stockpile more beer in the double wide refrigerator in the kitchen than he could in the boat's space-efficient model. If he was lucky, there might even be a few cold ones waiting there for him right now.

His momentary lift in spirits was scuttled by the thought that he was probably going to have to offer to share one of them with Ollie.

"I'd love a beer," Ollie said, responding to the lackluster offer Mitch felt obliged to make as they approached the house. His cheerfulness rubbed Mitch like beach sand on sunburn. As cheerful as he was, however, Mitch knew Ollie wasn't there just to be sociable.

The man was like a bulldog, he reminded himself, indefatigable when he had his sights set on something. And for whatever reason, Ollie clearly had his sights set on Mitch right now.

"The Sox playing today?" Mitch asked as he punched the security code into the alarm panel before unlocking the back door.

"I don't know. Since when are you a Red Sox fan?"

Mitch shrugged. "I'm not. I just thought we might be able to catch a few innings to pass the time."

At last the indulgent smile left his friend's face. Mitch didn't know whether to applaud or brace himself.

"I didn't drive all the way down here to watch television," Ollie admitted at last. "The truth is, Mitch, I need to talk with you."

"Yeah. That's what I was afraid of."

Mitch headed for the kitchen and pulled a couple of beers from the refrigerator, taking mental note of the contents as he did so. Three left. He was definitely going to have to make a trip to the store before long.

He popped the caps off both bottles and handed one to Ollie.

"So talk," he said, tipping his head back to take a long swallow from his bottle.

"It's about Mickey DelCosta."

Mitch straightened as if the countertop he'd been leaning against had caught fire. Every muscle in his body tensed. "See you later, Ollie."

"For God's sake, Mitch, will you listen . . ."

"Not if you're going to talk about DelCosta. There's nothing about that animal I want to hear, nothing more I ever need to know, nothing you could possibly tell me that could make me—"

"He killed someone else," Ollie interjected sharply.

Mitch quieted and tipped the bottle to his lips again. He swallowed, shook his head and wiped his mouth with the back of his hand.

"Guess I was wrong again," he said. "I was going to say there was nothing you could tell me that would add to my level of disgust where DelCosta is concerned, but you just managed to do it. Thanks for stopping by...pal."

"Don't you want to know who he murdered?" persisted Ollie, following him out of the kitchen toward the den.

"Does it matter?" Mitch retorted over his shoulder.

"It does to the guy's widow and family."

Mitch stopped in his tracks.

Had he always been this callous? This immune to other people's pain? Maybe so. Maybe he was...how had Angie put it? Isolated. Maybe she was right. Maybe ex-wives had a corner on being right about things like that. Mitch shook his head. What was he thinking? Of course Angie was right. If he was wrong, and everyone in the state old enough to pick up a newspaper knew how very wrong he had been, then it followed that Angie had to be right.

Reluctantly he turned to face Ollie. "Okay, who was he?"

Ollie immediately pulled a sheaf of folded papers from his inside jacket pocket. Prepared as always, thought Mitch wryly as he observed his former assistant. Oliver Bennett was lean and intense, with dark brown hair, tortoiseshell glasses and a keen sense of humor that Mitch hadn't expected to find lurking beneath that Ivy League exterior.

"His name was George Hanson, sixty-six years old, ran a store over in Plymouth—a mom-and-pop sort of place, everything from magazines to ice-cream cones and homemade fudge. From all accounts, Hanson was unanimously well liked, something of a town celebrity." Ollie narrowed his eyes quizzically. "Plymouth is only a stone's throw from here, maybe you've heard of this guy?"

Mitch shook his head, accepting and scanning the papers Ollie offered him without really wanting to. "I know the store you're talking about though, Hanson's."

More accurately, he remembered Angie and the girls dragging him in there one afternoon a couple of summers ago, during one of the family outings Angie was always complaining he didn't have time for. He remembered the endless wait as Becky and Nicole filled their bags with candy they selected one agonizing piece at a time from the baskets lining the wall. He remembered that he'd been like a leashed animal all that day, knowing he had a foot-high stack of notes waiting at home for a case he'd been preparing. And he recalled how he'd snapped when three-year-old Nicole had dropped her basket of candy and had to start all over again.

Ignoring the sudden tightness in his chest, Mitch shoved the papers back at Ollie. "So now I know who he was. Thanks."

"There's more," Ollie said to his back.

Wasn't there always? Mitch thought. A victim was always more than spilled blood and a page full of crime scene details. There was always the family left behind, mothers and fathers, widows and children, and all the little, seemingly inconsequential bits of personal history you learned during the investigation that made you aware of the precise size and shape of the hole the victim's death was going to leave in the world.

The memory of the victim's family, their tears and sorrow, had always ridden Mitch hard throughout an investigation, pushing him on even when it seemed as if he was facing brick walls on all sides. It's what had made success that much sweeter when he nailed someone he knew was guilty...and the dejection that much deeper when he failed.

Without waiting for Mitch's permission, Ollie began telling him all about George Hanson.

"He had six kids and fourteen grandchildren, and even with that many of his own, he volunteered to read at the local Children's Center a couple of days a week. He organized a food drive around the holidays and the kids in town all loved him because every Halloween—''

Mitch slammed his empty bottle down on a table in the den. ''Why the hell are you telling me all this?''

Ollie met his gaze, completely nonplussed by his fierce expression and tone. They'd worked together for a long time. ''Because I want you to care, that's why.''

''Why? I cared about the last guy DelCosta blew away and you saw how much good it did.''

''You made a mistake. It happens. When are you going to let yourself off the hook?''

''I'm not. I thought I made that clear when I resigned.''

''You're being an ass.''

''So what?''

''So if any one of the attorneys working under you had failed to file that motion in time and had let DelCosta walk on a technicality, you would have—''

''I would have chewed his butt for a week.''

''Exactly. And when the week was up, you would have told him to pick himself up and get back to work. You sure as hell wouldn't have demanded his resignation.''

Mitch cursed himself for plunging straight into Ollie's clever little word trap. ''Yeah, well, I'm not any other attorney.''

''Right, I forgot, you're the legendary Mitch Dalton. You don't get to make mistakes. You don't have personal problems that interfere with your concentration, you're the all-seeing, all-knowing, fearless foe of criminals everywhere, or at least throughout the state of Massachusetts. That's what the papers all said anyway, and that's what everybody believed . . . including you, unfortunately. The only problem is that someone forgot to tell you that legends are always a mixture of fact and fiction, and that underneath that ego the size of the national debt, you're still only human.''

Mitch leaned back in his favorite chair and clapped laconically. "Nice pep talk, Bennett. You get an A for delivery and a B+ for content. The Yale Debating Society would be proud. Now, why don't you go wage a war you have a chance of winning? Go build a case against DelCosta."

Instead of leaving, as Mitch had hoped, Ollie casually dropped into the chair beside him. "Love to. Only one little problem."

"What's that?"

"DelCosta's not charged with anything."

"I thought you said he killed Hanson?"

"He did. At least, I believe he did it. Unfortunately, at the moment I'm one of only two people in the world who do believe it. And the other person is the kid who happens to be charged with the murder."

"Kid?"

Ollie nodded. "Seventeen years old...and as dumb as dirt, Mitch. Kid was caught a block from the scene still carrying the murder weapon."

"So exactly where does DelCosta fit into this fairy tale?"

"Only in the kid's version of things. He claims he knows DelCosta from the Junction."

Mitch grimaced, familiar with the rough Boston neighborhood Ollie referred to because he had grown up there.

"Leo—that's the kid's name, Leo Belanger—Leo says that DelCosta invited him to go cruising with him. Getting to cruise with DelCosta is a big deal to Leo, which gives you some idea of the kid's IQ and social standing," Ollie remarked dryly. "They head out of the city toward the Cape, and only then does DelCosta tell him he knows a place where they can make some easy money. He plays it up to sound as if Leo is very fortunate to be his chosen accomplice for this operation."

Mitch's thin smile was bitter. "And the kid lapped it up."

"Like it was honey. You know how charming DelCosta can be."

"Yeah, a real sweetheart."

"So Leo was charmed. And scared. He says he knew about Mickey's temper and he was afraid if he didn't go along, Mickey would throw him out of the car and make him walk back to the city."

"Kid never heard of a bus?"

"That's a real possibility." At Mitch's incredulous look, Ollie added, "All right, that might be a slight exaggeration, but very slight. Mitch, the kid never made it past eighth grade and I understand from his parents and teachers that even at that, the last three or four grade promotions were gifts."

"All right, so he's not a Rhodes scholar...."

"He's not even a Romper Room scholar."

"He still had to know right from wrong when it comes to armed robbery and murder," Mitch insisted.

"Agreed. Except he had no idea DelCosta was even carrying until he pulled the gun on Hanson and fired. Leo says he tried to stop him, but it happened too quickly. He panicked big time and when DelCosta told them they better split up and run, he did."

"How did he end up with the gun?"

"He can't remember."

Mitch gave a harsh laugh. "Sure, right, but he remembers that DelCosta was involved, that it was all his idea, that—"

Ollie broke in, his quiet tone of conviction one that Mitch had come to respect. "I know how it sounds, but I believe him, Mitch. You would too, if you talked with him."

"That's not going to happen."

"Why not? What's the harm in just talking to him? You know you've always had a way of getting kids like Leo to open up and—"

"Have you forgotten? I'm no longer on the team. I'm out, finished, resigned."

"Technically you're still on the books as taking an extended leave of absence," Ollie reminded him. "You know as well as I do that Grayson would jump at the chance to have you back."

"I'm not going back, Ollie. So if that's why you drove all the way down here, you wasted your time."

"Evidently so. I thought that maybe six months of fresh air would have cleared your thick skull, that you'd come back rested and restless and ready to go another round with DelCosta. I guess I was wrong."

Mitch detected the slightly derisive edge in Ollie's tone and words. He knew it was intentional, intended to get to him, and it worked, dammit.

"Another nice speech," he snapped, "except I don't hear anyone offering me another round with DelCosta. All I hear is some farfetched story from a punk looking to slide off the hook on a murder one charge by claiming DelCosta is the real shooter."

"He is."

"Is that what the police report says, too?"

Ollie colored a little and adjusted his glasses. "You know how it is, Mitch, the police had this homicide logged in the closed column the second they slapped the cuffs on Leo Belanger. There's no advantage in their complicating the matter by looking for another suspect on his word alone."

"And Grayson? What does he think?"

"Same as always...he's too busy to think. And he says the investigative unit doesn't have the manpower to chase down every potential accomplice a suspect points a finger at."

"He's right."

"Not this time, Mitch. Grayson just wants me to hurry up and carve another notch in the department's belt by getting a conviction on Leo. My gut tells me the kid is innocent."

"So you came here hoping to involve my gut on the chance I'd help you save the kid?"

Ollie shook his head slowly. "Not exactly. I came here because a nice old man was killed for no reason and I thought that would matter to you. And because an innocent kid is going to take the fall for a guy we both know is a cold-blooded killer and I thought that might matter to you. And yeah, I thought you might help me try to save him. But most of all I came here because I wanted to give you a chance to save yourself." He got to his feet. "Thanks for the beer."

"Anytime."

"Sure."

Mitch didn't even make an attempt to see him to the door as any good host would do. He wasn't a good host, so why pretend? Hadn't Angie told him that time and again? Every time he forgot a dinner engagement or arrived home late for a party she had planned? Host was just one more thing he had failed at, right up there with husband and father and prosecuting attorney. And now, apparently, friend.

Damn Ollie for coming here and opening old wounds, he thought as he returned to the kitchen for another beer. And damn the storm that had wreaked havoc on the *My Way*'s electrical system and damn Howie for being the only one whom he trusted to work on her.

He jerked open the refrigerator door and instead of the beer bottles he expected to see there, Mitch saw the taunting grin of Mickey DelCosta, lowlife extraordinaire.

Mitch sighed and reached around his vision for a beer. The sight had ceased to surprise or alarm him. The fact was, he saw DelCosta's grinning face regularly, lurking in a crowd of strangers, haunting his dreams when he slept, drifting over the crystal-blue waters that surrounded him when he was alone at sea. He saw his squinted eyes and his crooked teeth, but most clearly he saw that smile that DelCosta had flashed him across the courtroom as the judge dismissed all charges against him because of a major screwup on Mitch's part.

At first Mitch had thought that, in time, the image would fade and eventually disappear entirely. It hadn't. DelCosta's grin had followed him south to the Keys and back home again. He used to wonder what, if anything, would free him from it. He didn't have to wonder any longer. Thanks to Ollie, Mitch thought grimly, he knew exactly what it would take to get DelCosta off his back once and for all. He wished to hell he didn't.

In spite of his earlier denial, the news of the Hanson murder had done more than anger him and remind him of the all-too-similar murder DelCosta had walked away from thanks to him. It had raised a possibility he'd rather not have to consider; if not for his mistake, DelCosta would be behind bars right now and George Hanson would still be alive. So what the hell was he supposed to do about it?

Walk away, said a voice deep inside. *You're out of it now.* He'd never asked for a second chance and he sure as hell didn't want one. That's exactly what this would be. Ollie was right when he said this was Mitch's chance to get even, to put DelCosta in prison where he belonged and to save a kid from being locked up in his place. And, just maybe, a chance to redeem himself at the same time.

The question was, did he really want to be redeemed?

Freezing with the bottle opener in hand, Mitch swore softly, then shoved both the bottle and opener aside and buried his face in both hands. He stood that way for a long time. Finally he dragged his fingers through his hair and reached for the phone. He dialed from memory.

"This is Dalton," he said to the switchboard operator who answered, banking on the fact that a six-month absence wasn't long enough to completely erode the power once associated with his name. "Put me through to John Grayson."

Chapter Two

Rachel was clipping coupons from a supermarket circular, engrossed in the weekly juggling of prices and nutrition, when there was a knock on the door. She froze with scissors in hand, eyeing a coupon for Bonnie's favorite cereal. Without the coupon, the cereal, like so many other things, would not fit into their meager budget.

A second knock brought needless reassurance that she wasn't hearing things. She also wasn't expecting anyone to come knocking on her door this afternoon.

They rarely had company. Rachel purposely refrained from getting too chummy with the neighbors. It wasn't easy, given her friendly nature and the loneliness inherent in her situation, but she'd learned to be aloof. Bonnie had made friends with a couple of children who lived nearby, but since they were all still too young to go off alone, their play times were always planned in advance by Rachel and the other parents. Nothing had been planned for today.

So, whoever was knocking was probably selling something, Rachel thought in an attempt to reassure herself as she stood and walked to the door. It didn't work. As she wiped her suddenly damp palms on her jeans, she wondered when these stomach-twisting jitters would begin to subside.

It had been over a week since the shooting at Hanson's. Mr. Hanson had been buried days ago and although Rachel hadn't attended the funeral service, she had cried for his wife and family. Her heart ached for them and she wished there was something she could have done to help. But there wasn't, she reminded herself. Not then and not now.

Mr. Hanson had died before reaching the hospital; his murderer, a teenage boy who had apparently been looking for some quick cash, had been caught with the murder weapon only a few blocks away from the store. It was an open-and-shut case. There was nothing to be gained from Rachel stepping forward to say Bonnie had been in the store when it happened. She was at peace with what she had done.

That didn't mean she wasn't constantly on edge. In some ways this past week had been as bad as those first months after they'd fled St. Augustine. She kept remembering the fear and helplessness she'd felt as they were shuttled from one safe house to another. In other ways, this was even harder. Until that afternoon at Hanson's, she had actually begun to believe that she and Bonnie had survived the worst of it, that they actually had a chance for a normal life here in Plymouth. This incident was a cruel reminder that they really weren't any safer now than they had been eighteen months ago, and that perhaps they never would be.

Since the shooting, both she and Bonnie had been having trouble sleeping. Rachel lived with the fear that Bonnie would innocently say or do something to arouse suspicion. She had spoken carefully with Bonnie about what she might have seen that afternoon in Hanson's... which actually turned out to be very little, since she was engrossed in her candy selection until the last instant. Without outrightly coaching her to lie, which Rachel steadfastly refused to do, she had explained to Bonnie that she shouldn't say anything to anyone about that day. Rachel was honest and forthright by nature, and one of the hardest aspects of their situation was not only the subterfuge she herself was forced to practice, but that she had often no choice but to involve Bonnie as well.

A slipup by Bonnie wasn't her only concern. She also worried that perhaps someone had seen them on Main Street that afternoon after all and that somehow the police would find out and come around wanting to talk with Bonnie. Her only consolation was that none of the news stories had made any mention at all of a little girl. Rachel could only hope that by some miracle, the young killer had been so nervous he hadn't even noticed her.

Of course, she wasn't so naive to discount the possibility that the police were purposely withholding the information about a possible witness. They might already be mounting a quiet search, methodically checking out every girl around Bonnie's age in the vicinity. She hadn't heard anything to make her think such a search was taking place, but then, she was hardly part of the local gossip circuit. If the police were out looking, then this or any other unexpected knock on her door could well mean disaster.

If this was a policeman, would she have the courage to look him in the eye and lie for Bonnie's sake?

Yes, Rachel decided without hesitation, drawing strength from that thought as she reached to open the door. For Bonnie's sake, she would dare anything, risk everything. She already had.

"Ms. Curtis?" inquired the man waiting outside.

The second-floor landing was small, with barely enough room for a welcome mat, but Rachel had a feeling that even standing in the Astrodome, this man would look big. As a novice reporter, she'd been sent to cover a lot of petty crime stories and interview a lot of investigating detectives, many of whom didn't want to be interviewed. She could zero in on a cop a block away. This guy didn't look like a cop, or a salesman. But he did look like trouble.

The sixty-watt bulb hanging behind him didn't provide the most advantageous backdrop for a close inspection, but Rachel's reporter's eye was accustomed to cataloging pertinent details under all sorts of conditions. Her visitor had broad shoulders and thick dark hair, and was wearing a suit she judged to be Italian and expensive. She noted that rather than a cookie-cutter white business shirt, his was a muted gray-green, nearly as dark as his suit. First glance also told her that the man had what some young gang members she'd once interviewed had called attitude.

Attitude, by its street definition, was a blend of savvy and swagger, backed up with whatever it took to back it up. Hard to translate into words, it was impossible to fake. If you had it, a member of the gang had told her, you didn't need to carry a gun. Nobody would mess with you anyway. This guy clearly had it. It wasn't difficult for Rachel to imagine him in jeans and leather instead of a shirt and tie, and the image made her grip the door a little tighter.

"What do you want?" she asked, trying not to invite suspicion by sounding overly wary.

"For starters, I'd like to know if I have the right address. You are Rachel Curtis, aren't you?"

Rachel hesitated for only a second before nodding. "Yes. I'm Rachel Curtis."

Before she got any further, he pulled a leather case from his jacket pocket and flipped it open to reveal an official-looking ID with the state seal in the top right corner. Rachel's stomach clenched.

"Mitch Dalton," he said. "I'm with the Attorney General's office. I'd like to ask you a few questions."

Rachel knew she was staring at the ID as if expecting to find the secret of immortality written there in fine print. She couldn't help it. She'd been moderately prepared to face a police officer, perhaps even a homicide detective, but not someone from the Attorney General's office. In terms of investigations, this was sending out the big guns. What did that mean? Nothing in her reporter's experience could provide the answer, only a warning that, under the circumstances, it couldn't be good.

"What sort of questions?" There, that seemed understandably cautious without sounding guilty, Rachel thought.

"Nothing too tough, I promise."

She shrugged. "All right. Go ahead."

"It might be better if I came inside."

"Better for whom?"

In the dimly lit hallway, Rachel couldn't tell if his eyes were gray or blue, but she did see the glint of surprise that appeared in them at her response. "Both of us, hopefully."

She kept both hands on the door, fighting a primal urge to slam it shut and run. Running wasn't going to work this time. She had to think her way through this.

"Actually, Mr...."

"Dalton."

"Mr. Dalton. I don't usually invite strangers into my home."

"Fine. I was simply trying to make this as convenient for you as possible. If you'd prefer to come down to the A.G.'s office, we can continue this—"

"No. I..."

Damn, damn, damn, she thought. She had refused much too quickly, sounding exactly how she didn't want to sound. Guilty. As if she had something to hide.

"It's just that I don't have a car," she explained. "So it probably would be best after all if we talk here." Reluctantly she swung the door open wider and stepped aside to make room for him to pass. "Come on in."

The door opened directly into the kitchen of the small apartment. Off the kitchen was a den barely large enough to accommodate a small television sitting atop the packing crate she had salvaged and painted glossy white and the blue-and-white-plaid sofa she'd bought for fifty bucks from one of her co-workers at the Y. A short hallway off the den led to the two tiny bedrooms beyond.

She saw Mitch Dalton glance in that direction and was suffocatingly conscious that Bonnie was in her room playing with her dollhouse, a secondhand affair that Rachel prayed wouldn't fall apart until she could afford to replace it. It was Bonnie's favorite toy and some days she would stay in there playing with it for hours.

Let today be one of those days, Rachel prayed.

"Sorry about the mess." She swept her hand at the newspapers strewn across the scarred pine table and the lunch dishes in the drainer by the sink, more in an attempt to distract him from the sounds coming from Bonnie's room than from any real sense of embarrassment. "I wasn't expecting visitors."

"Don't worry. I'm very unobservant."

Yeah, sure, she felt like saying, *that must be why they sent you out to question*... who? What was she exactly? A suspect? Potential witness? An obstructor of justice?

Ha, she thought, struck by the irony of that. If Mr. A.G. here wanted to talk about obstruction of justice, he'd sure come to the right woman.

Shivering slightly, Rachel warned herself to get a grip. After all, she still didn't even know what he wanted to question her about. It could be anything. Anything. She suddenly felt crushed under the combined weight of all the things she had to hide.

"Would you like a cup of coffee?" she asked, her mother's old advice about catching more flies with honey than vinegar running through her head. She wanted to get this over with as quickly and smoothly as possible.

Dalton shook his head. "No, thanks. I won't take any more of your time than necessary, Ms. Curtis. I can see you're busy."

"Fine," she replied, not denying it. "Have a seat."

When he was seated across the table from her, he pulled out a pen and small notepad and flipped it open to a fresh page.

In the sun-filled kitchen, Rachel was very aware that he was much better looking than either his ID photo or her first impression had indicated. He looked to be in his mid-thirties, his face lean and darkly handsome in a way that even women who ought to know better could never seem to resist. Rachel recognized the type. There was something about the way he narrowed his eyes and the haunted expression in them that suggested both danger and vulnerability. A compelling combination, to be sure. In another lifetime, she thought wryly, she might have been wildly attracted. Instead she was scared.

"I assume you're aware of the shooting that took place here in town last week," he began.

Rachel's heart thundered behind what she hoped was a calm outward appearance. *Stay cool, act normally,* she told herself, *as if you were just another citizen.* How would just another citizen react to a murder in town? She clasped her hands on the table in front of her and let a hint of sorrow and indignation creep into her expression.

"Of course I'm aware of what happened. Everyone in town knows about it. I think it's a shame about poor Mr. Hanson."

He nodded. "You were acquainted with him then?"

"Not really. We talked a little whenever I stopped into the store, but that was the extent of it."

"When was the last time you were in Hanson's Store?"

His eyes were blue, she realized suddenly. Ice blue. The contrast with his dark skin and hair was striking. Locked in the path of that ice-blue gaze, Rachel felt as fatally pinned as any specimen in a petri dish.

"Let's see," she replied, as if the time and date of that last trip wasn't branded into her mind forever. The shooting had taken place on Tuesday. "It was a week ago Saturday, I believe...no, no, now that I think about it, it must have been Sunday. Yes, it was Sunday for sure. I remember we stopped in to pick up a newspaper so I could check the bus schedule for Bonnie's first day of school."

"Bonnie?"

Damn.

"Bonnie's your daughter," he prompted.

It wasn't a question. Clearly he had already known about Bonnie, so she hadn't given anything away. Still, she was going to have to be more careful.

"That's right," she said simply. She no longer tensed or launched into long, unnecessary explanations when asked that question. For all intents and purposes, Bonnie was now her daughter, period.

"How old is she?"

"Five. She just started kindergarten."

"Some kindergartens are only in session a half day. Is that the way it works here?"

"Yes."

"Does Bonnie go mornings or afternoons?"

"Mornings," Rachel replied, wishing she could lie, knowing it would be senseless. Bonnie's school hours would be very easy to verify. "Do you mind if I ask what this is all about?"

"Not at all," he countered, then hesitated, eyeing her consideringly as if he really did mind and wasn't sure exactly how much he ought to tell her.

Rachel held her breath.

At last he leaned back in his chair and spoke. "It's come to our attention that there was a witness to the shooting, a little girl."

They knew. The knowledge beat inside Rachel. *They knew. They knew. They knew.*

His gaze was fixed on her, monitoring the reaction Rachel refused to give him in spite of the fact that she was trembling inside.

"I see," she said. What now? Should she ask what this had to do with Bonnie? Or should she just say as little as possible?

"It would help our case immensely," Dalton continued, "if we could talk to this little girl."

"How could it help immensely? I mean, why would you even need help? The newspaper said you've already arrested the killer. He was caught with the gun on him, wasn't he?"

"It's true that we have a suspect in custody who was caught carrying what we believe is the murder weapon. That's not necessarily one and the same as having the killer."

Why wasn't it? A week's worth of rationalization threatened to crumble beneath Rachel.

"I didn't read anything about this little girl in the paper," she said almost accusingly. "Or see it on the television reports."

Dalton's lazy shrug suggested that wasn't his problem. "We only learned of her existence recently ourselves. Now we have to find her."

"Do you have a description of her?"

"Not much of one. Obviously the suspect had other things on his mind at the time. Think again, Ms. Curtis. Is it possible you were there that day and it's slipped your mind?''

It was so ridiculous Rachel laughed out loud. ''Do you really think I'd forget it if I saw someone get shot?''

''I'm not suggesting that you saw it,'' he countered, his gaze intense. ''But Bonnie may have.''

''She didn't.''

''Do you mind if I ask her myself?''

Rachel's blazing green eyes met his frosty blue ones. ''Yes, as a matter of fact I do mind. She's already upset enough about what happened to Mr. Hanson. I can't see any need for you to remind her and force her to think about it all over again when I can tell you for a fact she wasn't anywhere near the store that day. Except for school, Bonnie is never out of my sight. She's not the little girl you're looking for, Mr. Dalton.''

For a few seconds, he said nothing, as if letting the echoes of her angry tirade fade.

''You said that Bonnie's upset,'' he commented finally. ''I take it she must have known Mr. Hanson pretty well for her to get so upset at the news of his death.''

''Not really. I already told you, we were customers of his, period. All the kids in town liked Mr. Hanson. He was always giving them free lollipops and letting them sit at his player piano. He was a wonderful man.''

''So I hear. That's why I'm going to make sure that the man who murdered him pays for it. The right man.''

''Do you really think they might have arrested the wrong man?''

''Let's just say that at the moment I'm less than convinced.''

Rachel slid her fingertip back and forth along the edge of the table. ''I wish I could be more help.''

''Maybe you can.''

''Look, Mr. Dalton, I already told you that I don't want you questioning Bonnie and—''

"And I'm willing to go along with that." He interrupted her. "For now at least. I'm hoping maybe you can help."

"I really don't see how."

"You told me you were last at Hanson's on Sunday. Is that the last time you were in that general area as well?"

"What do you mean by 'general area'? I live only a few blocks from the store."

"True. Let's say Main Street then. Was Sunday the last time you were on Main Street?"

Rachel hesitated, wondering where this was leading. "I . . . yes," she said at last. "I think so."

"Thinking so isn't good enough. I want you to be sure. Maybe you have a diary or a date book of some kind that you could check."

"I don't keep a diary, and I don't lead such an active social life that I need a date book . . . and I'm not so feeble-brained that I can't remember where I was last week. I wasn't on Main Street last Tuesday."

"You're sure?" he said, the cool blue lasers of his eyes unwavering. "The reason I ask," he added before she had a chance to speak, "is that this was found outside of Hanson's by one of the responding officers."

He reached inside his suit jacket and pulled out a magazine, holding it up for her to see.

"Do you recognize this?" he asked.

Rachel shrugged noncommittally, even as she went cold inside. "I've read that magazine, if that's what you mean."

"Actually it appears that you do more than read it, Ms. Curtis, you subscribe to it. The reason I know is that this particular copy has a label with your name and address on it."

Rachel felt her throat squeezing shut, making it hard to breath, not to mention think. She'd forgotten all about the magazine. She had taken it from the mailbox on her way out that day and it had slipped her mind in the furor that followed. She must have dropped it on the bench when she heard the shots.

She eyed the address label across the table. "So it does."

"Did you leave the magazine there, Ms. Curtis?"

"No..." She hesitated, shaking her head. "I don't think so."

"But you might have?"

"I suppose I might have," she replied, speaking rapidly. "It does have my name on it, after all. I might have carried it along with me on Sunday. Maybe it slipped out of my handbag."

"I don't think so... at least, not on Sunday. I checked with your mailman...Mr. Ianetta," he said, supplying the name as if he'd known the man all his life, "and he remembers delivering that magazine on Tuesday morning. The same day as the shooting. He claims he always remembers when the magazines arrive because those are extra heavy load days. So you see, there's no way you could have had the magazine with you on Sunday. Are you sure you weren't mixed up earlier, and that perhaps you were on Main Street on Tuesday after all?"

"No... I mean, yes, I'm sure I wasn't there," she snapped, straightening in her seat. "I wasn't anywhere near Hanson's after Sunday. As for the magazine, I have no idea how it got there. In fact, I don't think I ever even saw that issue. Maybe some kid stole it from my mailbox and tossed it on that bench."

"Did I mention that it was found on a bench?"

"I... Didn't you? You must have."

Rachel felt her face heating under the relentless weight of his gaze. She'd bet that stony, unreadable look of his must be a real professional asset.

He was silent for a moment before giving a slight nod. "You're right. I guess I must have." He leaned forward. "Tell me about Mr. Curtis."

The curveball hit Rachel broadside, stunning her momentarily. "Wh-what about him?"

"The basics. Where does he work? Was he around last Tuesday afternoon? Maybe he took Bonnie to the store with him without telling you. You know how dads and kids can be," he added in a tone so hollow Rachel surmised that *he* had no idea how dads and kids could be.

"No, he... Bonnie's father wasn't anywhere near here last week."

"Are you sure? Did you two discuss—"

"He's dead," she interjected.

"I'm sorry."

Rachel cast her eyes down at her tightly entwined hands, hoping she looked saddened and not panicked.

"Have you been widowed long?"

"Since Bonnie was an infant."

"That must have been really rough on you," he remarked.

Without looking up, Rachel had the sense that he was watching her closely, appraisingly.

"We've managed okay," she told him.

"I'm sure you have. Was Bonnie born here in Plymouth?"

She shook her head, willing herself to remember all the nice tidy details of the background she had created for herself and Bonnie. "No, we moved here only last year. I wanted to live near the ocean. We couldn't afford to do that in most of the places I checked out, but these old houses that have been broken up into smaller apartments are perfect for us. The neighborhood might not be ritzy, but it's safe... at least, I thought so until last week."

She fell silent, cringing inwardly. *Watch it,* she thought, warning herself to remember what she'd been taught. *Keep it simple and direct. Don't explain. Don't hedge. And for pity's sake, don't ramble.*

"I wouldn't worry. I'm sure this will turn out to be an isolated incident."

"I hope so."

"Where are you from originally?" he inquired.

"Indiana."

"Is that where you were living when your husband died?"

"No. We moved around a lot. He was in the service." Rachel felt all her carefully prepared facts evaporating in the face of her mounting anxiety.

"Army?"

"Navy."

"Ah. That must explain why you like being near the ocean."

Rachel folded her arms across her chest. "What does all this have to do with Mr. Hanson's murder?" she asked.

"Nothing," he replied levelly. "I was just curious."

"I see," she said, the tense curve of her lips more nerves than smile. "Well, as you said, I am busy, so if I've satisfied your curiosity, Mr. Dalton..."

She let the remark trail off expectantly, aware that his small smile was neither apologetic nor genuine. She had the same impression she'd had ever since he walked in, that she was under a microscope, being studied by a master.

"I'm sorry for the interruption," he said, rising and sliding a business card across the table to her. "This is my card. Please call me if you remember anything you think might help us, no matter how small."

"Fine, but I really don't expect to remember anything that could help."

"Let me be the judge of that. Sometimes something that seems inconsequential can make the difference between a conviction and a walk. I'd hate to see Hanson's murderer slip through the cracks on a technicality."

A frown creased Rachel's forehead as she reached for the card. "Could that really happen?"

"It has in the past, believe me," he said, his tone suddenly harsh. He turned at the door. "I caught you by surprise this afternoon. Sometimes after you think about something like this for a while, you see it differently." He stared hard at her and Rachel had the impression that his words were being carefully chosen. In fact, she had the feeling that all of Dalton's words were carefully chosen. "Call me," he said again, reaching for the doorknob.

Before he had a chance to pull the door open, a loud crash sounded in the other room, followed immediately by a high-pitched cry of anguish.

"Oh, no," Rachel gasped, starting for the bedroom. "Bonnie?"

The scene in the bedroom was one of disaster that only a mother could fully understand. Rachel knew instantly what had happened. Engrossed in her make-believe world, Bonnie had pushed the fragile dollhouse to the edge of the small table it rested on and it had toppled over onto the wood floor. It lay in pieces, the roof detached, the walls—held upright by brittle glue—crumbled. Her hodgepodge collection of tiny dolls and furnishings were scattered across the room and Bonnie was in tears.

"Oh, Bonnie, don't cry," Rachel soothed, wrapping her arm around the child. "We can fix it."

"H...h...how?" Bonnie sniffled. "It's all broke...the roof and the doors and the stairs all mashed down on top of each other. It's so broke we can never fix it, Mommy."

Crying even harder, she buried her face against Rachel. "Is she all right?"

Rachel froze. For a moment she had forgotten all about Mitch Dalton. He had followed her down the hallway and was standing in the doorway surveying the scene with a look of confusion quite the opposite of the steel-eyed control he'd exhibited in the kitchen.

"Her dollhouse fell," Rachel explained.

"Oh." He looked from the debris on the floor to Bonnie. "Did it fall on her?"

"No, it didn't fall on her," Rachel replied with a flash of impatience. "She's crying because it was her favorite toy in the whole world and now it's broken."

She bit her lip before she said too much, before she revealed to this dangerous stranger that a little girl who couldn't remember having a real home of her own needed a dollhouse and a bit of make-believe in her life.

"I see," he said, although clearly he didn't see and even after being told wasn't quite sure how to reconcile the broken dollhouse with the obvious depth of Bonnie's grief. He glanced around the room awkwardly.

Bonnie, still sniffling loudly, had peeled her face from Rachel's jeans to check out the stranger in her bedroom. Strangers were rarely permitted to get this close and she clung tightly to Rachel as she stared at him.

"Hello, Bonnie," he said. "I'm sorry about your dollhouse."

Bonnie sniffled.

"But I'll bet your mom has it all put back together in no time."

She sniffled again.

"Bonnie, honey," Rachel said, reaching to smooth the dark wisps that had escaped the barrettes holding Bonnie's hair off her face, "why don't you go into the bathroom and wash your face and blow your nose while I show Mr. Dalton out? Then we'll see about getting this all picked up and put back together."

Bonnie nodded and walked toward the door, keeping a cautious eye on Dalton the entire time.

"Goodbye, Bonnie," he said, smiling at her as she moved past him.

Bonnie hesitated, wavering between the caution Rachel had instilled in her and her good manners. "Goodbye."

Keeping his hands in his pockets, he leaned toward her slightly. "Hey, I really like those barrettes you're wearing . . . are those angels?"

With a sound somewhere between a sniff and a small giggle, Bonnie shook her head. "They're mermaids," she said, her tone questioning his intelligence the way only a five-year-old could. "They're the Little Mermaids. You know, like the movie."

"Ah, so they are. Little Mermaids. They're real pretty, Bonnie, just like you."

"Thank you," Bonnie recited automatically, then scampered from the room.

"Thank you," Rachel said when she was gone.

Dalton glanced at her quizzically.

"I half expected that you were softening her up to slip in a few questions."

His expression darkened, underscoring Rachel's initial impression of him as a dangerous man. "You told me you'd rather I didn't question her."

"That's right, I did."

"And I said I wouldn't, at least for now. I keep my word."

Yes, Rachel could believe that, and a sense of trepidation scratched at her as she recalled that he'd also told her he intended to find the little girl who witnessed Mr. Hanson's murder and see to it that the right man was punished for it.

"I just wanted to thank you for respecting my wishes," she said. "Especially after this." She glanced at the broken dollhouse and sighed. "She's already upset enough."

He looked past her, dubiously eyeing the heap of dry wood and bits of plastic that had been Bonnie's treasure. "Can you really fix it?"

Rachel picked up a part of a tiny window casing and placed it on the bed, already mentally evaluating what could be salvaged and what couldn't.

"I don't know," she told him. "But you saw how brokenhearted she looked. I sure have to try."

Chapter Three

Nice. The word hung in Mitch's mind long after he left Rachel Curtis's apartment and headed back to the office.

"Nice" was the word George Hanson's widow had used to describe Rachel and in spite of the wariness and cool reserve with which she had received his questions, Mitch agreed with the assessment. "Nice" summed up just about everything about the woman—her manner, her kitchen, the instinctive way she responded to her daughter's mishap. Another time, he might dismiss the description as pale and wishy-washy, but not where Rachel Curtis was concerned. She seemed to imbue the word with new and fascinating attributes.

He'd bet that under different circumstances, Ms. Curtis was the warm, friendly type. He'd also bet that soft-looking mouth of hers was capable of a killer smile. Several times during his visit, he'd caught himself thinking it was just a shame he'd probably never get to see it.

Mrs. Hanson had given him a list of names of girls she thought might possibly have been in the store the afternoon her husband was killed. Bonnie Curtis's name had been an afterthought, offered with the admonition that this particular child was always accompanied by her "nice young mother." Which was basically the same thing Rachel herself had told him.

How had Rachel put it . . . that except for the time she spent in school, Bonnie was never out of her sight. She'd said it with absolute certainty, but Mitch had been a prosecutor long enough to know that almost nothing in life was absolutely certain.

What interested him more than the remarks Ms. Curtis had made with such conviction, however, were the ones she'd made without it. It was her sporadic falters that aroused his curiosity about the woman and made him wonder what she was hiding behind all that nervous energy.

Aside from his professional opinion that she was being less than honest with him, he had also formed a decidedly unprofessional, inherently male impression of Rachel Curtis. His reaction to her had been instantaneous and gut level, momentarily challenging his gift for professional detachment. It had also been something of a surprise.

He estimated that during the six months he'd spent in Florida, he had viewed from the deck of his boat more firm, tanned, exposed female flesh than he had in the preceding thirty-five years combined. He'd taken note, admired, even indulged in a fantasy from time to time. He wasn't dead, after all. But all of it, fantasies included, had had an impersonal, almost clinical quality, and that suited Mitch just fine.

This thing with Rachel Curtis was different. More intimate—if the strained interrogation of a stranger could in any way be considered intimate, he thought with more than a touch of cynicism. Maybe it was due to the fact that he hadn't been eyeing her across a safe expanse of ocean, but rather sitting close enough to see her emotions reflected in her eyes as he questioned her.

Or maybe it was because she'd been dressed in jeans and a sweater instead of a string bikini that she had affected him less like a centerfold than like a real flesh-and-blood woman. He'd been more distracted by speculation about what was under that loose sweater than he'd been by anything freely offered him in the past six months. Which made so little sense it was scary.

Hell, the truth was he wasn't sure why it had been different with her, or why he'd reacted to her with a hormonal yank he hadn't felt since Angie walked out on him. His mouth crooked disparagingly. All right, so he hadn't felt it for a long while even before Angie walked. He'd sure as hell felt it sitting at Ms. Curtis's kitchen table. He supposed that, in a way, it was a hopeful development, a sign that maybe he wasn't as far gone as he'd thought. It was also alarming. For a prosecutor to have a yen for the mother of a possible witness wouldn't only complicate matters, it was downright unprofessional. And that made it off-limits as far as Mitch was concerned.

A man was only as good as the job he did. His father had taught him that. Harold Dalton hadn't been a warm man or a doting father. He'd never had the time or the inclination to teach Mitch to throw a baseball or bait a fishhook or land a punch. Most of what Mitch had learned about life, and survival, he'd learned on the streets. But after Mitch's mother left, old Harold had hung in there and worked nearly around the clock to support himself and his five kids. As far as Mitch was concerned, that had been lesson enough. He figured his mother might not have loved them worth a dime, but his father had. He'd proven that by sticking around and providing for them the best he could. That's what a man did for those he loved. He worked his butt off to provide.

Once upon a time, Mitch had understood the truth of that all the way to his soul. It was that conviction, the white-hot desire to someday make a better life for himself and his own family, that had gotten him through college and law school when most folks who knew him would have bet he'd end up behind bars, not putting others there.

Success was a game he'd been born to lose, and that made him determined to win. That determination was what had driven him to learn the rules and use them to his advantage. It had kept him on track at the A.G.'s office, where he had outsmarted and outhustled everyone around him. And it had worked. He had been a quick success and was headed for nothing but more of the same when it all fell apart.

He still wasn't sure why, whether the game had changed when he wasn't looking or whether Angie had simply tired of playing by the rules. After years of doing everything he thought he was supposed to do, he sure hadn't expected to come home and find out his wife had taken his kids and left him for the carpenter he'd hired to remodel the kitchen. A carpenter. Just the thought of it still made Mitch shake his head with bitter amazement. A guy not much better off than dozens of guys he'd left behind in the old neighborhood. The thought of losing his wife and children to such a man filled him with a mixture of rage and confusion.

Maybe he should have seen it coming, but he hadn't. Because he was never home enough to take a good look, Angie would say. Whatever the reason, the divorce had hit him broadside and it had thrown him hard enough so that he forgot that a man's work was his only real anchor. He'd let himself be distracted by his personal problems. And he had screwed up.

That was never going to happen to him again, Mitch thought with a resurgence of the bitter self-recrimination he'd been shouldering for months. He wasn't going to let it happen. No matter how sweet Rachel Curtis's behind looked in a pair of jeans.

It wasn't too long a drive from Plymouth to the neighboring town where he was temporarily based. Mitch knew that officially, he was considered back on full-time status at the A.G.'s office. State bureaucracies weren't big on contingencies and private deals. A private deal, however, was exactly what he had struck with his old boss, John Grayson. Grayson wanted him back, and despite his years as an administrator, he had enough of the old prosecutor's fire still in him to understand that the only way Mitch could ever return to his old job was if he was allowed to settle the score with Mickey DelCosta.

It wasn't that Mitch couldn't stand to lose. He'd lost cases before, cases he'd wanted badly to win. Hell, he wanted to win them all. But whenever he had lost before it was because the evidence just wasn't there or he'd had the misfortune to draw a judge with a particular ax to grind or simply because justice was sometimes a roll of the dice and that particular time his number hadn't come up. Blowing the DelCosta case last time, however, hadn't been the result of bad luck or bad evidence, but rather because he had messed up, pure and simple. The Hanson murder case offered him an unexpected second chance. Grayson understood that and, off the record, he had agreed to give Mitch his head in handling it.

For starters that meant Mitch could do things the way he liked best, his way. It also meant he wasn't going to be handling any other cases until this broke one way or the other, and it meant that for the time being he could work out of the local district attorney's office rather than driving into the city every day. That saved precious time because the local office was not only closer to home for Mitch, but closer to Plymouth.

This time around he was determined to stay on top of the details every step of the way. That meant spending a lot of time in Plymouth, chasing leads that he could legitimately ask the state police to handle. This time there would be no stone left unturned, no missed deadlines, no screwups and no compromises.

Mickey DelCosta had shot George Hanson in cold blood. After questioning Leo Belanger and reviewing the case, Mitch believed that as fervently as Ollie had the day he'd met him at the dock. Unfortunately he was still just as unable as Ollie had been to back up that belief with the cold, hard facts that were courtroom currency. He'd spent hours reading reports and double-checking facts and so far there seemed to be only one possible key to opening up the case. That key was the missing witness, the girl with the Little Mermaid barrettes whom Leo recalled being in the store at the time of the shooting.

Mitch was well aware that thousands, maybe even tens of thousands of little girls owned very similar barrettes. The Little Mermaid was a hot item with the preteen set. The only reason Leo had been able to recall the barrettes in such detail was that he'd recognized them as similar to a pair his niece wore. Even Mitch, who would be hard pressed to tell you anything else about his daughters' wardrobes, knew that both girls were the proud owners of Little Mermaid barrettes.

If he were to regard the matter analytically, the fact that Bonnie Curtis also happened to own the same barrettes wasn't especially significant. But law, at least the way Mitch practiced it, was a balancing act between logic and instinct, and when the chips were down, he went with his instincts. In this case, both logic and instinct told him that Bonnie was the odds-on favorite to be the little girl he was looking for.

It wasn't only the barrettes, or Rachel Curtis's slip about her magazine being found on a bench, a detail he was certain he never mentioned. There had also been something tense and unnatural about the way the woman had reacted to the suggestion that Bonnie might have seen the shooting. Not to mention the odd way she'd responded to questions about her late husband. Mitch had questioned a lot of people over the years and after a while he'd discovered that there was a normal pattern to the way people who didn't have anything to hide responded to routine questions.

In his experience, when asked about their husbands, women who had been widowed for even a short period of time automatically responded by revealing that their husband was deceased. Instead, Rachel Curtis's first response had been that Bonnie's father hadn't been anywhere near Hanson's store the week of the murder. That made perfect sense since the poor guy had been dead for five years, but she only saw fit to add that little piece of news afterward. True, her confusion could have been the result of nerves, and awkward answers weren't a prosecutable offense. But all together, it was more than enough to make Mitch decide to conjure up an excuse to pay her a second visit.

He asked Ollie to do a routine background check on Rachel. It would be quicker for Ollie to handle it through the central office, and besides, he trusted Ollie almost as much as he trusted himself. Ollie got back to him later that afternoon with some preliminary information, social security number and the like, including the information that Rachel worked as a swimming and aerobics instructor at the Plymouth YMCA.

Mitch wasn't surprised. She looked like an aerobics instructor, he thought, recalling the graceful way she'd moved around her small kitchen. Ollie promised a detailed report would follow as soon as possible. In the meantime, Mitch decided that first thing the next morning he was going to visit the Plymouth Y for round two with Ms. Rachel Curtis.

* * *

He found her dripping wet, just finishing a swimming class with a group of noisy preschoolers. The woman at the front desk had responded to his official ID with typical willingness to help, providing him with directions to the pool and the information that this was Rachel's last class for the day.

Mitch stood outside the glass partition for a few moments, observing her easy manner with both the toddlers and their parents. Her relaxed expression was quite a change from the tight-lipped, arms-crossed civility she'd accorded him yesterday. He'd thought she was pretty even then, but now, watching her break into a smile, he realized she was closer to drop-dead gorgeous. Of course, the snug red one-piece bathing suit she was wearing might have something to do with his revised opinion. It was a real stretch to try to convince himself that he would have stood there, watching her just as intently for just as long, even if she wasn't beautiful and sexy.

Rachel's brand of beauty was both wholesome and delicate. She looked strong and feminine. And intelligent, thought Mitch, recalling the intensity of her gaze and his feeling that there was more going on behind it than she wanted him to know.

He waited until the youngsters and their parents had all disappeared into the locker room before stepping inside the pool area. The warm, humid air in there was a perfect match for the feelings that watching Rachel had stirred inside him, feelings he was working hard to ignore. She was alone, hanging up the last of the bright orange life preservers as he approached.

She turned and caught sight of him, quickly masking her alarm with a disapproving frown.

"You can't come in here with shoes on," she told him.

"Says who?"

"It's a rule. See for yourself."

Mitch barely glanced at the posted list of rules she indicated with a sweep of her hand. "I don't put much stock in obeying rules."

"That's odd, since I thought your job was to enforce them."

"You're confusing rules with laws. And my job isn't to enforce them, only to see to it that anyone who breaks the law pays the price. I never let rules get in the way of doing that."

"That sounds a little like vigilantism."

"Not at all. Being unorthodox doesn't make me a vigilante, any more than wearing my shoes in here makes me pond scum."

"I never said it did."

"No, you just looked at me as if that's what I was."

"Then I apologize. I certainly don't know enough about you to judge whether you're scum, pond or otherwise."

Their eyes met. Catching the glint of defiance in hers, Mitch felt a sudden, intense, absolutely insane urge to taste the drops of water that fell from her hair to her smooth-looking shoulders.

Instead, he glanced around, then moved to sit on one of the benches lining the wall.

"What are you doing?" she asked as he hitched one foot up on the opposite knee and began unlacing his shoe.

"What does it look like? I'm taking my shoes off, just like the rules say to do."

"I thought you didn't obey rules," she said as he let the first shoe drop and prepared to remove his sock.

"Then you weren't listening. What I said is that I never let rules get in my way. When it suits my purpose, I can follow them just fine."

"I see. And exactly why does it suit your purpose now, when it didn't a few minutes ago?"

"Because now," he said, stopping what he was doing to look up at her, "it might get me what I came here for."

"Which is?"

"A few minutes of your time. I need to talk with you," he added.

"I said everything I have to say yesterday."

"Maybe not. I have a few more questions."

It was hard to hide body language when wearing only a skintight swimsuit, Mitch observed, noting the instinctive tensing of her shoulder muscles. She ran her fingers through her hair.

"Look, Mr...."

"Call me Mitch," he interjected. "It'll make me feel less like I'm the Gestapo."

"How nice. Now if only something would make *me* feel less like you're the Gestapo."

"Just a few quick questions, I promise."

She shook her head, succumbing to a small smile that wavered between amusement and exasperation. "Scout's honor?"

"Far from it," he countered dryly. "But I will cross my heart, if you like."

"Forget it. Just hurry up and put your shoes back on. I don't feel like having to explain what I'm doing in here with a barefoot man in a flashy business suit."

"You making fun of my suit?" he asked, eyes narrowing.

She arched her brows, openly amused now. "European cut, hand-tailored wool-silk blend? What's to make fun of?"

"It's just a suit," he muttered.

"Right, like a Blackgama is just a coat."

"You sound like you know a lot about expensive clothes."

Her scowl came quickly. "Not from personal experience, trust me."

Trusting her, thought Mitch, was the one thing he was not prepared to do.

"Look, I'll make a deal with you," he said. "I'll put my shoes back on and fade into the woodwork out there—" he indicated the hallway outside "—if you promise to join me so I can ask you a few questions."

Rachel hesitated.

"All right," she agreed finally, looking about as pleased as if he'd just suggested tying her to the rear fender of his car and dragging her a few miles. "Just let me change and I'll meet you out there."

While he waited for her to get dressed, Mitch came up with a better idea than sitting on the Y's uncomfortable, molded plastic chairs to do their talking. He had a strong hunch that Rachel's anxiety was due to her reluctance to let Bonnie become involved in a murder investigation. Actually it was more of a hope than a hunch. He'd walked in there determined to handle Rachel with cool professionalism and had wound up being mesmerized by her smile, shucking his shoes just to please her, like some overeager sixteen-year-old.

"What are you doing?" she had asked him. And for a split second, he'd had absolutely no idea. Ordinarily he wasn't an impulsive man. Ordinarily being the operative word. This whole case was out of the ordinary—too many variables, too many hidden cards. That bothered him. Rachel Curtis bothered him...and in more ways than one. The way he was reacting to her bothered him most of all.

He didn't like being impulsive. He liked to plan his strategy beforehand and stick with it as closely as possible. That was the way to win. The only way he knew how to win. Most of the time it worked. But not always, he thought, inadvertently rousing the memory of his failed marriage and the kids he hardly ever saw anymore. He quickly shoved the image away.

Snap out of it, Dalton. This is work, dammit, not the time or place for self-pity... or for acting on impulse. Kicking his shoes off had definitely not been part of his careful strategy for this meeting. It had just happened. Some instinct had told him that bit of horseplay would make Rachel smile, and for one foolish instant, that had mattered to him more than anything else.

He shook his head in disgust.

The problem was that, in spite of his suspicions and doubts, he found himself liking Rachel. And not liking the fact that he had to harass her with more questions and see the wariness that invaded her eyes at the mere sight of him. He liked even less the prospect of catching her in a lie. It would be nice if she could turn out to be exactly what she appeared to be: a beautiful young mother with a cute kid and nothing to hide. He wanted to believe that she wasn't guilty of anything other than fear...and maybe putting her kid before everything else.

It was possible. In fact, a parent shielding a child was a common situation. He'd run into it on other cases and knew from experience that the only way to overcome it was to convince the parents that their fears were groundless. He had to make Rachel understand that no harm would come to Bonnie no matter what she had witnessed, and that it was perfectly safe for her to answer questions and even testify in court if it came to that. To do that, he first had to get Rachel to relax and listen to him. And believe what he had to say.

What was it going to take, he wondered, to get Rachel Curtis to drop her guard around him?

"That was quick," he said, standing as she emerged from the women's locker room.

"No, it wasn't," Rachel retorted. "I purposely took my time, hoping you'd get bored and give up."

"I never give up when I want something badly enough."

She fussed with the strap of her black nylon gym bag before meeting his gaze. "All right, Mr. Dalton..."

"Mitch."

"All right, Mitch, shoot. What is it you want to know so badly that you forgot to ask me yesterday?"

"It's just something that occurred to me after I left your place and I thought I might run it by you for your reaction. Why don't you let me buy you a cup of coffee at that doughnut shop around the corner and I'll tell you about it?"

She was shaking her head even before he got the invitation all the way out.

"No. Thanks anyway. Can't you just tell me right here?"

"It's complicated. And," he added, unraveling a slow smile. "I could really use a cup of coffee. I haven't quite mastered the art of coffee making, I'm afraid."

She arched her brows and gave him the same sliver of a smile she had earlier, by the pool. It was a look that a man might easily interpret as a come-on, thought Mitch, but that man would be wrong. Rachel wasn't flirting with him. She simply thought he was full of crap and she wasn't about to hide that opinion. He had a strong feeling that such directness came naturally to Rachel, that she was a woman given to speaking her mind, and that all the rest, the hedging and reticence, was a sham.

"You mean you have yet to master the art of pouring boiling water into a cup and stirring in some instant coffee?" she inquired.

"I don't like instant coffee," he explained.

"I'd say a man who doesn't like instant and hasn't figured out the workings of a coffeemaker has a problem."

"Not as long as there's a doughnut shop around. Come on, let me buy you a cup."

She sobered instantly. "Sorry. I have to get home to meet Bonnie's school bus."

"What time does the bus come?"

"Around twelve."

"Then you have nearly an hour—that's plenty of time. I promise you'll be home to meet the bus."

"I don't know," she said, obviously stalling as she ran her fingers through her hair the way Mitch noticed she did when she was uneasy.

Wet, her hair had looked almost auburn, but as it dried it gradually lightened to the shade he remembered, a shade that reminded him of golden ripe peaches. As a rule, he liked long hair on women. Angie had always worn her hair long and loose and it was one of the things about her he'd found most sexy. Right this minute, however, he couldn't imagine anything sexier than Rachel's short, tousled hair. The way it fell softly across her forehead and brushed her temples called attention to the finely sculptured lines of her face and to eyes that were greener than any Mitch had ever seen. Except for Bonnie's. Bonnie's hair was darker and curlier than Rachel's, but she had her mother's eyes.

"Come on, I'll even throw in a doughnut," he prompted. "I'll bet a jelly doughnut would really hit the spot after all that exercise."

"A jelly doughnut would sort of defeat the purpose of all that exercise."

"All right, since I haven't exercised this morning, I'll eat the doughnuts and you can watch."

"Now there's a gracious invitation," she remarked dryly.

"I tried being gracious. It wasn't working. In case you haven't noticed, I'm also trying to make up for being so hard on you yesterday."

"You weren't all that hard on me," she countered with a shrug. "It is your job, after all."

"You're right, it is my job...and sometimes when I'm doing it, I forget that not everyone is a hostile witness."

"Not everyone is a witness, period," she added pointedly.

"True enough. Now how about that coffee?"

She shook her head. "You're not very good at taking no for an answer."

"No," he agreed without apology, "I'm not good at it at all." Taking the gym bag from her hands, he hitched it over his shoulder, and when she didn't protest, considered the matter settled in his favor.

Outside the Y, they turned right and headed toward The Country Kitchen Doughnut Shop. Mitch felt an unexpected and unexplainable satisfaction having her by his side. He told himself it had to be because questioning her meant he was that much closer to finding out if Bonnie was the girl he was looking for, and that much closer to bringing down DelCosta.

Rachel's long legs easily matched his pace, even walking down a steep hill like the one where the Y was located. At the foot of the hill was Plymouth Harbor and the tree-shaded park that had been established there in honor of historic Plymouth Rock. Nearby was docked the replica of the Mayflower. Together they were the town's direct link to the country's first settlers, and its greatest claim to fame.

"Do you work only mornings?" he asked as they walked.

"Are you asking as a prosecutor or simply out of curiosity?"

Mitch slanted her an assessing glance. "Does it matter?"

"I suppose not," she replied. "I work mostly mornings, but occasionally I'll take on an afternoon or evening class or cover a shift for someone else."

"Who baby-sits for Bonnie when that happens?"

"Ahh, now we're getting to the prosecutor questions."

"Sharp lady."

"No one baby-sits her. I bring her along with me. I can't afford to pay anyone, for one thing, and besides, I don't really trust anyone else to look out for Bonnie."

"Why's that?"

She tossed her head as if annoyed. "I don't know, I just don't. Is it so odd for a mother to prefer to look after her child herself?"

"Not at all. I just figured most mothers also like having a break once in a while. I know my wife did."

She met his gaze, her surprise evident. "You're married?"

"I was," Mitch explained, wondering if she really had looked disappointed as well as surprised, or if he was letting his imagination run herd over his common sense. "I guess I should have said my ex-wife."

"I see. How many children do you and your ex-wife have?"

"Two. Both girls. Becky is the same age as Bonnie, five, and Nicole is seven."

"Do they live with their mother?"

"Yeah. She remarried, so her place is like a real home for them, and with the crazy hours I was working at the time we split up, it just seemed they were better off with her and...who am I kidding? The truth is I was—am—a pretty lousy father."

They had reached the doughnut shop, but instead of going inside, Rachel stopped with her back to the door and looked up at him, her green eyes narrowed in contemplation. "Somehow I find that hard to believe."

Mitch grimaced. "Why? Because I wear a suit and earn a decent living?"

"No," she returned, her tone growing harsh. "None of that has anything to do with being a lousy father. I know that for a fact."

"A fact...is that another way of saying you know it from personal experience?"

"Something like that," she said, shrugging, her lips pressed tightly together as she reached for the door handle.

"Not so fast, lady," Mitch said, stopping her by taking hold of her arm. "You haven't answered my question."

Chapter Four

"I have no intention of answering your question, counselor," Rachel retorted, glancing pointedly at his grip on her arm. "My personal experience is none of your business."

"I meant my first question," he explained. "Tell me why you find it hard to believe that I'm a lousy father."

"Oh, that. I don't know." The panic that had flashed briefly in her eyes began to fade. Now she looked more ill at ease than hostile. "It was just a comment. My impression of you is...you look like someone who cares, all right? You seem to care about poor George Hanson and his family, and even about the kid who was arrested for killing him, about the possibility that he might not have done it. It seems to me that a man who cares that much about strangers would certainly care about his own flesh and blood."

Mitch felt a lump the size of an egg in his throat and he wasn't sure exactly why.

"Yeah, well." He ground out the words as he released her to reach for the handle and pull open the door, "maybe caring isn't enough."

"It has to be," Rachel insisted staunchly. She hesitated as she brushed past him to go inside, so that for just a split second their gazes met and held. "Sometimes that's all there is."

At Mitch's suggestion, they got their coffee to go and carried it across the street to the park. Rachel demurred at first. It seemed to Mitch that was her automatic reaction to everything, but she finally acquiesced to his reasoning that the park was more or less on the way to her house anyway. They stood by the railing that surrounded the famous Plymouth Rock, staring down at it in silence for a few moments.

"You know," he said, "the first time I ever came here was on a school field trip. I was about nine, I guess. We had been studying the Pilgrims for weeks and I was dying to see the rock that they had first set foot on. We had to take turns filing past to see it, and when my turn finally came, all I could think was how small it was."

"Me too," Rachel exclaimed, an incredulous laugh in her voice. "Of course I was much older when I first saw it, but I had that same reaction."

"Disappointment?"

"Yes, and I hated feeling that way because it is a historic monument after all, but I had been expecting something more..." She extended her arms to illustrate as she searched for the right word.

"Impressive?"

"Exactly. At the very least, I was looking for something boulder size. This," she said, gesturing at the rock below, "looks like just an ordinary rock."

"Not so ordinary," Mitch argued, "when you think that centuries later, thousands of people still come here to see it."

"True. I guess that, in a sense, the fact that it is so ordinary looking makes the story all the more inspiring. When those first settlers stepped off the Mayflower here, they couldn't have dreamed of how significant and revered this spot would someday be."

"My bet is that after crossing the Atlantic in a wooden ship, they were too happy to be getting off to much care." As Rachel smiled and nodded agreement, he added, "It sort of makes you wonder about your own life, doesn't it? I mean, we get up in the morning and go about living our lives, without thinking that something we do or say that day might have repercussions we never imagined."

Mitch was thinking of himself, and of things he'd done—and failed to do—that had brought repercussions he wouldn't wish on anybody, but the sudden tightening of Rachel's jaw told him his words had touched a personal chord within her as well.

"What choice do we have?" she asked. "If we stopped to consider all the possible repercussions of everything we did, we'd never do anything. Sometimes you just have to do what you think is best and worry about the consequences later."

Mitch studied her over his raised cup, wanting to uncover whatever it was that gave her comment its steely edge and knowing instinctively that cornering her about it was the surest way to make her retreat even further.

"Speaking of later," she said, hurriedly downing the rest of her coffee, "I have to run if I'm going to be home in time for Bonnie...and you still haven't asked me what you wanted to ask me."

"That's right, I haven't," Mitch replied, scrambling to come up with a feasible question. "You said that you and Bonnie didn't go to Hanson's store the afternoon he was killed. I know this is a long shot, but I just wanted to double check with you to make sure there was no possibility that Bonnie might have wandered up there on her own. She seems like a bright kid.''

"She is," Rachel agreed, her tone turning crisp and defensive.

"Bright enough to find her way to the candy store alone, maybe?''

"She might be bright enough to find her way there alone, but she would never attempt it. Bonnie is not only bright, Mitch, she's also cooperative and obedient. What you're suggesting just didn't happen.''

He smiled. "Fine. Just double-checking.''

"That's it? That's all you wanted to ask me?''

"That's it." He took note of her reaction, surprise overlaying an unmistakable sense of relief, and his curiosity grew even stronger.

"Then I guess I'll be going," she said.

"Hold on, I'll keep you company," he replied, taking her empty cup and sliding it inside his own before tossing them into a nearby trash barrel.

"That's really not necessary.''

"I know it's not necessary. I want to walk you home.''

"Why?''

"Because it's a nice day to be outside. Why are you so suspicious of me?''

"I guess because you're so suspicious of me," she snapped back.

"Fair enough," he agreed, slanting her a wry smile as he fell into step beside her. "At least we have no illusions about each other.''

"Right," she agreed, staring straight ahead. "No illusions at all.''

Her apartment was located several blocks from the Y, on a hill that ran parallel to the one they'd walked down earlier.

"I thought I was in pretty good shape," Mitch commented when he began to feel the steep climb in his lungs and the back of his legs, "but this hill has me thinking otherwise."

"Maybe you ought to sign up for one of my classes," she teased, then bit her lip as if her spontaneity had been a major slip and she regretted it.

"Might be interesting," Mitch replied, hoping to restore the easiness of a moment ago. Recalling the gentle way she had supported her tiny students' bodies in the water, he was sure that taking lessons from her would be interesting. "Unfortunately I already know how to swim. It's a prerequisite for sailing."

"You sail?" she asked, excitement lighting her eyes as she turned to him.

Mitch nodded. "Have you ever been out on a sailboat?"

"A few times. Not recently, though."

"Maybe someday before the weather turns cold, you'd like to come out with me."

"I don't know... I already told you that I don't like to leave Bonnie with a baby-sitter."

Mitch was growing accustomed to her refusals, and to overriding them.

"Then we'll bring Bonnie along with us. I'll bet she'd love it."

"She probably would," Rachel admitted.

"Is that a yes?"

"A maybe. I'll think about it, okay?"

"Fair enough."

Behind his attempt at a smile, Mitch cursed himself. He wasn't sure what had prompted him to invite her to go sailing, but he didn't like it. It was one more impulse, one more lapse in judgment, and each time it happened, he liked it less. Not that it really mattered. He had no intention of following up on the invitation, no intention of taking Rachel, or any other woman, out on the *My Way*.

In fact, he had no intention of taking Rachel Curtis anywhere.

Aside from the very real possibility that she might yet prove to be involved in this case, he wasn't ready for another emotional involvement. He had a hunch he never would be. And if he were looking for a purely physical outlet, he sure wouldn't pick a woman with sad eyes and a daughter who reminded him too painfully of how much he missed his own little girls.

They were approaching Rachel's house when Mitch thought to ask how the salvage attempt on Bonnie's dollhouse was going.

"Not good," Rachel confided with a sigh. "In fact, it's downright hopeless, but I haven't had the heart to break the news to Bonnie yet. I'm hoping I can find a reasonably priced replacement before I have to."

"It meant that much to her, huh?"

"That much."

"Well, if I hear of any small-scale real estate deals, I'll be sure to let you know."

"Thanks," she said, laughing. "I appreciate that."

She had a great laugh, Mitch thought, realizing that this was the first time he'd heard her really laugh. It was loose and easy, like music. The kind of laugh that rippled over you and made you want to laugh along. It struck him that her laugh, like the spirit that flashed in her eyes from time to time, was at serious odds with the tense, guarded woman Rachel seemed determined to be.

The yellow van that transported the kindergarten students to and from school rounded the corner just as they reached the front steps of the white two-story house where her apartment was located.

"Look at that," he said as it rolled to a stop beside them. "Perfect timing."

Bonnie came bouncing down the van steps as soon as it came to a complete stop.

"Look, Mommy," she exclaimed after returning Rachel's enthusiastic hug. "I made a picture."

"It's beautiful," Rachel told her, holding up for closer inspection the picture of a sunny sky above a cluster of trees. "Did you do this all by yourself?"

Bonnie beamed and nodded. "All by myself. I even put the birds in their birdbath."

"Well, I'm very impressed. You're becoming quite a little artist, sweetheart."

Rachel glanced at Mitch. "Thanks for the coffee."

"Anytime. Would you mind if I came in for a second?" He watched her begin to tense and quickly added, "I'd just like to use your phone to check in with the office. It will save me from having to find a pay phone."

"Sure," she agreed, doing a fair job of hiding the reluctance Mitch sensed she was feeling. "Come on."

As they walked up the stairs, Bonnie revealed that she'd been invited to a friend's house to play for the afternoon. Her friend's mother was going to phone in a while to arrange it.

"And I want to bring my Berenstain Bear books," the little girl told Rachel. "All of them."

"All of them?" Rachel replied with mock surprise. "Bonnie, you must have at least ten Berenstain Bear books."

"I know. And I want to show them all to Sheila."

"All right, I just hope we can find them all."

Inside the kitchen, Rachel pointed to the wall phone next to the door. "There's the phone. Help yourself," she told Mitch. "I'm going to help Bonnie look for her books."

As she and Bonnie disappeared into the other room, Mitch quickly placed the call to his office. His temporary secretary was eager, but not very efficient. While he waited for her to locate his messages, he examined the collage of photos hung on a nearby wall. Most of them were of Bonnie, with a couple of Bonnie and Rachel together mixed in.

The cheerful voice of his secretary interrupted his study of them.

She quickly read his messages to him and Mitch thanked her and hung up. There was nothing urgent requiring his attention, which meant he had time to make a few other planned stops before driving into Boston to meet with Ollie. He was anxious to find out anything new that his search into Rachel's background might have turned up.

He turned to find Bonnie standing behind him, watching him warily, the way she might watch a wild animal that had wandered into her home and didn't belong there.

"Did you find your books?" he asked.

She nodded. "All except for *The Berenstain Bears Go On Vacation*. And that's my favorite."

"Sounds like a good one."

Did Becky and Nicole like the Berenstain Bears as much as Bonnie did? he found himself wondering. He was pierced by the realization that he had no idea what his daughters liked.

"I could read it to you," she offered.

Mitch smiled at her. "I'd really like that, Bonnie, but I can't hang around today, and I think I heard you say you're going out, too."

"I am. To Sheila's. She lives over there," she said, pointing behind her, "and she has the same dress I have." She held out the skirt of her pink dress. "Except hers is blue."

"That's quite a coincidence."

She furrowed her brow. "What's a coincidence?"

Mitch's brow furrowed, too, as he struggled for a suitable explanation. "It's when two friends both pick the same dress to wear on the same day."

"Only Sheila's is blue."

"Right. I'll let you in on a little secret, though. When it comes to little girl's dresses, pink is my favorite color."

"Me too. Except for yellow 'cause that's my most favorite color of all. My favorite dress was yellow, but I don't have it anymore," she told him with a forlorn look.

"I guess it got too small for you, hmm?" he asked gently.

Bonnie shook her head. "Nope. It wasn't too small. My mom had to burn it 'cause it got stains on it. Right here," she added, pointing to her chest.

"Bonnie." Rachel's sharp tone instantly drew both Bonnie and Mitch's attention.

Mitch met her gaze with a searching look. Bonnie's innocent comment about her dress had raised all the hair on the back of his neck, as if he were a dog picking up the scent of his quarry.

"Sweetheart, I can't find that book anywhere," Rachel said to Bonnie, still staring directly at Mitch as she spoke. "Why don't you go check the pile beside your bed?"

"Okay," Bonnie replied, hurrying from the room.

When they were alone, she squared off against him with her arms folded tightly across her chest. "When I heard your voice, I assumed you were still on the phone."

"No, it only took a minute to check in. Bonnie was keeping me company."

"I guess what I meant to say was that I assumed that after I let you into my home, you wouldn't stoop to grilling my daughter against my wishes... and behind my back."

Mitch felt a flash of anger. "I didn't."

"Don't lie to me. That's exactly what you were doing."

"The hell it is. We were talking about her favorite book and her friend Sheila. Period. I wasn't grilling her about anything."

"That's not what I heard."

"Then you heard wrong."

"Come off it, Mitch, she was telling you about her dress when I walked in."

"Right, she was telling me. I wasn't asking. But as long as we're on the subject, why did you burn her dress, Rachel?"

"Because she spilled something on it and ruined it," she snapped back. "Not that it's any of your business."

"But why burn it? Why not just toss it into the trash? Or use it for a dust rag? Why did you have to burn the dress, Rachel?"

"I didn't have to. I chose to."

"Why?"

"I told you."

He took a step closer. "What are you hiding, Rachel?"

"Nothing," she retorted, moving back until she was pressed up against the sink with nowhere to go.

"What are you afraid of?"

"Nothing."

"There's no need to be afraid, you know. We have specialists who deal with young witnesses. Believe me, a kid's safety and peace of mind come first every step of the way. If Bonnie saw something in Hanson's that day, we can help her deal with it."

"No."

"Let me help, Rachel."

"Why won't you listen to me? Bonnie didn't see anything and she doesn't need any help."

He took another step toward her. One more would bring his body against hers and the realization that that was exactly what he wanted washed over Mitch like a wave of heat, stopping him in his tracks. "How about you, Rachel? Do you need help?"

"I don't know what you're talking about."

"I think you do." He saw his breath feather the hair across her forehead. He was that close. Too close, he warned himself.

"Well, you're wrong, counselor."

He shook his head, not moving any closer, but not moving away, either. "I think you're hiding something from me because you're afraid."

"I am not hiding anything. And I'm certainly not afraid. Not of anything... or anybody," she added, folding her arms across her chest as she lifted her chin to stare defiantly at him. "Now please leave."

He stared at her in silence.

Rachel gripped the edge of the counter behind her, certain that he was looking straight through her, that he could see the shaky tower of lies and distortions piled atop one another inside her.

"Okay," he said at last. "I'll go."

He took a step back from her, and Rachel, shivering, swore she could feel the loss of heat from his body. At the door, he turned to look at her, his expression dark and unsmiling.

"You know where to find me," he said.

Rachel stood as if rooted to the floor as his footsteps faded on the stairs. Not until she heard the front door close behind him did she allow herself to sag with relief.

She'd spent all last night reassuring herself that in spite of her nervousness yesterday, she had managed to convince Mitch Dalton that she and Bonnie had been nowhere near Hanson's Store the day of the shooting. She had almost talked herself into believing it, too. That scene a moment ago had put an end to that little flight of fancy. It had also left Rachel feeling breathless, and not sure whom she was most afraid to tangle with... Mitch Dalton the prosecutor, or Mitch the man.

She wasn't entirely sure which one of the two had just backed her up against the sink and begged her to trust him. Not that it mattered, she reminded herself, shaking off the lingering spell of his closeness. She couldn't afford to trust either side of him. She couldn't afford to trust anyone but herself. If she didn't forget that for an instant, she just might make it through this all right.

After all, Dalton had no way to prove that she and Bonnie were at the store that day. If he had a witness to contradict her, surely he would have produced him by now. So it came down to a question of her word against Mitch's suspicions. She only wished she hadn't left that magazine on the bench, but if that was all they had on her, she could handle it. All she had to do was stand her ground long enough and it would all go away.

Until the next time.

Oh, she didn't expect that she or Bonnie would witness another murder anytime soon, but she was smart enough to know there were hundreds of other things that could go wrong and endanger their safety. Time and again during the past week or so, she had cursed herself for getting into this whole mess in the first place. She had gone back over everything that had happened in the past two and a half years, reanalyzing it from every angle and getting enraged and depressed all over again in the process. Finally, when she'd hit her emotional low point, she had reminded herself that the one and only reason she'd gotten herself in this impossible situation was that she'd had no other choice. She'd done it for Bonnie, and if it were to happen all over again tomorrow, she'd do it all again.

All except for going to Hanson's that afternoon, she thought with a rueful sigh.

She would still take Bonnie and run away, although until the very last, desperate moment, that had never been her plan or her intention. From the start, from the very first moment when her sister, Donna, had arrived crying on her doorstep, she had tried to remain calm and find a reasonable solution to an insane situation.

It hadn't been easy to stay calm when she looked at the bruises on Donna's face and shoulders and stood holding an ice pack to Donna's eye, which had been nearly swollen shut. They were bruises that her brother-in-law had put there. Rachel had never been crazy about Randy Parnell. She considered him to be too good-looking, too spoiled and too glib for his own good . . . and certainly for Donna's.

Donna, however, had fallen hard for him on their very first date. That in itself was a switch, since usually it was guys who fell for Donna. She was the uncontested femme fatale in their family, the flirt, the cheerleader, the homecoming queen. Rachel, smarter, more ambitious, and with no inclination to hide either her intelligence or her ambition, wasn't nearly as popular with the opposite sex. In high school, she sometimes longed to be more like Donna, but in the years since, she'd come to the cynical conclusion that maybe not having a man around wasn't such a big loss.

As Donna's big sister, older by two years, it had been hard for her to bite her lip about her opinion of Randy, but she had tried. Her opinion was that Randy was a know-it-all and a braggart and overly demanding. She'd also long had an unsubstantiated hunch that he drank too much and cheated on Donna, but she had never had reason to suspect that he physically abused her sister. If she had, she would have spoken her mind much sooner.

With Rachel and their mother, the only family Donna really had, living in St. Augustine, fifty miles away from the small Florida town that was practically owned by the Parnell family, it was easy for Donna to hide from them the painful evidence of how bad things had gotten in her marriage. She simply didn't visit them whenever she had visible bruises or black eyes and was extra careful not to incur Randy's wrath in the days before she knew for sure she would be seeing them.

According to what Donna had told Rachel that last weekend she'd stayed with her, the physical abuse was only part of it . . . and not always the worst part. Randy's drinking and cheating had humiliated her and broken her spirit, and his constant criticism had her walking through life on eggshells. Rachel had been horrified to see the nervous, fearful woman her once self-confident and care-free younger sister had become.

Sitting there on her living-room sofa, with two-and-a-half-year-old niece Kim asleep in the spare bedroom, she'd wanted to kill Randy Parnell. For the sake of her sister, who unbelievably still had mixed feelings for her jerk of a husband, Rachel had struggled to put her rage aside and help her work through those feelings until she decided what she wanted to do.

In the end, Donna had decided she wanted to leave Randy, and Rachel had to restrain herself from standing up and applauding. By talking about it, Donna had finally acknowledged that nothing would change unless she took drastic steps to change it. It was a lesson Rachel wouldn't have expected her sister to need to learn a second time. She'd have thought they both had had an indelible lesson in that regard during the years of being bullied and shoved around by a stepfather whom their mother refused to leave.

It was because of their family history that Rachel was so amazed Donna had put up with Randy's abuse for so long. Her stepfather's treatment had fired within Rachel the conviction that a bully couldn't be appeased or waited out, that he'd just keep pushing and pushing until somebody bigger and stronger pushed him back, or until you smartened up and got out of his way.

Donna wasn't nearly big enough to challenge Randy physically, which meant she had no choice but to get away from him as fast as she could. The problem was, she was afraid that Randy would never agree to a trial separation, that it would be a divorce or nothing and that if they divorced, he would fight her for custody of Kim. Donna feared losing Kim most of all.

Rachel had well understood her wanting custody of Kim. Judging from what she'd seen of Randy's behavior as a husband, she didn't think he'd make much of a father and she told Donna that no judge in his right mind would give him custody of Kim.

Donna was convinced otherwise. She'd told a shocked and incensed Rachel story after story of how the Parnell family ran things in their hometown, and how what the Parnells wanted, the Parnells got. Although Donna agreed that Randy wouldn't win any dedicated dad award, she was certain that he would demand custody simply so she couldn't have Kim with her. And she was certain that, thanks to his influential daddy, he would get it. Worse, she was terrified that if she dared to fight him openly, she might end up with no visitation rights at all.

It had been Rachel who steadfastly insisted to Donna that even the Parnells didn't control the justice system. How naive she'd been, she thought now, grimacing in sorrow as she packed Bonnie's books into a bag for her to bring to her friend's. It had also been Rachel who finally convinced her sister that the first step was to confront Randy directly, tell him she wanted a trial separation and see what his reaction was. She had even offered to go with her, but in the end, Donna had decided it would be best if she talked with him alone.

Rachel closed her eyes and surrendered to the same question she'd asked herself a million times since then. Why hadn't she insisted on going with Donna?

Instead she had agreed to Donna's request that she mind Kim so that the little girl wouldn't be subjected to any argument that might take place between her and Randy. Donna decided to return home late Sunday afternoon, after Randy got home from the obligatory Sunday dinner at his parents' house and before he went out drinking with his buddies. He never drank much in front of his folks and so she figured that would be the best time to approach him.

She'd left Rachel's at four-thirty. Rachel could still picture her driving off as the mantel clock chimed the half hour.

On the way out the door, she'd turned to Rachel with a shaky smile and said, "Wish me luck, okay?"

"Good luck, sis," she said, hugging her. "You promise you'll call me tonight and let me know how it goes?"

"I promise. And you promise you'll take good care of Kim for me?"

"Of course, I will, you idiot. We're going to order a pizza and watch Cinderella ... again."

"I don't mean tonight, Rachel ... I mean, promise me you'll always take care of her, I mean, if something happens to me."

"Donna, please let me come with you. We can call Mom to come over and ..."

Donna shook her head, cranking her smile up a notch. "No, I'll be fine, really. I'm just being silly and sentimental. Shoot, you know I've never even left Kimmie alone overnight before. So just sort of promise me, okay?"

"I promise, Donna."

It was the last promise she ever made to Donna. The last time she ever saw her sister alive.

Rachel drew a sharp breath, grinding the heels of her fists against her closed eyes. Oh, Donna ... I promise ... I promise ... I promise.

"Mommy?"

She quickly dropped her hands to her sides at the sound of Bonnie's voice, and from somewhere deep inside she dredged up a smile for her sister's little girl.

"What's up, Ki—I mean, Bonnie?"

My God, she thought, how long had it been since she'd called her by that name? She couldn't afford to make a slip like that in front of the wrong listener, like Mitch Dalton, for instance.

"Are you okay, Mommy?" Bonnie asked her.

"I'm fine, sweetie."

"I thought you were crying."

Rachel shook her head, reaching out to stroke Bonnie's face, which was arranged in a very concerned frown. "Nope, I'm not crying. Just thinking. But now I'm ready to help you find that book."

"I found it already," she said, holding it up for Rachel to see. "Under the bed."

"So you did." Rachel took it from her and blew on it. "My goodness, was all this dust under there, too?"

Bonnie nodded, giggling.

"Hmm," Rachel said, "I see some serious sweeping in my future, before these things get so big we have to give 'em names."

"Can we?" asked Bonnie, clearly tickled by the facetious suggestion.

The ringing of the phone spared Rachel from having to make any foolish promises. It was Sheila's mother, offering to pick Bonnie up, feed her and Sheila lunch, and drive her home again around four. For once Rachel agreed without insisting that she walk Bonnie one way. Next time she'd invite Sheila to get off the school bus with Bonnie and have lunch here and it would all balance out in the end.

It was strange, she thought, after Bonnie had left. Loving Bonnie as if she was her own child and putting her well-being ahead of everything else in her life had come naturally to her. It was all the peripheral details of parenthood—setting bedtimes and learning what to feed a kid and how to interact with other parents—that had been tough to get the hang of. Probably because she'd had no time for pregame warm-ups. One day she had been comfortable in her role as doting aunt, the next she had been the full-time mother of a toddler...with absolutely no one she could ask for advice. She had no friends, joined no play groups, and she didn't dare do what other new mothers did and consult her own mother for help.

Rachel paused in the act of sweeping under Bonnie's bed, her first chore in an afternoon she had decided to devote to housecleaning in the hope that it would be therapeutic . . . for both the house and her. Of all the things she had given up and left behind, she missed her mother the most. That had surprised her at first. God knows, they'd had their differences. Her mother couldn't understand how Rachel could put her career as a television reporter ahead of marriage and a family. Rachel could never understand how a woman could stay with a man who hit her and her kids, simply because she was afraid to stand up to him.

For all those years when Rachel was growing up and making her plans to be independent and successful and resenting her mother for looking the other way while her stepfather made life hell for all of them, she hadn't known that that was not what her mother was afraid of at all. That what she really feared—much more than she feared being punched by a man twice her size—was trying to make it on her own for the sake of her daughters and failing them.

Rachel hadn't known that until it was too late for her and her mother to make amends. She hadn't known until the morning she went to see her mother to tell her that things had reached a crisis point with Kim, that in spite of all Rachel's efforts through both the courts and the press to get someone to acknowledge that Randy was mistreating his daughter the same way he had mistreated his wife, Kim was in grave danger every minute that she spent living under his roof.

She almost hadn't gone to her mother's that day at all, half afraid that she would once again only resort to wringing her hands and telling Rachel to be patient and see what happened with the latest court motion. Afraid that, as always, her mother would opt for the path of least resistance. But Rachel had been desperate after the early morning visit from one of Randy's neighbors and she hadn't known where else to turn to. And in the end, she thought, returning to her sweeping with a vengeance, her mother had surprised her.

"Leave," she'd told Rachel after she heard what the neighbor had told her. Rachel recalled that her mother's voice had been almost like a stranger's at that moment, stronger and more determined than she ever remembered hearing it. "Take Kimmie and go someplace where he'll never find you. It's the only way, Rachel."

Her mother had reached out and taken her hands in a solid clasp. Rachel would never forget the look on her mother's face at that moment, or the pain in her eyes as she blinked back tears, her eyes swimming with regrets, for both the past and the future.

"Don't make the same mistake I made," she implored. "You're young and strong, so much stronger than I ever was, and you're the only hope Kim has left. Go now, honey, and never come back."

Her mother's words had pushed front and center a worst-case contingency plan Rachel had been nursing for weeks. At that moment, with Kim's arm still in a sling from what Randy was successfully passing off to everyone else as the result of a fall down the back steps, it had seemed to Rachel that her mother was right. There was no other way out for Kim. And so they had run, and it seemed as if they'd been running ever since.

Even now, when she had thought they had finally found a place they could call home for longer than a few, nerve-racking months, Rachel was running once again. Only this time she was running in place, she thought wryly, running from the suspicion in Mitch Dalton's eyes.

And maybe, suggested a small, instigating voice within, from something much closer to home, a feeling that she hadn't let herself feel in quite a while.

A longing.

A constant, gnawing speculation about what things might be like if she wasn't running and Mitch wasn't suspicious and they could have met under different circumstances. What if she was just any woman and he was just any man and there weren't all these secrets and lies and fear stacked between them like a solid brick wall?

Rachel took another break from her cleaning and moved to gaze out the window of Bonnie's room, where only the tiniest strip of ocean was visible above the roofline of the houses on the hill below. There was no denying that buried under everything else there was a certain attraction between her and Mitch. At first it had been no more than a flicker of awareness, purely physical, nothing more than she might feel passing a good-looking guy on the street or running into one at the Y.

But she and Mitch hadn't just passed on the street. They had talked, spent time together, played mind games with each other, she thought wryly. And perversely, for all the tension and duplicity, it had served to fan that small spark of awareness into something much more distracting.

She'd realized that when she stood beside him at the pool earlier that morning. She had suddenly been acutely conscious that she was wearing only a form-fitting swimsuit, and aware that he was aware of it as well. Oh, sure, his gaze had stayed politely fixed on her face, but in a way, all that forced self-control had made his interest even more obvious. She had known, in the way a woman always knew these things, that he had already checked her out and hadn't forgotten what he saw.

Her body had always been decent, but working at the Y had greatly improved her muscle tone, creating more pronounced curves and angles. Rachel had appreciated the way that increased her stamina and gave her more energy, but today, under Mitch's disciplined gaze, was the first

time in two and a half years that she had taken pleasure in
her body for the sake of pure, sensual vanity.

Unfortunately it didn't end there. If the sparks between
her and Mitch were only physical, she wouldn't be dwell-
ing on it this way. She was as susceptible to a pair of broad
shoulders as the next woman, but her actual hands-on
sexual experience had been decidedly limited and some-
what less than earth-shaking. Truthfully, when it came to
sex, she wasn't sure what the big deal was.

Back in what she'd come to think of as her other life, she
had refused to let her relationships with men get in the way
of what mattered most to her...her career. It was the same
now. She certainly would never let a physical attraction to
Mitch Dalton or any other man endanger Bonnie's safety.

But Mitch's appeal was more insidious than that. It was
subjective and intellectual and emotional and she was a
sitting duck for all of it. Her mouth curved into an instinctive smile as she recalled how it had felt to do something as simple as stand beside him in the sunshine and sip
a cup of coffee. When they had traded first impressions of
Plymouth Rock, their shared disappointment had been
tantamount to a symphony playing inside her. It had been
an instant of understanding and companionship and that
was one instant more of it than she'd had in years.

The fact was, she was lonely. And that, more than anything else, made her vulnerable to a man with Mitch's
charm. Unfortunately, knowing that she was like the bull's
eye on the dart board didn't make it any easier for her to
get out of the line of fire.

Sighing, Rachel reached for the glass cleaner and paper
towels and prepared to attack the mirror above Bonnie's
dresser. If she was lucky, Mitch had run out of questions
and wouldn't be coming around to harass her again. Then
she could go back to being lonely, and safe. For now, she

was going to cling to that hope, and not think about the fact that, judging from everything that had happened in the past few years, she wasn't anywhere near that lucky.

Chapter Five

Rachel never received calls at work. So when Peggy, the Y's receptionist, caught her between classes to tell her that Bonnie's kindergarten teacher had phoned and wanted Rachel to call her back when she had time, her first thought was that something had happened to Bonnie.

"Calm down," Peggy urged as Rachel hastily punched out the number of the school. Peggy had fluffy red hair and a round, no-nonsense face, which currently sported a reassuring smile. "If it was an emergency, the woman would have said so. All she said was for you to call her when you had time. When you had time," she stressed. "That's doesn't sound like any emergency I ever heard of."

Rachel knew that Peggy was probably right. If anything had happened to Bonnie, surely her teacher wouldn't have been so casual about the return call. What Rachel couldn't reveal to Peggy was her fear that perhaps it wasn't an emergency in the usual sense. As she made the call to the school, her ever-present concern that the private detectives she was sure Randy Parnell must have hired to find them had somehow traced them here to Plymouth rose to take center stage, glazing her mind to all other thoughts the way frost ices a windshield on cold winter mornings.

The short wait while the school secretary summoned the teacher to the phone seemed years long. Finally Ms. Trenton, Bonnie's teacher, came on the line.

"Ms. Curtis?" she said.

"This is Rachel Curtis," Rachel replied, achingly alert to any nuance in the teacher's tone.

"I'm so sorry to bother you at work, but..."

"It's no bother," Rachel interjected. "Has something happened to Bonnie?"

"Goodness, no. Bonnie is just fine. I should have mentioned that to the woman who took my message, so that you wouldn't think the worst."

"I'm afraid that's exactly what I did think when I heard you had called."

"I'm sorry. I probably would have thought the same thing myself. Mothers... we're all alike, right?"

"I suppose so," Rachel murmured, glad that the teacher couldn't see the ironic twist of her lips. "How can I help you, Ms. Trenton?"

"You can't really. I'm calling in case what I have to say might help you."

Rachel nervously wound the spiraled phone cord around her finger. "In what way?"

"I'm not sure. I just want to let you know that a man from the Attorney General's office came to the school yesterday, asking questions about you and Bonnie."

She wasn't calling because Randy's detectives had found them. Rachel felt an instant of sheer relief, which quickly gave way to renewed fear about her more immediate predicament.

"I see," she replied. "What sort of questions?"

"Nothing very personal...not that I could have answered that sort of question even if he asked. I explained to him that Bonnie has been in my class only for a very short while."

"Is that what he wanted to ask about? Bonnie?"

"Mostly. He just wanted some general information from her school records from Mr. Bello," she explained, referring to the principal. "Date of birth, inoculations, that sort of thing. And he asked me about Bonnie's behavior in class since the beginning of school.

"As I said," she continued, "it was all very innocuous. Mr. Bello and I weren't even sure it was worth mentioning to you, but I thought you had a right to know. Then, when the mother of one of Bonnie's classmates stopped in this morning to tell me that she'd also been questioned about you and Bonnie, well, I just told Mr. Bello that I, for one, thought you should be informed. So he told me to go ahead and give you a call and that's exactly what I did."

"I'm so glad you did call me," Rachel replied, a red haze of irritation slowly filling her head.

"I hope by telling you this I haven't alarmed you unnecessarily."

"No. No, not at all." On the contrary, Rachel was certain that her alarm was very necessary indeed.

"Good. As I said, I'm sure it was exactly as he said...routine."

"I'm sure," Rachel agreed, conscious of the note of hesitant curiosity in the teacher's tone. She hoped Ms. Trenton didn't expect her to proffer an explanation as to what sort of routine would bring someone from the prosecutor's office around to ask questions about a kindergarten student, because she had no intention of doing so. "Thank you for letting me know about this."

"You're certainly welcome. I know I'd want someone to do the same for me."

"I just have one question, Ms. Trenton."

"Yes?"

Rachel really didn't even need to ask, but she went ahead anyway. "Do you happen to recall the name of the man who questioned you?"

"As a matter of fact I made sure to have his card right here with me, in case you asked. It was Dalton," she said. "Mitchell T. Dalton."

Mitchell T. Dalton.

The name might as well have been branded across Rachel's forehead. Her face felt that fiery. The nerve of the man. Questioning Bonnie's teacher and the mother of her classmate... make that mothers, plural, for all she knew. Had he questioned the parents of every child in Bonnie's class? How about their neighbors? The landlord? She had no idea how many people he had visited, gathering fuel for his suspicions.

But she was going to find out... and put a stop to it.

Passivity didn't come naturally to Rachel, and she'd had a lot of it thrust upon her in the past two and a half years. Time after time, she'd had no choice but to be quiet and nonconfrontational and blend into the background for safety's sake. And she was sick to death of it. This was one time when she wasn't going to blend... and she wasn't going to run.

For just one fleeting instant as she listened to what Ms. Trenton had to say, she had thought of running, of rushing home right now and having their suitcases packed when Bonnie stepped off that school van today and catching the next bus out of town and simply disappearing. Fortunately she remembered in time how very difficult it was to "simply disappear" and resurface with a whole new identity... the planning and research that went into securing new names, new birth certificates, new social security numbers.

Now that Bonnie had started school, it would be even more complicated. School records would present yet another problem, and a difficult one, the women she'd met through the underground had warned her. That was the reason Rachel had been so determined to find a safe place for them to settle down before Bonnie started kindergarten. And she'd thought she had succeeded in doing just that, until Mitchell T. Dalton came barging into her life.

Lord, she thought, how many bad breaks could one woman take?

Seething inside, she turned away from the phone. Peggy had just finished registering a new Y member. She dropped the completed forms into the appropriate basket and glanced quizzically at Rachel.

"So was I right? Was it an emergency?"

"No. At least, not the kind I was imagining. I do have to run out for a while, though." She reached for the clipboard hanging from a wall hook beside her and glanced at the schedule for the week. "Good. Dottie's here this morning. I'm going to ask if she'll cover my Beginners' Step class at 10:00, if I take her Jazzercise at 2:00."

"Sure thing, hon," Peggy said. "Just let me know what you two arrange, in case anyone should ask. It's hard enough to keep up with who's coming and going around here as it is."

"I will," Rachel promised.

Dottie was happy to switch classes with Rachel, since it meant getting off a little earlier than usual. Rachel informed Peggy of the schedule change, as she had promised, and hurried out of the building, confident she had plenty of time to get to Mitch's office, put him in his place, pick up Bonnie at home and get back to the Y in time for the two o'clock class. Plenty of time, that is, provided she spent an outrageous sum of money taking a taxi to his office, which was located in a nearby town. Money that she really couldn't afford to spend. On the other hand, the bus, which was a lot cheaper, was also a lot slower. All things considered, Rachel concluded ruefully, she really couldn't afford not to splurge on a taxi.

The forced expenditure only added to her ire, however. All the way to his office it built, until she felt like a water balloon, filled to the danger point with all the things she had to say to Mr. Mitchell T. Dalton.

She never considered that he might not be waiting there to hear it.

Inside the red brick building, which housed a variety of state offices, she followed signs to the offices of the District Attorney and asked for Mitch, only to learn that he wasn't available.

"When will he be available?" she inquired of the young woman to whom she was referred. She was young and blond and pretty in a breezy way that didn't sit real well with Rachel at the moment.

The blonde blinked and appeared as perplexed as if Rachel had asked her for the chemical formula for monosodium dioxinate.

"Dalton. Your boss," Rachel prompted. "When will he be back?"

"Oh, Mitch isn't my boss." Her smile widened to display yet more perfectly straight white teeth. "I'm a floater. That means I float from one department to another," she explained in her own, inimitable singsong way, "going wherever I'm needed at the moment. Right now, Mitch needs me."

Rachel could believe that. What man wouldn't? The question was, what kind of man would waste his time visiting grade schools and hassling her when he had a Barbie doll personified waiting here to do his bidding? The answer was, a man with a mission. It wasn't a very reassuring thought.

"I could take a message, if you like," offered "Barbie."

"Fine. Tell Mr. Dalton that..."

"Wait, I have to find a pen." She rummaged in the top drawer of her desk. "Not this one . . . it leaves blotches. I just hate when you get those ink blotches on your knuckles, don't you?"

"With a passion," Rachel retorted in a voice totally devoid of any. She gritted her teeth until the floating secretary had located a pencil, sharpened it, opened her message book to a fresh page and glanced up at her with an expectant smile.

"All set?" Rachel asked, just to be sure.

"Whenever you are."

"Good." She leaned forward and planted her hands on the desk. "Just tell Mr. Dalton that—"

"From the tone of your voice, I think maybe this is something you ought to tell me yourself."

She spun around to find Mitch standing behind her, wearing a red flag of a smile. Rachel longed to eradicate it from his face by whatever means necessary.

"Gladly," she said through clenched teeth.

He reached to push open the door, which had a piece of cardboard bearing his name taped to it. Temporary quarters to match the temporary secretary, she thought.

"In here," he directed quickly. To his smiling secretary, he added, "Hold all my calls, will you, Darlene?"

Inside the office, after closing the door behind them, he rested his hips on the corner of the desk and waved her toward the chair nearest him.

Rachel ignored his silent invitation and remained standing, arms folded across the chest of the white nylon warm-up jacket she'd tossed on over her exercise clothes, black leggings and a tropical print leotard. For the second time she was conscious of what a disadvantage it was to square off against a man dressed in a business suit while she was wearing clothes that fit like a second skin. She was only thankful that at least this time she wasn't also wet.

"To what do I owe this visit?" he asked.

"To the fact that I have enormous self-control," Rachel snapped. "Otherwise I'd have just paid the cabdriver to wait outside and run you down when you came out."

"You seem upset with me."

"Brilliant deduction. Perry Mason, move over."

"The question is, why?"

"The answer is that you are the most stubborn, close-minded, shortsighted, mulish man I have ever had the misfortune to have to deal with."

He tilted his head thoughtfully. "Care to be more specific?"

"What gives you the right to go around to everyone I know asking questions about me?"

"The laws of the state of Massachusetts," he replied without missing a beat. "Is that what all this fuss is about?"

"That's exactly what all this fuss is about. The last I heard, this was still a free country, where a person's private life is just that, private."

"To an extent."

"What does that mean?"

"It means your life is private in so far as it doesn't impede the constitutional rights of someone else. For example, the right of Leo Belanger to a fair trial."

"I'm not impeding his right to a fair trial," she countered irritably. "I wish him the very fairest trial any man ever had. I just don't have anything to do with it. How many times do I have to tell you that?"

"Three."

Rachel's eyes narrowed. She hadn't expected a numerical answer. "What?"

"Three. You asked how many times you have to tell me that you're not in any way involved in the Hanson case and I answered. Three."

"What kind of answer is that?"

"A specific one, which is more than I usually get from you. I've questioned you three times about that afternoon and your story is always the same."

"Are you saying you finally believe me?"

"I'm saying I have no real reason not to. I admit I've had the feeling that you're being . . . let's just say, less than forthright with me, that maybe you're afraid of something, but I accept the fact that as long as it doesn't pertain to this case, it's really none of my business."

Alleluia, thought Rachel.

"Exactly," she said out aloud. Catching her lower lip between her teeth, she wavered between relief and apprehension. "But then why did you question Bonnie's teacher? And the mothers of her classmates?"

"Verification. You told me that Bonnie was in school that day, and department policy—not to mention my own policy—demands that every fact be verified. As for her classmates, I'm looking for a little girl around Bonnie's age, remember? Believe me, I've interviewed lots of mothers."

"You have?" she asked, relaxing a bit as she offered him a subdued shrug. "Somehow I felt that I'd been singled out for that honor."

He shot her a wry smile. "Not by a long shot. I will confess, though, that you're by far the most...interesting mother I've questioned."

"I see," Rachel countered, wondering exactly what the word "interesting," uttered with that rough inflection, might mean. She was not about to ask. Shrugging a second time, she took a step backward, toward the door. "Well, I hope you solve this case soon . . . for everyone's sake."

"I will," he countered, his square jaw tightening with familiar determination. "There's no way DelCosta's going to walk twice."

"Twice?" she echoed frowning.

He scowled, as if he regretted the remark, and nodded. "That's right."

Straightening, he circled the desk and picked up a folder lying in the center. He tossed it down across the desk, open so that Rachel could see the photo on top of the thick stack of papers inside. It was a police mug shot of a man who looked to be in his late twenties. He had stringy dark hair, narrow eyes and a smile that even in a still photo had the power to make Rachel shiver.

"Meet Mickey DelCosta," he drawled in a contemptuous tone, "the man who killed George Hanson."

"But that's not the man they arrested," Rachel protested.

Mitch smirked unpleasantly. "Fancy that, will you."

"So when you said you thought they had arrested the wrong man for the murder, you weren't just taking a stab in the dark. You've known all along who really killed him."

"That's right."

"Then if you know who really did it, why haven't you arrested this man?" She slapped the photo. "Mickey De— De..."

"DelCosta," he said, the syllables rolling easily off his tongue, as if he'd said the name a thousand times. "Because without a witness to corroborate Belanger's story— and my suspicions—arresting him would be a waste of time. Mickey is one slippery son of a bitch."

"Is that what you meant when you said he wasn't going to walk twice?"

He nodded.

"What happened?" she asked. "The last time, I mean."

"What happened?" he repeated with a sound that she might have interpreted as a laugh if she hadn't been able to see his face and the shuttered look of anguish that darkened it in the second before he averted his gaze to stare out the window behind him at the passing traffic.

"What happened," he went on, after pausing for so long Rachel had almost resigned herself to the fact that she wasn't going to get an answer to her question, "is that a couple of years ago, Mickey DelCosta walked into another store in another town and shot another man in cold blood and, thanks to me, he got away with it."

"What do you mean, thanks to you?"

"I mean I screwed up." He spat the words out, wrenching his head around to face her as if he wanted to see the shock or condemnation he clearly expected his words to elicit. "I let DelCosta walk."

"So you lost a case," she said, puzzled by the strength of her sudden urge to console this man who only a few minutes ago she'd wanted to throttle. "You know what they say, you can't win them all."

"You're not listening. I didn't lose this case," Mitch said, holding her gaze. "I blew it. I failed to file a critical motion on time and because of that the judge had no choice but to dismiss the charges."

Rachel shrugged feebly, uneasy with the depth of emotion he was clearly struggling to suppress. "Anyone can make a mistake."

"Yeah, right." He glanced out the window and then back at her. "I was making dozens of them at the time. Fortunately the others were all so small they didn't matter or else they got fixed before it was too late. I was so busy wallowing in my own misery, I didn't even realize how many people were mopping up after me until the crap hit the fan with DelCosta."

He lifted his brows, watching her puzzled expression with harsh amusement. "You're wondering what sort of misery, right?"

"No," she said quickly, wondering exactly that. "It's really—"

"The divorce kind."

"None of my business."

"Don't worry, I'm not going to bore you with all the gritty details."

"I'm not afraid of being bored. I just didn't want you to feel I was questioning you about things you'd probably rather not tell me about."

"There's not that much to tell, actually. We were happy enough—at least I thought we were—two kids, nice house, money in the bank, and then I came home one day and she was gone. She and the kids. My daughters."

Pain shadowed his face, the pain of loss mingled with confusion, stirring a response deep inside Rachel. She understood that kind of pain.

"I'm sorry," she said, hating the inadequacy of the only words she could think of to offer him.

He shrugged. "Me too. For a lot of things. Not the least of which," he added, the brief suggestion of vulnerability giving way to the stubborn look she'd come to know, "is letting DelCosta squirm off the hook once already."

"Under the circumstances, I don't think anyone would hold you responsible or blame you—"

"You don't get it," he said, cutting in sharply. "*I* blame me. I hold me responsible."

"Maybe you shouldn't. After all, you had to have been under a great deal of emotional strain at the time and—"

"Emotional strain doesn't count for squat," he said with undisguised disdain. "When a man has a job to do, he doesn't sit around wasting time wondering what the hell went wrong with his love life. He gets the job done, period. I let myself forget that once, but never again. This time around, I'm going to do whatever it takes to get him."

"At least now I understand why this case is so important to you, and why you seem to take it so…personally."

"It is personal with DelCosta," he said, his eyes flashing dangerously. "Damn personal."

"Maybe it shouldn't be."

"What does that mean?"

"Nothing really," she replied, realizing that she should be saying goodbye and thanking heaven he was off her back, instead of standing there prolonging a discussion of something that was not her concern. "I just wonder if you aren't setting yourself up for another fall. Do you think that convicting DelCosta will somehow bring your family back?"

"Not quite," he said, his small smile sardonic. "Since she remarried as soon as the divorce was final."

"I see."

"You do raise an interesting question however." He came around the desk to stand much too close for Rachel's peace of mind.

"What question is that?"

"For a woman who was threatening to run me down when she first walked in here, you sounded downright concerned for me just then."

"Well, I'm not," she retorted. "For some reason, I just felt obligated to warn you about the obvious."

"I'll consider myself warned." His eyes gleamed in a dark, unsettling way. "And maybe you weren't that far off after all. Maybe a part of me does hope that if I can settle this thing with DelCosta, just maybe I'll be able to figure out what went wrong with everything else in my life."

"I should think there would be a much simpler, more direct way to do that," she countered. "Didn't your ex-wife ever tell you why she left you?"

Mitch shrugged. "I never asked."

I never asked.

Strange as it sounded—and it must have, Mitch decided, judging by the look Rachel gave him as she made a hurried exit—it was the truth. He had never actually asked Angie why she'd left him. He'd never asked her at which exact moment she had stopped loving him . . . if she'd ever really loved him at all, that is. He'd come to the conclusion that what had brought him and Angie together in the first place had less to do with love than with convenience . . . on both their parts.

Angie had been the daughter of a successful attorney who was also a visiting lecturer at Mitch's law school. She was bright and pretty and well connected, and a newfound honesty with himself forced Mitch to acknowledge that in those days, that was all he required in a wife. As for Angie, he supposed that, on the surface at least, he was enough like the father whom she adored for her to talk herself into believing she was in love with him. And it all worked, for a while.

He leaned back in his seat and propped his feet on the desk, amazed that his heart hadn't begun to pound and his temples to throb. This was a change. When had he become able to think about the failure of his marriage—his failure—without a resurgence of the blinding resentment and raw pain he'd felt at the time?

It was hard to say for sure, since for months now he'd done his best to avoid thinking about it at all. He'd forced himself to forget he ever had a life before he sailed south, and he'd spent all his time down there concentrating on nothing more significant than how many fish he might catch and toss back that day, letting the fire of the sun overhead anesthetize him from the outside in. He'd had no choice; it was either stop thinking about the past and reliving it, or go crazy.

For months after Angie left and announced that she wanted a divorce, he had walked around in a silent, crushing fury. Oh, he'd continued to function all right, at least he'd thought he had. The debacle with the DelCosta trial had put a very public end to that delusion. During that time, he'd thought almost nonstop about losing Angie and the girls, about how it was possible that he had done everything a man was supposed to do, given his wife everything he thought she wanted and needed to be happy, and had lost it all anyway.

It didn't make any sense to him. He had followed all the damn rules and he had still lost and it left him feeling like he was free-falling through a world of darkness with about a hundred tons of lead strapped to his back. A small, detached part of him, which had stood aside and watched his descent into emotional chaos, hadn't been at all surprised at how hard he landed.

He'd been too angry and bitter back then to even consider asking Angie for answers, too angry even to miss having a family to come home to. He'd only realized how completely he'd shut down inside when another attorney, a man he knew only slightly and who was also divorced, had asked him one night in a bar if he missed tucking his daughters into bed at night. He'd confided to Mitch that that was what he missed more than anything else, more than having someone cook his meals and deal with his laundry, more than the companionship or the available sex. He missed kissing his kids good-night.

Even through the alcohol haze he usually retreated into when work was done for the day, Mitch had been stunned by the comment. The man's words had driven home to him the uncomfortable fact that he'd been so busy feeling sorry for himself, he hadn't even had time to miss his kids.

He missed them now, though. Swinging his feet back to the floor, he unconsciously rubbed his chest near his heart, the spot where the pain of missing them seemed to be centered. Alone on the boat all those months, he had missed them like hell. He'd missed them to the point where he tried so hard to conjure up their faces that his mind would go blank and he'd panic and have to get out of bed and turn on the light to stare at their pictures tacked over his bunk until he had recommitted each tiny detail to memory and could fall asleep in peace. He'd missed them so much he had several times changed directions and docked with the sole intent of phoning just to hear their voices, only to chicken out at the last second.

He hadn't known what to say. To Angie or to his daughters. That's really what he'd been thinking of when he told Rachel that a part of him hoped that settling the score with DelCosta would help him settle other things in his life. Just maybe, if he was able to look himself in the eye in the mirror without seeing a failure, he would be able to think of the right words to say to his little girls. Maybe he would find the guts to ask them if there was still room in their lives for him.

At the moment, that seemed a monumental task. So he was concentrating instead on something he did know how to do. Work was always what he'd been best at. Far better than he'd been at being a husband or father. If he couldn't fix this, Mitch thought, he couldn't fix anything.

The small office he'd been given on a temporary basis suddenly felt even smaller and more airless. Deciding he'd get more done if he worked at home, he stood and tossed a couple of folders from the top of his desk into his briefcase. One of the folders on the desk had Rachel Curtis's name on it. Mitch flipped it open and glanced idly at the one-page report Ollie had faxed him that morning.

Everything looked all right with her, according to Ollie. Which is exactly what Mitch had wanted to hear. Reading the report, he had finally acknowledged to himself that his preoccupation with Rachel, which he'd been writing off as a professional hunch, was probably something else entirely...something more personal than professional. Somehow, Rachel had awakened in him a need that he'd thought had died. He wanted to get to know her better, and since it seemed Bonnie wasn't the kid he was looking for after all, that was no longer a problem.

Opening the bottom drawer of the desk, he shoved the folder with Rachel's name beneath a plastic zip bag containing a paper coffee cup. He glanced at the cup with a

perplexed frown. He'd returned and fished it out of the
trash barrel near Plymouth Rock after walking Rachel
home the other day. If he wasn't going to have it dusted for
prints, as he'd initially intended, he might as well get rid of
it.

The buzz of the intercom on his desk interrupted him as
he reached for the cup and he turned to punch the Listen
button instead.

"You have a call on line two," Darlene told him. "It's
Mr. Grayson."

"Thanks," Mitch said, the cup forgotten as he automatically shoved the drawer shut with his foot and reached
for the receiver to take the call. "John, Mitch here. What's
up?"

Grayson explained that reporters were asking questions
about how soon they would be ready to go to the grand
jury with what was turning out to be a very prominent
case. It took fifteen minutes and all of Mitch's stalling
tactics to avoid having to tell Grayson the truth, that he
really had no idea. He wasn't any closer now to having the
evidence he needed to charge Mickey DelCosta with murder than he had been the day he sailed back into Massachusetts waters. Just more frustrated.

Knowing he wouldn't be able to stall Grayson indefinitely, he hung up feeling even more restless and cooped up
than he had earlier, and decided to get out of the office
before he was stuck taking more phone calls and fielding
more questions for which he had no answers. He needed
to be alone so he could do what he always did when he was
stuck on a case, spread out his notes and go back over
every detail of it. He needed time to think and regroup. But
what he needed most, he thought as he strode toward the
parking lot, was to find the kid who saw DelCosta pull the
trigger.

He slid behind the wheel of his black BMW, equipped
with every extra feature and luxury the car company of-

fered, and pulled from the lot. Once, he had derived immense pleasure from driving this car. Not because the car itself was such a pleasure to drive, but rather it was a BMW and that had signified something to him. It had been a symbol of achievement, his own, a trophy, a milestone along the way to the next trophy and the next milestone.

No longer. These days, it was just a car...and at that, he thought as he revved the engine to pass a pickup truck, a car with such tight suspension it didn't deliver a very comfortable ride. There were lots of things that no longer held the same significance for him that they once had. The half-million-dollar house was just a place to sleep, the hand-tailored suits were just clothes. Even the *My Way*, secured at its mooring out back, no longer brought him the pleasure it once had. Maybe because it was tough to take milestones very seriously when you no longer had any idea where the hell you were going.

He was halfway home, stopped at a red light in the center of town, when he happened to glance at the row of stores on his left and noticed the Magic Hours Toy Shop. More specifically, he noticed the dollhouse in the shop's front window. He immediately thought of Bonnie and her broken dollhouse. He wondered if Rachel had found a replacement yet.

At that moment the light changed. Mitch hesitated for a second, just long enough for a car parked beside him to slide out, freeing a parking space. Omen or impulse, Mitch wasn't sure exactly which of the two was guiding him as he quickly pulled into the spot and turned off the engine.

He stopped in front of the store window to check out the dollhouse more closely. He hadn't actually seen Bonnie's dollhouse intact, but from what he'd seen of the ruins, he surmised that it resembled this beauty only in name and basic structure. The dollhouse in the window had bay windows, French doors and a turret. There was a grandfather's clock in the front hallway and tiny flowered dishes set atop a lace-covered dining-room table. The Cadillac of dollhouses, Mitch thought with amusement. Imagining Bonnie's expression when she saw it made him smile broadly as he entered the small shop.

Inside, he had to wait for the teenage clerk to finish her phone conversation and hang up.

"May I help you?" she asked, tucking a wad of gum in her cheek and a lock of straight blond hair behind one ear.

"I hope so. I'm interested in the dollhouse in the front window."

The girl smiled. "That's the Marieville, our top model. It's a Victorian style and comes complete with carpeting and wallpaper and with operating doors and windows."

"How about the furniture?"

She shook her head. "All the furniture is sold separately. That's so you can choose the style and pieces you like best. Is this a gift?"

"Yes. And since I have no idea what she'd choose, I'll just take it exactly as it is in the window."

"All of it?" she asked, eyes widening with surprise.

Mitch smiled and nodded. "All of it."

"Don't you want to know what the total cost will be?"

"Only so I can write the check," he replied, reaching into his inside jacket pocket for his checkbook.

"Fine. I'll just check the stockroom to make sure everything is available and I'll ring it up for you."

She returned to tell him that everything except for the canopy bed in one of the bedrooms was in stock. She offered to wrap up the one from the display model and Mitch agreed. While he waited, he wandered around the shop looking at dozens of stuffed animals and dolls and jewelry-making kits, all of which reminded him of Becky and Nicole.

It seemed obvious that if he was buying something for a child he barely knew, he ought to buy something for his own kids as well. But what? Both the girls had had their own dollhouses in their rooms when they lived at home. That word again, he thought, wincing slightly. When they had lived in his house, he corrected himself, thinking that as far as they were concerned, "home" was probably where they lived now.

They'd taken the dollhouses with them when they left, along with their dozens of stuffed animals and the tiny bicycles he was always tripping over in the driveway. He gazed at the shelves of stuffed bears and rabbits and puppies, wondering which breed and color his daughters would choose if they were here, and which ones they already owned. After much deliberation, he added a pair of soft, floppy-eared dogs to his growing pile on the counter, swapped them for a goose and a turtle, and then swapped back again.

When it was all packaged in several cardboard cartons, and paid for, the salesclerk held the door open for him as he carried it to his car. Although it took him two trips, Mitch was surprised at how compact it was, none of the cartons looking quite as big as the dollhouse itself. Probably because the roof was packed separately, he decided as he drove away.

He did a U-turn at the next corner and drove straight to Rachel's apartment. He lugged the first carton up to her door, only to discover she wasn't home. He debated leaving it all there in the hallway, but he wasn't sure all the boxes would fit. Besides, he was really looking forward to seeing Bonnie's reaction. And Rachel's, too, he admitted to himself.

Back in the car, he decided maybe it was a good thing they weren't home after all. This way he could check out the dollhouse ahead of time and make sure all the parts were there. Nothing was worse than giving a kid something she couldn't play with right away. While he was at it, he'd get that roof attached. If it turned out to be complicated, he'd rather tackle it in private than in the middle of

Rachel's kitchen, with her and Bonnie looking on impatiently. He wasn't sure why, but the idea of appearing in-
ept in front of Rachel made the skin at the back of his neck
prickle uncomfortably.

At home, he brought all the cartons into the den and
then used a screwdriver to pry loose the heavy-duty staples securing the first. He reached in, carefully peeling
away sheets of foam packing material, and frowned at
what he uncovered. Walls. A stack of them, bound together with plastic rope. Not standing upright and covered in a rainbow of different wallpapers, as they had been
in the store window, just a pile of plywood walls with
gaping holes where the doors and windows should be. The
operating doors and windows, Mitch reminded himself, a
heavy sense of foreboding setting up shop in his belly as he
reached for the phone and punched out the number on his
sales slip.

"Magic Hours Toy Shop," announced the female voice
he recognized as belonging to the girl who'd waited on
him.

"My name is Dalton," he said. "I was just in your store
and I bought a dollhouse, with furniture."

"Hi, Mr. Dalton. Is there a problem with it?"

"Yes. It's in pieces."

"You mean there are pieces missing?"

"I mean the problem is there are pieces, period. I bought
a dollhouse."

"No, you bought a dollhouse kit."

"What?"

"A kit. You have to put the pieces together yourself. I
thought you knew that, since kits are all we sell."

"No. I saw a dollhouse and that's what I thought I
bought."

"I'm sorry, Mr. Dalton. You can return it, if you like.
But it's really not that hard to assemble. In fact, I did the

one in the window myself, in one day, in between customers.''

Customers, thought Mitch irritably. More like victims.
There ought to be a law against stuff like this.

"You should have told me it was a kit before I bought it
and dragged it all the way home," he grumbled.

"I really am sorry," she said again. "There's a sign
above the counter saying that all the dollhouses are sold in
kit form, and it's also stamped on the box."

He checked the box. It was stamped there all right,
making him feel even dumber, and madder.

"Mmmph," he said.

"I'll be more than happy to give you a refund if you
want to return it."

He thought about it. "Can I exchange it for the one in
the window?" he asked.

"I'm afraid not. The display model has already been
sold."

Figures, he thought, eyeing the cartons with disgust.
"All right, thanks anyway."

"You're welcome . . . and Mr. Dalton," she said, before
he could hang up, "just one piece of advice. Make sure you
hang the wallpaper before you install the walls. It's much
easier that way."

"Thanks."

He hung up the phone and went to the kitchen. Shoving aside the beers that had been there since he returned
home, he grabbed a can of cola and returned to the den to
open the rest of the cartons. At least the roof was already
shingled, he noted. That was the good news. The bad news
was the directions were three pages long. The fact that half
of each sheet was printed in Spanish didn't console him
even a little bit.

He glanced at the first of the forty-seven numbered as-
sembly steps. Sort and check pieces against the diagram on

back, it read. He flipped the page over and groaned at what looked like a diagram of a nuclear reactor.

This, he thought, was exactly why he always bought everything from the girls' bikes to disposable razors already assembled. It prevented headaches like the one he felt coming on now.

He wondered if the girl at the toy shop would be willing to put it together for him if he offered to pay her. Then he wondered how foolish he would feel asking a teenage girl for help with something he couldn't figure out on his own.

Maybe he ought to just forget the whole thing.

Before the thought had even cleared his head, he thought of Bonnie's heart-wrenching expression that day in her bedroom, the pieces of the shattered dollhouse lying all around them. And he thought of the determination that had sparked in Rachel's eyes when she told him she had to try to put it back together. And she had tried, in spite of the fact that it was obviously hopeless.

He glanced again at boxes full of pieces, thinking that he had an advantage over Rachel. At least he had all the pieces intact, and directions to follow. And he'd always been really good at that, following directions. With a sigh, he reached for them once again. Do Not Use Nails. Do Not Trim Excess Molding. Use Only Staples Provided. He had to admit, the instructions looked pretty simple. What's more, they promised success or his money back. Now there was an offer he couldn't refuse.

He put down his soda can and picked up the stack of walls. Step-by-step directions for success, he thought, his mouth slanting in a rueful smile. The story of his life.

Chapter Six

Each autumn, the town of Plymouth sponsored bicycle races, which drew serious bicyclists from throughout the country. The race course encompassed several city blocks, including two steep hills and a hairpin turn, and it passed right in front of Rachel's apartment house. She had never known that a bike race could be such a big deal, much less had she witnessed one, but it was free entertainment and these days, that was the kind that suited her budget best.

Her job as a television reporter in Florida hadn't been all that lucrative, but it had paid twice what she earned at the Y and back then, she'd had only herself to support. Pinching pennies was one more adjustment she'd had to make. Still, if she ever resented the chronic shortage of cash, it was for Bonnie's sake, for all the things she couldn't provide her with and all the places she couldn't afford to take her. Even something as simple as a trip to the movies, which she used to take for granted, was a rare treat. That's why free outings were never to be missed. As

soon as she heard about the bike race, she told Bonnie and
began making plans.

Bonnie's first reaction had been to wish for a bike of her
own so that she could race, too. When Rachel explained
that she was too young to enter and that all the racers
would be riding special, multispeed racing bikes and passing right in front of their house, she gradually came
around to thinking that having a front-row seat for the
excitement would be the next best thing to racing a bike of
her own.

To make the day even more fun for Bonnie, Rachel invited her friend, Sheila, to sleep over the night before the
race. The next day was Saturday, and the first of the many
scheduled races was to start at ten. By nine-thirty the girls
had their place staked out on the front lawn, blanket
spread, and a small cache of sodas and treats alongside.
Rachel, dressed in faded jeans and a yellow cotton-knit
sweater, claimed the rocking chair on the spacious front
porch.

"Can we walk to the corner to see if they're almost ready
to start, Mommy?" Bonnie asked, hopping from one foot
to the other in anticipation. Sheila's smile was equally im-
ploring. Sheila had strawberry-blond braids and freckles
and as the first real friend Bonnie had ever had, held a
special place in Rachel's heart.

"Sure, come on," she replied, abandoning the peaceful
comfort of her rocking chair.

They headed down the hill, where they would have a
view of the grandstand set up on the edge of the park
across the street. Rachel only half listened to the girls'
chatter as they walked, her own thoughts turning to the last
time she'd walked down there, the day Mitch had pres-
sured her to have coffee with him.

She'd mulled over that meeting more than once since
then, especially after her visit to his office this week. It still
baffled her why he'd been so determined to see her to ask

such a seemingly trivial question. She couldn't help spec-
ulating that he might have wanted to see her for other reasons, reasons that had nothing to do with his job or the
Hanson case. And as dangerous as that prospect was, Rachel felt a small jolt of excitement each time she considered it.

It was more than dangerous really; it was downright
reckless. And impossible. She couldn't chance a relationship with any man, at least not right now. Maybe when
Bonnie was a little older, after time and distance had lessened the risks involved. Even then, however, she couldn't
imagine a less suitable man than Mitch Dalton. A woman
in her position wasn't exactly the perfect match for a man
who'd dedicated his life to putting criminals behind bars.

The fact was that, even though she didn't feel like a
criminal, or think of herself as one, that's precisely what
the law said she was. Kidnapping was a felony, and if no
one had been willing to listen to her about what had happened to Donna, she didn't fool herself into thinking anyone would be interested in hearing the reasons she'd been
forced to take Bonnie away from her father.

It was a warm September day and the street was as
crowded as it usually was during the summer months. A
local radio station was broadcasting live from the site and
street vendors were hawking everything from hot dogs to
balloons.

"Look, Mommy," Bonnie cried, "cotton candy."

"So it is."

"Can we have some? Please, Mommy."

"Yes, but it's a little early for it right now. How about
after lunch?"

"Okay," Bonnie replied, and Rachel gave thanks, as she
frequently did, that she was such an easygoing child. If
not, the fallout from the shooting might have been even
harder to deal with.

Rachel had done her best to make Bonnie understand what had happened and at the same time shield her from details of a senselessly violent world she was too young to have to deal with. An occasional question when they were alone was evidence that she hadn't recovered completely, but five-year-olds were resilient and always eager to turn their attention to something new, and after her assurances from Mitch yesterday, Rachel was even more confident that Bonnie was going to get through this all right.

They walked a short way down the street, to where those entered in the race were gathering. There were hundreds of them, both men and women, most young and trim and dressed in sleek bicycle pants and tops in team colors ranging from black and red to neon pinks and greens. The mood was one of festive excitement as the announcer called for those registered in the opening race to line up at the starting point.

Rachel made sure to keep the girls safely on the curb beside her as the starting gun sounded and the racers exploded into action, and afterward was glad she had. Like any racers, they jockeyed for position, cutting the corner where Rachel and the girls were standing so close that she felt the rush of wind as they passed and could have brushed against them simply by leaning forward. Bonnie and Sheila laughed and clapped along with the crowd. Most of the races consisted of several laps, so they stayed there to watch the entire first race, then decided to return home for a soda and watch the rest from the comfort of their front lawn.

For safety's sake, roadblocks had been set up on the perimeter of the race course, closing the area to traffic for the day. There were none of the usual parked cars on Rachel's street, providing her with a clear view all the way to the top of the hill as she turned the corner, and at first she thought she couldn't possibly be seeing what she thought she saw.

Squinting from behind her dark glasses, she studied the man walking down the hill from the opposite corner, who was carrying something bulky draped with white cloth. There was something instantly familiar about his loose, long-legged gait. As they drew closer, her pulse quickened with the realization that it was who she thought after all. Mitch Dalton. But what was he carrying? And just as interesting, where was he headed with it?

That question was answered as he reached her front walk a minute before she did and turned in there. He climbed the porch steps and lowered whatever he was carrying to the table there with what looked like a smile of relief. Then he turned and leaned on the porch railing to watch them approach. His short-sleeved white polo shirt emphasized his tan and the snug jeans, molded to the lower half of his body, emphasized his masculinity in a way only wear-softened denim could.

"Hello," he said to Rachel as she reached the steps, then shifted his smile to Bonnie. "Hi, Bonnie. And who's this? Wait, let me guess, Sheila."

Both girls giggled and scampered onto the porch.

"That's right," Bonnie said. She pointed at the sheet-draped mystery beside him. "What's that?"

"Shh, Bonnie," Rachel admonished quietly. "That belongs to Mr. Dalton."

"Actually it belongs to Bonnie," he said correcting her.

"To me?" Bonnie asked, eyes widening in surprise.

"That's right, honey. Go ahead and uncover it." He grinned at Rachel. "Can you do a drum roll?"

Laughing, she attempted one, only to break off abruptly when Bonnie pulled away the sheet and uncovered a dollhouse unlike any Rachel had ever before seen.

Bonnie and Sheila both squealed with delight.

"It's beautiful," Bonnie cried. "It has doors...and dishes...it has everything!"

It did indeed have everything, Rachel noted with dismay, all the elaborate—and costly—details that she couldn't afford. She looked at Mitch to find him staring at her, his eyes narrowed, head tipped slightly to the side, as if he was trying to interpret her reaction.

"It's a beauty all right," she said to him. "But you never should have bought it."

"Why not?" he asked, breaking into a smile.

"Because it's much too expensive."

"How do you know how expensive it was?"

"Because I've looked at dozens of dollhouses in the past week or so and I know there's no way I can afford anything close to this one."

"Then it's lucky you don't have to, because I can."

"Mitch, I can't let you just give this to Bonnie."

His smile reversed into a perplexed frown. "Why not?" he asked again.

The girls were busy standing up all the furniture that had tipped during the trip there and were totally oblivious to her discussion with Mitch. Still, Rachel searched carefully for words. There were lots of reasons he shouldn't have done it, but she knew that at the root of her protest was the fact that she wasn't used to accepting help from others and she wasn't comfortable doing it. What she didn't know was how to explain that to him without opening up to scrutiny parts of herself and her past that were strictly off-limits.

"Because it's too expensive for one thing, and you don't even know us for another, and...and it just isn't right. I'll have to pay you for it," she insisted, wondering how in the world she was going to manage it.

"That's not possible."

Now she was the one to ask, "Why not?"

"Because I wouldn't know what to charge you."

"Simple. I'll pay whatever you paid for it."

"That would cover materials, but what about the cost of my labor? Do you know what an attorney earns an hour?"

"Probably too much," she muttered, then as what he'd said penetrated, she looked at him incredulously. "Labor? You don't mean you built this?"

"From scratch," he told her, pride lurking beneath his attempt to appear offhand about it. "Or rather, from a kit."

For some reason the fact that he'd built it both touched and disturbed Rachel even more.

"Mitch, it's beautiful," she said, staring with fresh respect at the incredible dollhouse, a creation much too fancy to be called a toy. "I can't believe you actually built it."

"Truthfully, neither can I." He ruefully explained to her how he'd bought the kit by mistake and tackled it grudgingly.

"All night?" she asked when he was finished his story, sympathy creeping into her tone.

"Most of it. I think I finally wired the doorbell around four-thirty this morning."

Rachel's brows arched. "Wired the doorbell?"

"Sure. How else would the dolls who live there know when a salesman was at the door?"

Rachel shook her head, laughing. "You're right, of course. You're also crazy." She stopped laughing and shaking her head and smiled warmly at him. "And, in spite of everything I've said or thought about you in the past, you're also a pretty nice guy."

He stared at her, a look of pleasure and satisfaction in his dark eyes. "I knew it," he said quietly.

"Knew what?"

"That if I ever got you to smile at me, I mean really smile, just for me, that this is how it would feel."

"How?" Rachel asked, her own voice pitched low, probably because she knew how foolhardy she was being. "How does it feel?"

"Good. Too good maybe." He took a deep breath and exhaled. "Anybody ever tell you that you have a killer smile, lady?"

She shook her head, afraid to speak, afraid to hear any more, mostly afraid of the pleasure bubbling inside her. How long had it been since she'd felt this way? How long since a man had flirted with her and made her feel something besides fear and suspicion? Too long, came the answer from deep inside, much, much too long.

"Well, you do," he said to her. "A real killer smile. A smile like yours could make a man do a lot of foolish things."

In spite of the rough caress of his tone, his words had a tempering effect on Rachel. Thank goodness. A woman could do a lot of foolish things, too, she reminded herself.

"Like buying an expensive dollhouse and staying up all night to build it?" she asked, trying for a light, teasing tone.

"For starters."

"Is that why you did it?" she prompted, heedlessly backpedaling into the emotional quicksand all around.

His mouth quirked into a rueful smile. "I should probably say yes, but the truth is, I did it for another sort of smile entirely. That one right there."

With a movement of one broad shoulder, he indicated Bonnie, who was indeed smiling as if all her dreams had suddenly come true. Which wasn't far from the truth, Rachel thought with a new rush of affection for the man responsible. At that moment Bonnie had everything she wanted in the world right there within her grasp. Rachel was thrilled for her. What would it be like to feel that way, she thought wistfully, even for just a little while? If only her own problems could be solved with such relative simplicity.

"You have no idea what this means to her . . . to both of us," she told him. "It's more than just a replacement for a broken toy. There's so little in Bonnie's life to cherish and hold on to and . . ." She caught herself venturing onto treacherous ground and stopped short. "You just can't imagine what it means."

"I think I can. I saw how she looked the other day when her old dollhouse broke. It was as if her whole world had collapsed."

"It just about had. And now look at her . . . I don't know how I can begin to thank you."

"I do," he said.

Rachel braced inwardly, wondering if she had misjudged him and this act of kindness. What did he want in return?

"A cup of coffee would square things, as far as I'm concerned," he said before she had a chance to ask.

"You've got it," she returned with a laugh. Relief seeped through her on several levels. She was relieved that the dollhouse wasn't an attempted bribe of some sort. Even more, she was pleased that Mitch's motive hadn't been calculated. "In fact, I made a fresh pot just a while ago. It's still in the carafe. I'll just bring down a couple of cups . . . that is, if you don't mind sitting out here."

"Out here is fine."

"Good, because after all the hype I'm sort of interested in seeing these bike races." She glanced at the girls, knowing they weren't going to want to leave the dollhouse even long enough to accompany her inside.

"Don't worry, I'll keep an eye on them," Mitch said, as if reading her mind. "That is, unless you don't trust me."

"Don't be silly, of course I trust you. I just don't want them to go near the street. Those bikes are really tearing past here."

She hurried upstairs and quickly filled two mugs with hot coffee, remembering that Mitch took his with cream. She shook her head at the irony of his questioning whether she trusted him alone with Bonnie. She didn't, of course, but not for the reasons she suspected he had in mind.

When she returned with the coffee, the girls were still absorbed in their play. Rachel had a hunch they would remain so for hours. And that Bonnie, at least, would have to be dragged away to eat lunch and collect on the promised cotton candy.

Mitch had settled himself on the wide porch steps. Rachel handed him his coffee and then slipped into the space between him and the railing, leaving room for people to pass on their way in and out. For the moment, they had the porch to themselves, but she expected that to change as the day wore on.

She took a sip of coffee, then turned to look up the hill as the sound of rubber on pavement announced the appearance of another group of races. Spectators on neighboring porches and seated in lawn chairs scattered along the sidewalk cheered them on.

"See the guy in green?" Mitch asked, pointing at a rider on the side of the pack closest to them. His black bicycle pants and jersey were striped with a screeching green.

Rachel nodded. "Mmm-hmm."

"He's been moving up with every lap. I'll bet next time they pass us, he's in the lead."

"Unless this is the final lap for this race."

"It's not."

"How can you tell?"

"From watching the guy with the flags down there." He nodded toward the end of the street, where a man dressed in shorts and a T-shirt was holding up a white flag with a black number four on it. "He signals the number of the lap to the riders and flashes a black flag when they're starting the final lap."

"I can see you're an old hand at this."

"Nope. This is a first for me."

"Then how did you know about the flags?"

He turned to her. "Just naturally observant, I guess."

That's exactly what she was afraid of, Rachel thought, feeling a little shiver in spite of the sun overhead.

"Here they come," he warned, leaning forward to get a better view of the corner in a way that pressed his shoulder against Rachel's and set off another sort of heat shiver entirely.

"You were right," she exclaimed. "That guy's taken the lead. Way to go, green," she shouted, caught up in the shouts all around them.

"Wow. Where'd you learn to whistle like that?" Mitch asked when the racers had rounded the next corner and sped out of sight.

"You mean like this?" she said, once again placing a finger at each corner of her mouth and producing a shrill whistle.

Mitch pretended to tap his eardrum. "Yeah, that's the one, all right."

"I don't know. Just naturally talented, I guess."

He shot her a sardonic smile in recognition of her play on his earlier comment.

She returned her attention to the street. "How long do you think it takes them to circle the entire course?"

"About two minutes and ten seconds. I clocked it," he explained when she looked startled by his exactitude. "You were right, they really are moving fast enough to hurt anyone who steps in their way."

"This is my first time watching a bike race, too," she said, "and I had no idea how fast they went . . . or what a big deal these races are."

"Me, either," he agreed.

"I'm surprised. . . . I mean, since you've lived here in Massachusetts for a while . . ."

"All my life," he interjected.

"And from what I've heard this week, this race is one of the biggest in the country."

He shrugged. "I guess that's the way it goes sometimes...you keep chasing after the big score, the trip to Europe, the Super Bowl tickets, and overlook the special things right under your nose. I knew about these races, of course, but I was always...too busy," he concluded, his faint smile grim.

"Well, I'm glad you weren't too busy today."

"Me too," he agreed. "Even though it wasn't planned. I had no idea the races were scheduled for today until I had to park my car a mile away and hike all the way here carrying that thing."

"Was it heavy?" Rachel inquired sympathetically.

Mitch shook his head. "Just bulky."

"Still, a mile is a long way to carry something that size. You should have waited until tomorrow."

"I couldn't," he countered, his tone wry. "Once I had finished building it, I couldn't wait to see Bonnie's reaction. I think she likes it."

Rachel felt a dangerous rush of emotion as she watched him glance at Bonnie and smile with rekindled pleasure.

"I don't think 'likes it' comes close to describing her reaction," she told him. "She's in heaven. All thanks to you."

"I'm glad I could do it."

"Why did you, Mitch?" she asked quietly. "I mean, I know that hers was broken and you knew how much I wanted to replace it, but why did you go out of your way to help? Not only buying a new dollhouse, but spending an entire night putting it together for her?"

He shrugged, watching in silence for a moment as Bonnie carefully opened and closed the French doors before finally turning to look at Rachel.

"I don't really know. Maybe just because I knew I could. Because I knew what it would take to make Bonnie smile again. And, I guess, maybe, because I wish I knew that much about my own kids."

"Are you... having problems with them?" she asked, not sure if she was intruding where she wasn't welcome.

"I guess you could say that, if not seeing them counts as a problem."

"Mitch, that's awful. Don't you have visiting rights?"

"I have all the rights in the world," he said gruffly, shifting his gaze to a flag waving from a flagpole across the street. "Angie's been fair... or she's tried to be. She'll let me see the girls whenever I want to. I just... don't know what to say to them anymore."

"What did you used to say to them?" she asked gently.

He met her gaze, his own burning with self-recrimination. "Not much."

"I see." She rolled her mug between her hands. "That's no reason things can't change. When was the last time you saw them?"

"Six months ago. It's not as bad as it sounds," he added quickly, wincing at the shock in her expression. "I was away most of that time. After the DelCosta fiasco, I handed in my resignation and took off on my boat. I got back only a couple of weeks ago."

"And your job was still waiting?"

He nodded. "Thanks to some good friends."

"So you got back just in time to take on the Hanson case," she observed.

"That's the way it turned out. As a matter of fact, that case is the only reason I'm back at work at all."

Rachel was sorry she'd mentioned it, since the last thing she wanted to do was spoil the day by talking about the Hanson case. "A couple of weeks back home is still enough time to visit your daughters," she said pointedly, hoping to return to that subject.

"I know that. It's just that I've been busy," he said, shifting with obvious discomfort. "I'm working every night and they're both in school now and..." He shook his head, his sigh rough with self-disgust. "That's bull, right?"

She nodded with a matter-of-fact expression. "Sure sounds like it to me."

"All right, the truth is, I'm afraid to go over there and see them." His laughter was harsh. "That's a joke, huh? I've gone head-to-head with some of the toughest guys in the state, in court and out, and I'm afraid to go see my own kids."

"Afraid of what?" asked Rachel, her tone gentle.

He lifted his shoulders. "Damned if I know. Screwing up again, letting them down again. Not being there when they need me. Again." His grip on the mug tightened. "Maybe I'm most afraid that I'll find out that this time, I'm the one who needs them, and that it's too late."

"That's not going to happen. You're their father," she reminded him, her tone fervent.

"Yeah, right. A father who stands in a toy store with absolutely no idea what his kids might want. You said it, I know more about a virtual stranger."

"That's all incidental right now. There's more to being a father than buying presents."

Rachel heard the sharpness that had shot into her tone and wasn't surprised when Mitch swung around to look at her with a startled expression.

She quickly looked away, cursing herself. "I just meant that what's important is that you are their father...presents and saying the right thing, that's all secondary."

"Maybe. But I wonder sometimes if I ought to just leave well enough alone. Maybe their new father, the man Angie married, is all the father they need."

"More bull."

"Easy for you to say. Being a parent seems to come so naturally for you. You've made Bonnie the center of your life, and you always know the right thing to do and say."

"Not quite," she countered, unable to avoid the hint of dryness in her tone.

"Well, it sure looks that way. I saw how you reacted that day with the dollhouse. You were great."

"Damage control," she retorted with a sweep of her hand. "You're the one who knew how to make her smile again. So let me return the favor." She met his gaze and held it. "You want to see your kids smile? Go see them. It's as simple as that, Mitch."

His brow furrowed. "You really think so?"

"I know so. I'm a natural at this, remember?"

"Right," he said, returning her smile.

"So you'll do it? You'll go to see them?"

"I'll go. I planned to anyway, but—"

"Soon?" she said, interrupting him.

He laughed. "Soon...I promise."

"Good."

He stared at her satisfied smile and shook his head. "You know something? You'd make a great lawyer."

"Me? A lawyer?" she asked, looking pleased.

"Absolutely. Ever consider it?"

She shook her head. "Never."

"Always had your sights set on being a swim instructor, hmm?"

"Not quite. The job at the Y simply suits my needs for now."

"So what did you always want to be . . . when you grew up," he added teasingly. "A mother?"

"No." Rachel folded her arms atop her knees and watched the bikers do another lap, without cheering this time. "Not really. It just sort of turned out that way." She turned to him abruptly. "Would you like some lunch or something? All of a sudden I'm famished."

Mitch accepted her evasion tactic much more gracefully than she executed it. He agreed to lunch and insisted he buy, treating the girls to hot dogs from a stand at the center of the festivities. Rachel opted to join him in ordering chowder clam cakes at the take-out window of a café nearby. They found an available picnic table in the park and ate with a view of the street and the ongoing races.

As they were walking home, Bonnie tugged on Rachel's hand and reminded her about the cotton candy.

"Are you sure you still have room in your tummy for it?" she asked Bonnie.

"Mmm-hmm," replied Bonnie, nodding vigorously. "The hot dog went in the hot dog compartment of my tummy and the cotton candy goes way over here in the candy compartment." She used her index finger to indicate precisely where those specialty compartments were located on her anatomy.

Mitch looked both intrigued and amused, as if he'd never before heard that particular theory of digestion. Although how that was possible for the father of two young girls was beyond Rachel. She laughed at the two of them, feeling loose and buoyant, as if cotton candy and bicycle races were the only things in the world that mattered.

"All right, cotton candy for everyone," she declared. "Now, where is that cart?"

She did a slow, three-hundred-sixty-degree spin in an attempt to locate the peppermint-striped cotton candy cart they had seen earlier and finally spotted it on the opposite corner, half-hidden behind the bunches of balloons tethered to the cart beside it.

"There it is . . . and this time it's my treat," she said to Mitch as she stepped off the curb. "Just wait here and I'll—"

Rachel wasn't sure which came first, the frantic shouts of the people nearby, the rush of air as the pack of bicycles rounded the corner coming straight at her, or the sensation of being lifted off her feet as Mitch grabbed her from behind and pulled her back to safety. She only knew that when she finally understood what had almost happened, how close she had come to being plowed down and seriously hurt, she was shaking.

Trembling.

Breathless.

And Mitch was a solid wall of strength and protection.

He kept his arms around her and she couldn't pull away. She didn't want to pull away. It felt too good to lean on him. For no reason she could name, Rachel wanted to stay in his arms forever. The years of fear and running had created a backlog of need; the close call with the bikes had opened the floodgates and she was having trouble bringing it all under control.

He turned her so that she was resting her head against his hard chest. It was an undreamt-of pleasure, soothing and warm. Feeling his hand stroke her back and cradle the back of her head was more comfort than she'd received in years. His touch was strong and gentle and, Lord, how she needed both. All the loneliness and need she had tried so hard to deny and ignore and suppress broke free and suddenly her throat ached and tears stung her eyes. Her shoulders shook with silent, unspeakable pain.

"Hey, it's okay," Mitch crooned, his lips in her hair, his arms still tightly around her. "Didn't anyone ever tell you that close calls don't count?"

Somehow, Rachel rallied enough to force her head upright, thankful all the way to her toes that she was wearing sunglasses to hide her eyes. She wasn't strong enough, however, to move away yet, or to brush Mitch's hands from her shoulders.

"Feel better?" he asked softly.

"No, actually. I feel like an idiot. I can't believe I did that. Me, who's always so careful, always warning Bonnie to look both ways. My God, what if she had been the one who got hurt?''

"Take it easy. No one got hurt, that's what counts. And Bonnie wasn't anywhere near the street.''

"But she could have been, for all I knew. What was I thinking of?''

"Cotton candy?'' he suggested, giving her shoulders a playful shake.

"Right, when I should have been thinking of Bonnie.''

"Stop blaming yourself for something that didn't happen," he ordered. "I was here to look out for Bonnie and Sheila, and you knew it.''

"Bonnie's not your responsibility,'' she snapped.

His smile faded. "I know that. She's yours. And for once you let someone else shoulder a little of that responsibility. Is that so wrong?''

"Yes," she retorted, finally finding the strength to shrug off his hands. "It is.''

She just couldn't tell him why. She couldn't tell him that letting someone else share her responsibility would mean letting that person close to her. It would mean letting down her guard. It would mean trusting and letting someone trust her in return, and that was something she could never do.

Chapter Seven

Mitch left Rachel's shortly after their late lunch. Reluctantly, since to his surprise, he was enjoying the day immensely. He was having fun watching the races and watching Bonnie and her friend playing with the dollhouse. Most of all, he was having fun just being with Rachel. Not until he was hiking back to the car did it occur to him that he hadn't thought even once about the stack of reports and other work awaiting him back home.

He hadn't wanted the day to end so soon, but he also didn't want to wear out his welcome. Besides, Rachel's mood had changed after the cotton candy incident. She had been shaken by her close call and he could understand that. But even after she had calmed down, the easiness that had been between them earlier was gone. She had remained distracted and distant, and when he suggested leaving, she hadn't protested.

It was almost, he thought now, as if she regretted those brief seconds she had spent letting him comfort her. No, more than regretted it. It was as if she blamed herself for needing comfort in the first place, and maybe she even blamed him for providing it. In some ways, she was a tough lady to figure out. In others, she was the most beguiling woman he'd ever known.

Maybe he was just a sucker for an air of mystery. Call it an occupational hazard. Whatever the reason, he was having a hard time keeping Rachel Curtis off his mind. And he had a hunch that the embrace they'd shared was only going to make the task more difficult.

True, the contact had been brief, and not even remotely sexual. Her body had rested against his delicately, almost reluctantly. For sure there had been none of the pressing, grinding contact that he'd been drawn to speculate about after the fact. For all its innocence, holding her had been the most powerful aphrodisiac he'd ever known.

What's more, he knew that for that minute or so, Rachel had liked having him hold her as much as he had liked having her in his arms. It had almost made him glad she had stepped off the curb just as that pack of riders was rounding the corner. He had a hunch that dragging Rachel into his arms was the only way he was going to get her there.

For sure, he couldn't envision himself dating her and progressing through all the increments of intimacy he associated with that, holding hands, a good-night kiss, working up to taking the chance of sliding his hand inside her blouse. He couldn't help thinking about that as he walked, imagining how soft and firm her breasts would feel, wondering if her body would be quick or slow to respond to his touch. As slow as cold honey, if you judged strictly by the signals she gave off. But something deep inside Mitch wasn't buying that. It told him that beyond all the prickly defenses Rachel had erected, waited something soft and hot and worth working for.

Rachel's demeanor wasn't the only reason he couldn't imagine them growing closer over a period of dating. He also couldn't imagine himself settling for a good-night kiss at her door. He already wanted more than that, much more, and based on the way he'd felt this afternoon, holding her in full view of Bonnie and her friend and hundreds of strangers, he suspected that it wouldn't be easy to stop touching Rachel once he got started.

Just thinking about it made him restless and edgy. He slid behind the wheel of the BMW and realized that the last thing he wanted to do was return to an empty house and read police reports. For sure he didn't want to end his first good day in a long time thinking about Mickey DelCosta. He frowned and whacked the steering wheel with his fist and thought about Rachel instead.

Before leaving, he'd insisted on carrying the dollhouse upstairs to Bonnie's room for her. Bonnie had thanked him all over again and for just a second as he was leaving he thought the little girl might barrel into his arms for a big hug. She'd hung back however, and Mitch couldn't help thinking, like mother, like daughter.

He wondered what they were doing now. What sort of things did mothers and little girls do on warm September afternoons? As neatly as A leads to B, that question led him to thoughts of his own kids, bringing with them the usual dose of guilt, as sharp and burning as a shot of whiskey on an empty stomach. What were Nicole and Becky doing right now, he wondered. Maybe Angie had even brought them here to watch the bike races today. It was the sort of thing she always used to nag him to do on the weekends. The sort of thing he'd never had time for. He sighed. More guilt.

He sat without starting the car and tortured himself by following that train of thought. What would have happened if they were here and he'd run into them? Nicole and Becky, along with Angie and her new husband. Their new

father. What was his name? Steve Bannon. That was it.
How could he have forgotten after writing so many checks
to the man?

Steve Bannon was Bannon Construction, the firm he'd
hired to renovate his kitchen, and steal his wife. Only the
second part hadn't been written into the contract. It had
just happened. That's what Angie told him anyway. No
matter how unhappy she'd been, she told him, she'd never
cheated on him before, never even considered it. Then
good old Steve Bannon had arrived on the scene, with his
tool belt slung low and his expert carpenter's hands, Mitch
thought bitterly, and she had offered him coffee, the way
any friendly housewife would have, and they had started
talking and somehow it had just happened.

Just happened, he mused, not feeling nearly as good as
he had a few minutes ago. Like an earthquake or a tidal
wave, it had just happened, destroying his life in the process.

He shook his head and curled his fingers over the wheel.
This wasn't getting him anywhere. Hadn't he done enough
rehashing of something that was over and done with to last
him several lifetimes? Yanking his keys from his pocket,
he started the engine with no more idea of where he wanted
to go than he'd had a few minutes ago, only a slightly bigger chasm in his gut, which all the thinking he did about
his lost family never seemed to fill.

So stop thinking about it, chided a voice inside, *and do
something about it.* But what? He could no longer pretend not to know the answer to that question. Rachel had
put it in terms so simple even a screwup of his magnitude
could understand. Stop worrying about what to say when
you get there and just go see them, she had told him.

Rubbing his jaw, Mitch thought about that frightening
prospect. Could he trust Rachel's advice? Did he have the
nerve to drive over there, walk up to the door alone, and
find out once and for all what place, if any, remained for

him in his little girls' lives? Well, he wouldn't be exactly all alone, he rationalized, glancing in the rearview mirror at the two buff-colored stuffed puppies, their black button eyes bright and eager as they stared back at him.

He'd tossed the stuffed toys he'd bought for Nicole and Becky into the car along with the dollhouse without really knowing why. Fate, he decided now, as he pulled away from the curb.

He found their new house without any trouble. He'd wondered if he could, since all the other times he'd driven by there had been after dark and after a few stiff drinks. Now he was thankful he'd never stopped as he'd intended on any of those other occasions. He had a lot to make up to the girls, six months of only occasional postcards for starters, but at least there weren't any ill-spoken words between him and their mother.

Angie and Mitch had parted on as amiable terms as could be expected under the circumstances. From the start he hadn't been able to argue with her assessment that he was suffering more from hurt pride than a broken heart. Wherever the pain had been located, however, it had still hurt like hell. And the fallout, the aftereffects on his work, had been just as devastating.

He recognized Angie's Toyota parked in the driveway, with the oversize pickup with Bannon's company logo parked behind it. Mitch pulled to the curb in front of a house located kitty-corner across the street. He didn't mind walking a few extra steps to their front door. In spite of Rachel's pep talk, he needed time to think of his opening argument. He smiled ruefully and corrected himself; he needed time to think of a way to say hello. And I'm sorry.

The house was a standard raised ranch, modest and neat and nowhere near as impressive as his own. But Mitch had long ago overcome the shock of knowing his wife had left him for a man with less money, less power, less every-

thing. No, that couldn't be right. Bannon obviously had
more of something, Mitch conceded, his ex-wife and kids,
for starters.

Twin baskets of yellow mums flanked the front door
and a bright-pink bicycle lay across the walk. With a sharp
tug of wistfulness, he wondered if Steve Bannon shouted
at the girls every time he tripped over it the way he used to.

He reached over the front seat for the stuffed toys,
gathering them in his right arm as he went to open the car
door with his left. Before he could step out, however, Nicole and Becky came dancing down the driveway toward
the truck, their long hair like golden-brown streamers behind them. Mitch's heart lurched, then pounded fiercely.

Nicole was still a couple of inches taller than her sister,
he noted, and Becky still had to be out in front no matter
what they were doing. They looked beautiful, he thought,
thanking God that they hadn't changed or grown up too
much in the months since he'd last seen them.

How could he have done it, he wondered with a rush of
self-contempt as he stared at them. How could he have
squandered one moment with them, much less all these
wasted months? And that didn't even begin to account for
the hours and days he'd squandered when they were young
and he was always busy. Hours and days that he could
never reclaim.

But at least he could claim those that lay ahead, he told
himself, his heart swelling with love for them. He would
take whatever he could get, whatever they and Angie
would allow him, he vowed. Even as he thought it, Angie
and Bannon came into view. Angie looked pretty much the
same, too, he thought.

She was dressed in jeans, her shirtsleeves rolled to the
elbow, her long dark hair loose and falling to her shoulders in soft waves. She looked good, and in spite of all that
was between them—or rather, what was no longer be-

tween them—he felt affection for her. The interesting thing was that that was all he felt.

Mitch took his hand off the door handle and watched as Bannon swung open the driver's-side door of the truck and lifted first Becky, then Nicole onto the seat. They were leaving, he thought frantically, torn between disappointment and the urge to get out and shout for them to stop. Of course, he didn't. He simply watched.

Bannon was tall and rugged and he lifted the girls as easily as if they were sacks of feathers, swinging them around before depositing them in the truck. Both girls threw back their heads and laughed. Bannon grinned at them and said something that made Angie laugh as well. It looked as if Mitch was the only one who didn't get the joke. But then, what else was new?

He saw Bannon turn to Angie, who circled his waist with her arms as he bent his head to give her a quick kiss. Then he swung into the driver's seat and slammed the door. Angie stood at the end of the driveway as he backed up the truck, waving until it was out of sight.

Watching, Mitch couldn't help wondering if she had ever stood and waved goodbye to him that way. It struck him that he had absolutely no idea. How could he? He'd never glanced back to see; he'd never been concerned with what he was leaving behind, only with where he had to be. He felt a sudden yearning for... what? Not the past. As badly as he felt, he couldn't pretend that was the case, any more than he could blame Angie for what had happened. He wasn't sure exactly what he yearned for or what he wanted, other than to see his kids again.

Unfortunately it didn't look as if that was going to happen today. He exhaled a deep breath he hadn't been aware of holding. He needed to get out of there. Angie turned to go back inside, but as she did so, she seemed to notice a dandelion growing at the edge of the lawn and walked over to yank it out. Same old Angie, he thought wryly. As she stood, she caught sight of Mitch's car.

His smile froze.

At first, she appeared startled to see him there, but she quickly broke into a familiar grin and started toward him.

Reluctantly Mitch stepped from the car.

"Hi, Mitch," she said, stopping a few feet away and suddenly looking as awkward as he felt, as if she had just remembered the exact nature of their new relationship.

What was the proper way to greet an ex anyway? he wondered. With a handshake? A kiss? Angie settled it by reaching out to tug the ear of one of the dogs he was still clutching beneath his right arm.

"Who are your friends?" she teased.

"What? Oh, these, they're dogs."

"So I see."

"Puppies actually. I thought—"

He broke off. What could he say? That he'd thought the girls might be happier to see him or forgive him more easily if he brought them a present? That he'd always thought buying things for people, even things they already had enough of, meant something, that it was a way to say all the things he wanted to and never did.

"I know," Angie said, a quiet understanding in her voice. "They're for the girls, right?"

Mitch nodded. "Yeah."

"I'm afraid you just missed them."

"I know."

Her brows lifted. "You were here when they left? Why didn't you say something? I'm sure they'd have rather seen you than gone to the store with their..." She halted, her gaze freezing. "With Steve."

The realization of what she'd been about to say—that they'd gone with their father—lodged like a knife in Mitch's chest.

"I guess I should have called first," he said, wondering how the hell to get out of there.

"It would save mix-ups in the future," she agreed.

"Right. I'll remember for next time."

"Thanks." She rocked on her heels and smiled at him. "So. How've you been?"

"Fine. Great."

"You look good. Tanned and healthy."

"I've been out on the boat."

She nodded. "Yes, we got your postcards. The girls liked the one of the monkey in the hot-air balloon."

That brought him a smile. "They did? Good. That's good."

Angie's expression grew solemn. "They miss you, Mitch." She cocked her head to the side, eyeing him with growing amazement. "You don't believe me."

Mitch found it difficult to speak, not only to find the words, but to get them out. "I want to," he admitted at last. "I want it to be true so damn bad, I guess maybe I'm afraid to believe it."

"Believe it," she countered. More softly, she added, "They miss you more than you'll ever know."

Mitch made a sound of disgust. "I can't imagine why. Or how. I was hardly ever there for them."

"I won't argue with that," she said, lips pursed wryly, "but you're still their father."

"Are you going to try to tell me that's all that counts?" he challenged.

She shook her head, not even a hint of a smile visible now. "No, that's not all that counts by a long shot. I'm afraid it all counts, Mitch, dance recitals and learning to ride a bike and bedtime stories."

"All the things I failed at."

"All the things you missed out on. Nicole and Becky still danced and heard stories and learned to ride bikes. They just did it all without you."

Her quiet words crystallized a truth that Mitch had been edging closer to for some time. In this tragic drama, he was the real loser.

"I really screwed up, didn't I?" he asked, his attempt at a smile doing little to hide his despair.

Angie smiled. "You're here now. Today. In the scheme of things that count, that counts most of all."

"Yeah, now I'm here and they're not."

"They'll be back. We're planning a barbecue and they went to pick up more rolls. Why don't you stay and join us? You know me, there's always plenty of food."

Mitch was stunned by her invitation. "But what will . . . your husband say?"

"Steve won't mind. He'll be glad, really. You know, he feels awkward about everything that happened."

He should, thought Mitch, but he resisted the urge to say so. It wasn't as hard to bite his lip as it would have been a year ago, even a few months ago. Another surprise.

"I know I've told you all of this before, but we didn't plan for any of this."

"I know. It just happened," he countered, unable to keep the edge of sarcasm from his voice. He could only go so far.

Angie ignored it. "That's right. And while we wouldn't change the way it turned out, I know Steve isn't proud of what happened. He'll be glad to see you . . ."

"Yeah, right," he interjected.

"I mean it. He'll be glad because it will be a chance to clear the air . . . for all our sakes."

"How about you?" he persisted. "How can you want me here? After some of the things I said."

She shrugged. "That was then. You were hurt and angry and I know how that feels. You were wondering what the hell happened to your life . . . hell, I was wondering the same thing. We both made mistakes and said things we wished we hadn't."

"I don't remember your saying anything all that bad . . . at least, nothing that wasn't true."

"Well, you should have heard what I was thinking about you."

Mitch leaned against the car, his arms clenching the toys. "I guess it was easier for me to blame you," he said, thinking back to the time of their divorce, "than to try to figure out what I did wrong. The way I saw it, I'd supported you and the kids, given you everything I thought you wanted, and you had just used me until someone more interesting came along." He met her slightly bemused gaze. "I remember telling you that as far as I was concerned you had just married a paycheck."

"I remember that, too," Angie replied. "Boy, did it make me mad."

"Good," he said with a short laugh. "That's what I wanted to do at the time."

"And now?"

He shrugged. "Now I'm not really sure what I want, but making you angry's not part of it anymore."

"What a relief." She grinned briefly. "You know, Mitch, you were wrong. I never saw you as a paycheck. But the reason it made me so angry when you said that was because, even if I had, it would have been because that's all you ever let me see. All you wanted me to see, a man who could buy me expensive cars and big houses and beautiful jewelry."

"What's so bad about that?" he demanded, exasperated.

"Nothing. Unless that's all there is between two people. For us, at the end anyway, that's all there was. I felt as if I was living with a total stranger."

"Come on, Angie. I admit I worked a lot of hours, too many maybe, but we lived in the same house, shared a bed . . . for God's sake, we had two kids together. We weren't strangers."

"Not literally," she replied, remaining unruffled, "but I always felt there were so many things I didn't know about you, and so many things you weren't interested in knowing about me."

"I was interested," he protested, "but I was busy."

"Steve's busy, too," she told him in a quietly matter-of-fact tone. "Heck, I'm busy, with the kids and house and my job at the florist, but we make time for each other...to find out what's happening with each other. You and I, we never did."

"I knew what was happening. You were home with the kids. And you knew where I was, either at the office or in court. It's not as if I ran around on you."

She sighed, shaking her head at him with a gentle smile. "You still don't get it. I'm not talking about an activity log. I'm talking about knowing someone, really knowing them, all the way to their soul, Mitch, knowing what they love and hate and dream about, knowing their secrets and their fantasies." She laughed at his perplexed expression. "All right, here's an example. We lived together all those years—tell me what I'm most afraid of in the whole world."

His frown deepened. He stared at her, trying to remember any time she'd ever been afraid of anything in their years together. She used to grumble about his long hours, but afraid? All he could think of was that one time in the garage at the old house.

"Mice," he said triumphantly.

"Wrong," she retorted. "By a long shot."

"Then what are you most afraid of?"

"It doesn't matter. I was simply making a point. If it makes you feel any better," she added, "I have no idea what you're most afraid of, either."

Somehow, it didn't make him feel any better at all.

"I'm sorry, I really didn't mean to drag up the past. How did we get off on that anyway? I know," she said, smiling, "I was asking you to stay for dinner and you were trying to find out if I really meant it.

"And I do," she continued. "Please believe that." She offered him her hand, laughing when she noticed she was still gripping the dandelion. Mitch found himself laughing with her as she tossed it toward the gutter.

"I'm willing to make a fresh start, if you are," she said.

Mitch closed his hand over hers to shake it, and the familiarity of her filled him with a warm feeling. Relief, he realized. He was relieved that he and Angie could talk without arguing.

"I'm willing, too," he told her.

"Then you'll stay?"

"I'm not sure about that, Angie. Maybe another time. You ought to check it out with the rest of the family first."

"I told you, Steve won't mind, and the girls will be thrilled, trust me. Do it for their sake, Mitch."

He nodded slowly. "Okay, I'll stay...even though I'm still not sure why you're doing it."

"Why? Because I'm finally happy," she said, and looking at her, Mitch could see that was the absolute truth. "And the only thing that would make me happier is for you to be happy, too. I think spending time with your children is one way to do that. So, maybe this will be a start."

"Maybe," Mitch agreed, his tone gruff and his heart hopeful.

He wasn't disappointed. If he could have scripted and directed the evening, it couldn't have turned out any better.

As he and Angie sat on the deck behind the house, drinking lemonade and waiting for them to return, he tried his best to ignore a worry that assailed him frequently— that somehow the girls would have forgotten all about him, that they wouldn't even recognize him when they got there, that they would hang back from him the way Bonnie did, that they would treat him as if he was a stranger. And that he deserved it.

But they did remember him.

"Daddy... Daddy's here," they squealed when they caught sight of him. They bolted across the deck and into his arms and Mitch had to fight back tears as he hugged them tightly. They wanted to show him their swing set and their rooms and the new moves they'd learned in gymnastics class, and Mitch wanted to see it all.

His other worry, that in spite of Angie's assurances, Steve Bannon would be annoyed or resentful of his presence, was equally unfounded. At first they were both awkward and nervous. Gradually, over the course of the evening, they grew more relaxed. They probably would never be friends, but the evening established that they could be civil and, for the sake of Nicole and Becky, they would. The fact that Steve would do that for children who were not even his own earned him Mitch's grudging respect.

It wasn't until Mitch was leaving that he even remembered to give the stuffed toys to the girls. They liked them, but their reaction to them didn't come close to the joy he'd seen in their faces when they'd walked in and seen him there. It was a lesson he was late in learning, but at least, thought Mitch, he was learning. For the first time in far too long, he got to kiss his kids good-night, and before he left he made plans to see them again. They were to have the following Monday off from school and he promised to take them sailing if the weather was good.

He climbed back into his car feeling better than he had in months, and he thought immediately of Rachel. He really owed it all to her. He never would have gone there to see the kids today if she hadn't urged him to and made him believe he could handle it. He owed her big time, and he wanted to make it up to her.

But how? Maybe flowers, he thought as he drove toward home. Roses, dozens of them. No, too flamboyant. Something more subtle. Daisies? In autumn? Maybe flowers weren't the way to go. Candy? Dumb. Perfume? Too cliché. And too personal.

He caught himself midway between a book and a simple gold bracelet. Damn, he was thick-skulled. Here he was doing it again... reducing everything to material terms. Rachel had helped him make peace with his kids and find a missing piece of himself. She'd given him a gift of the heart and that couldn't be repaid by writing a check.

So what could he do to show her how much he appreciated her help? What did Rachel need as much as he'd needed this visit with his kids?

The answer came to him immediately. As much as he needed to see his kids, she needed to get away from her own. She was a great mother and her love for Bonnie was obvious to anyone who saw them together, but that was the problem. They were always together, and when they weren't, Rachel was working. Angie was also a great mother, but as he'd told Rachel once before, he recalled that she needed some time for herself once in a while.

He had a feeling Rachel needed a breather now, only she refused to admit it. Her reaction to her near-calamity this afternoon only reinforced his opinion. Losing one's perspective was one of the first signs of stress. He ought to know. The more he thought about it, the more convinced he was. Rachel needed a break and whether she liked it or not, he was going to give it to her.

Arriving home, he went straight to the den, picked up the phone and called her.

"Hi," he said when she answered. Her voice was pitched low. Nice, he thought.

"Mitch?" she replied.

That was nice, too, having her recognize his voice.

"Yes. I'm not calling too late, am I?"

"No, no, not at all. I just tucked Bonnie into bed."

"Is that why you're whispering?"

"Am I whispering?"

"Uh-huh. I like it."

"Why? Do I usually shout?"

Mitch grinned and settled back in his chair, enjoying this. "No, I like your usual tone just fine, too, but whispering is sort of... intimate, don't you think?"

"I don't usually think about it."

"Maybe that's your problem."

"Assuming I have one."

"Of course."

"Is that what you called to talk about? My problems?"

"Is that my cue to get to the point?"

"Only if there is one," she said, chuckling. Mitch had a feeling she was making herself comfortable on the other end of the line.

"Actually there is. I called to thank you."

He explained about going to see the girls and about being invited to stay for dinner. Rachel was clearly thrilled for him. She wanted to know how it had gone and listened as he went into what he realized later was probably much too much detail. But she didn't fall asleep on him and she didn't sound the least bit bored and when he finished sharing the news with her, somehow he felt even better than he had earlier. Something he wouldn't have thought possible.

"I'm so glad it worked out so well for you," she said when they had discussed everything from Becky's scraped knees to the new wallpaper on their bedroom walls. "And I refuse to pass up this opportunity to say I told you so, so... I told you so."

"Why do I have the feeling you're sticking out your tongue as you say that?"

"Probably because I am."

"I dare you to try that when I'm around sometime."

There was an interval of very intense silence.

"Maybe I will," she said finally, softly. "Seriously, Mitch, I am happy for you. And I'm glad you called to tell me about it."

"Actually I also had another reason for calling." He wondered if he just imagined her catching her breath apprehensively, or if he already knew her well enough to predict her reactions. "I want to return the favor."

"What favor?"

"Come on, Rachel, you know as well as I do that I wouldn't have gone to see them today if not for your little pep talk."

"Maybe not today, but you would have gone eventually."

"That's my problem, I've had years of eventually. I needed a push and you gave it to me."

"So now you want to push me back?" she countered, her tone light.

"Drag you is more like it, I'm afraid. Kicking and screaming, if I have to, but I am going to take you out to dinner. Just the two of us. Tomorrow night."

"Mitch, that's really sweet of you, but I already told you that I..."

"Don't leave Bonnie with baby-sitters," he finished along with her.

"That's right."

"That's crazy."

"Just the same..."

"Just the same, you need a break once in a while. You need a night out."

"With you?"

"That's what I had in mind."

"Thanks, but..."

"No buts. Tell me your main objection to leaving Bonnie with a sitter."

"I just don't feel comfortable leaving her with someone I don't know."

"What if I could produce a sitter whom you do know?" he countered, prepared for her objection. "What if I could promise to deliver to your door tomorrow night a baby-sitter extraordinaire, someone you couldn't possibly object to. Would you have dinner with me then?"

"Mitch, I..."

"Answer the question, please."

"Yes, sir, counselor," she retorted, laughing. "I suppose that I would, yes."

"That's all I wanted to know. Be ready at seven-thirty."

"But..."

"Night, Rachel."

He didn't even replace the receiver in the cradle, just pressed the button for a dial tone and punched the number from memory. He'd called it often in the past few weeks, but never before on a personal matter.

"Hello?"

"Hello, Mrs. Hanson," he said. "This is Mitch Dalton."

"Oh, Mr. Dalton, hello."

He heard the tension that invaded her voice and very gently said, "I'm sorry, Mrs. Hanson, I don't have any news about the case. I'm calling about something else entirely... a personal matter."

"I see. What matter is that?"

"Do you remember when we were talking the other day at the store, and you told me the days are bearable, but the nights are so long for you now?"

"Of course, I remember, it's all too true."

"Well, I have a favor to ask of you, and if my hunch is correct, I just might be doing you a favor in the process."

She gave a soft chuckle. "You've piqued this old lady's curiosity, Mr. Dalton. Please, don't keep me in suspense."

"I won't, as long as you promise to say no if you're not feeling up to this or if you're simply not interested in what I'm about to suggest. Promise?"

"You have my word on it."

"Okay," Mitch said. "Here's the deal...."

Chapter Eight

Rachel couldn't believe she was alone in a car with a man. On a date, of all things. And with this man, in particular. The absolute wrong man for her, she reminded herself, not for the first time in the past twenty-four hours. Unfortunately Mitch Dalton was also the man who, for those same hours, had occupied her thoughts almost exclusively. There was something about him. Something alluring and irresistible . . . and dangerous.

She had promised herself that this was not going to happen. She was an adult. She didn't have to have dinner with him or do anything else she didn't want to do. The possibility that deep inside she did want exactly this, to be sitting next to Mitch as they drove to his favorite seaside restaurant, was something she'd rather not think about. Thinking about it made her crazy, and tonight, she needed to be in full control of all her senses.

All day she had planned and schemed and rehearsed her objections to any baby-sitter he could possibly produce, only to be struck dumb when she'd opened the door to find Mitch and a smiling Mrs. Hanson on her doorstep. She could hardly speak, much less object. Especially not after Mitch took her aside and explained how letting the older woman spend a few hours with Bonnie would be an act of kindness on Rachel's part. He told her that all the Hanson children and grandchildren were doing their best to keep her spirits up, but they were also suffering from the loss of a man they adored. They needed a break and Mrs. Hanson was looking forward to a fresh young face. Think of Mrs. Hanson, he urged.

Rachel was sick to her stomach. Not only was she on her first genuine date in years, but she was dating the man who could, and might yet, put her behind bars. Meanwhile, Bonnie was home alone with a nice old woman who just might get her to talk about things that would spell disaster. Was it a plot they had cooked up together? she worried briefly. A case of divide and conquer?

Something told her it wasn't. After her phone conversation with Mitch last night, she couldn't believe he had ulterior motives for asking her out. And Mrs. Hanson just wasn't the undercover type. That made her feel only marginally better, however. Even without plots and traps, there were plenty of ways that tonight could prove to be her undoing.

The Lighthouse Tavern was in the neighboring town of Falmouth. Without a car, Rachel had little opportunity to venture outside of Plymouth, and in spite of her anxiety, she savored the changing scenery along the way. Mitch had tuned the radio to a classical station, which also helped her to relax. By the time they turned into the restaurant parking lot, she was feeling a whole lot calmer. She was even looking forward to dinner. How long had it been since she'd eaten in a real restaurant with another adult?

She straightened the short black skirt she had worn with a black silk T-shirt and muted challis print jacket. At least she hadn't had to anguish over what to wear. Her wardrobe was limited, and geared toward time spent at work and playing Mom. When it came to dressing up, this was it. Mitch was wearing khaki slacks and a navy blazer over a lighter blue shirt and strangely, he struck Rachel as being even more dressed up than when he was wearing a suit. There was something about the unmistakable look of a man who had just showered and shaved, the scent of subtle after-shave still clinging to his skin, that was very appealing, especially when you knew he'd done it just for you.

The car's tires crunched on the crushed shell drive as Mitch pulled into a spot facing the water. A light breeze ruffled the ocean, creating small, moonlight-kissed swells on its surface. Even with the windows rolled up, a slight bite of sea tang spiced the air.

Behind them, Rachel glimpsed the flicker of candlelight inside the tavern, prompting a memory of her former life, of good food and fine wine and leisurely evenings spent with friends. In spite of the fact that it wasn't safe to categorize Mitch as a friend, she suddenly found herself looking forward to the next couple of hours more than she would have dreamed possible.

Mitch turned off the car's engine. They'd spoken only intermittently on the ride there, both lost in their own thoughts. When they had spoken it had been trivial. Mitch had pointed out landmarks they passed en route and told her about his favorite dishes on the menu at what he described as his favorite restaurant anywhere.

Now he turned to her, a hint of wry amusement lurking behind his solemn expression. "I have to confess," he said, "that I'm a little rusty at this dating stuff."

Her lips curved in rueful understanding. "Me too. Want to start a club?"

"I think I'd rather get in some warm-ups, if you don't mind."

"Warm-ups?" she countered, growing curious. The dark, feral gleam in his eyes and the lazy way he stretched his arm across the back of her seat sent a quiver of anticipation through her.

"That's right. Warm-ups. The thing I remember best about dating is also the thing I hated most."

"What was that?"

"Waiting?"

Rachel arched her brows. "I beg your pardon?"

"Waiting for the climax."

"I wouldn't hold my breath if I were you," she said with sweet finality.

"Not that kind of climax," he told her, a smile of amused admiration shaping his wide, full lips.

Why was she suddenly obsessed with staring at his mouth? Rachel wondered.

"I meant the climax of the evening...the moment when you walk your date to her door and find out if she's going to let you kiss her good-night and if she does, how good a kisser she is. Did you ever wonder that?"

"I never walked a date to his door," she replied. "But I suppose I did speculate on technique a time or two in the past."

"A woman after my own heart. So," he continued as so much electricity raced through Rachel she was surprised she wasn't lighting up the entire parking lot, "for the sake of relieving both our curiosity so we can enjoy dinner...come here."

Rachel cocked her head. It had been a long time, granted, but she never had been easy.

"It was your idea," she said. "You come here."

He did, leaning over the space between the bucket seats and taking her face in his hands. He bent his head slowly, watching her, watching the excitement Rachel was certain was dancing in her eyes, only closing his in the last heartbeat before his mouth claimed hers.

There was no other word for it...he claimed, possessed, controlled. It was like no good-night kiss she had ever experienced at the end of a date. This kiss wasn't the end of anything...other than her illusion that she could keep this night—and this man—under control. For the duration, she felt like occupied territory, uncertain only whether he had conquered or she had surrendered.

He kissed her slowly, lightly, thoroughly, as if learning the shape and texture and nuances of her mouth was all he had to do for the rest of his life. Gradually the kiss grew deeper and harder and Rachel was leaning forward, kissing him back, her arms finding their way around his neck. Finally, gently, he lifted his head, leaving her wanting more, his stormy gaze telling her in no uncertain terms that he wanted the same.

Rachel spoke first, in an effort to defuse the tension they had generated. "So, did you find out what you wanted to know?"

He unfurled a slow, wicked grin, for a second looking exactly the way she imagined the teenage Mitch who'd waited through dates wondering about the good-night kiss had looked.

"Sure did. You let me...and you're good. Damned good."

His fingers tightened around the back of her neck as he dipped his head for seconds.

Rachel stopped him with a palm flat against his approaching chest.

"Uh-uh," she said with a smile. "I only kiss once on the first date."

Mitch frowned. "Once? But what about..."

She didn't wait to hear his question, or for him to come around and open her door. Swinging it open for herself, she stepped out of the car and into the crisp night air. She was sure he was asking what about later...and she didn't have any answers.

When he met her at the back of the car, he was grinning.

"We'll see about that" was all he said.

Dinner was as good as Mitch had promised. The atmosphere at the Lighthouse Tavern was rustic and relaxed. He ordered a mellow white wine, reminding Rachel of one more thing she was doing tonight for the first time in a long time, drinking wine. He also recommended the lobster casserole. The only flaw in the entire evening, reflected Rachel several times, was in his innovative variation on dating tradition.

Mitch's theory was wrong. Dispensing with the goodnight kiss at the start of the evening did nothing to lessen her anticipation... or prevent the stomach flutters that resulted. If anything, the kiss in the car had stirred her imagination and funneled the prospect of what was to come to the front and center of her thoughts. Regardless of her teasing remark about allowing only one kiss on a first date, she couldn't help looking forward to being in his arms again. Her mind kept wandering ahead to the end of the evening, and by the time dessert arrived, she could no longer feign indifference, not even to herself. She wanted Mitch to kiss her again.

After settling the check, he smiled at her across the table.

"Time to go," he said, his voice pitched low in a seductive way that told her his mind hadn't been riveted on the lemon mousse, either.

Rachel half expected him to make a move the instant they were alone in the car. After all, if she was feeling like a teenager, maybe he was, too. He didn't, however, and her anticipation continued to mount as they drove, edging steadily toward impatience. By the time they arrived back at her place, her entire body was humming, ready, eager.

Again he surprised her by getting out of the car without so much as touching her. She wet her lips nervously as he opened her door and when he placed his hand lightly on her back as they climbed the porch steps, she felt his touch all the way to her curled toes.

Now, now, she thought, as he held open the door for her to enter first. Make that now or never, since Mrs. Hanson was waiting upstairs for Mitch to drive her home. But he let her pass and followed her inside. She was beginning to think that he had taken her earlier warning too literally, or that she was rustier than she thought at reading signals and he simply wasn't interested. No, she decided, no woman was ever that rusty. The way he'd been looking at her all evening sent a message that was the same at any age and in any language. Mitch Dalton was definitely interested.

Confirmation of that came a second later. As she placed one foot on the first step, he caught her from behind, his arm curling around her waist to pull her back against him. The sudden contact with his hard, masculine body was all it took to overheat the longings already simmering inside Rachel. The longing to be held . . . to be touched . . . to be loved.

He turned her slowly so that she was facing him. Watching her with hooded eyes, he backed up until he was leaning against the door behind him, their only point of contact his fingertips resting lightly on her shoulders.

"This time," he whispered roughly, irresistibly, "you come here."

Standing there, waiting for her to do his bidding, he looked darkly handsome and cocky and overwhelmingly male. For so long, her life, her whole world, had been so totally devoid of any male presence, that his effect on her was magnified, like the wine she'd sipped with dinner. Her eyes shimmering with pleasure and expectation, she moved toward him.

With one arm he drew her even closer, with the other he reached to flick off the hall light, leaving them in near darkness. Only for an instant did Rachel even consider what the neighbors would think if any of them should come upon them right now. Then Mitch was kissing her and all thoughts of neighbors and Mrs. Hanson and tomorrow drifted out of reach, like helium-filled balloons on a windy day.

Their mouths came together as explosively as a match and dry timber. Their kiss exploded in the darkness, rough and raw and endless. They panted for breath, sipping air from each other. Rachel heard her own small whimpers of delight, interwoven with Mitch's coarser sounds of surprise and hunger.

Her arms stole around his waist, clinging for support in a world that seemed to be spinning around her. Her senses drummed with forgotten desire. She'd forgotten how it felt to kiss like this. No, that was wrong, she thought in spite of the sensations clouding her concentration. She couldn't have forgotten because she'd never before been kissed quite like this. She'd never felt like this. Hot and shivery at once, racing and floating, with no idea of where she was going and even less of how to stop. She felt out of control. She felt wonderful.

Mitch's hands moved over her body like a sheet of velvet, everywhere at once. The skimming pleasure of his touch blurred her senses. Her spine, her throat, the back of her thighs . . . he was bringing her to life bit by bit. Her own hands kneaded the ridged muscle of his back, thrilling to the feel of pure, rampant masculinity.

Only vaguely was she aware of him lifting her into his arms and turning so that when her feet touched the floor once more, it was her back against the door and Mitch's hard, hot body holding her there with the pressure of his hips and the sure, steady caress of his hands.

"Rachel . . . Rachel," he breathed against the ultrasensitive skin of her throat.

She arched her neck, breathless, trembling, wanting . . . more and more and more.

His rough chuckle close to her ear was her first warning that she had made the demand out loud.

"Ah, baby, I want more, too," he whispered. "I want all of you . . . right now. Unfortunately this isn't the right time or place."

Rachel froze, suddenly vividly aware of the fact that he had scrunched her knit skirt all the way to her waist and had his hand resting between her thighs.

"My God, what am I doing?" she muttered. She felt him go still.

"Nothing to merit that tone of despair," Mitch countered.

"Maybe not for you," she snapped. "But I don't do this sort of thing."

"Well, I didn't plan it, either, if you want to get technical."

The cynic in her snorted as she pulled away and yanked her skirt back into place.

"It's true," he told her. "I didn't expect this to happen when I started this."

"What did you expect?"

"A good-night kiss. All right, maybe a few kisses, maybe a little more. I sure as hell didn't expect to wind up so hard I can hardly walk and damn close to taking you right there against your front door."

"That never would have happened," she said through gritted teeth.

He snapped on the light, pinning her with a long, speculative gaze. "If you say so," he said at last, sounding every bit as unconvinced as he looked. "But one thing you can't deny. This thing between us . . ."

"There is no thing between us," she interjected, a little too desperately to be taken seriously. "Nothing. Do you hear me?"

"I hear. I just don't agree. There's plenty between us, Rachel, and there'll be more. I promise you that. There's been something there since the first day I walked into your kitchen. And what almost happened tonight just proves that it's not your ordinary, run-of-the-mill attraction.'' He reached out and ran his fingers through her hair, using his hold to make her look him in the eye. ''When it happens, the first time is going to be fast and furious.''

''Don't count on it,'' she said, giving her jacket an efficient tug.

Mitch gave her another of his sardonic smiles. ''Whatever you say.''

''I say that Mrs. Hanson probably heard us pull up and she's wondering what we're doing down here all this time.''

''Mrs. Hanson has lots of kids and grandkids. I'll bet she's not wondering at all.''

''I still think we should get up there.''

He indicated the stairs. ''Ladies first.''

Rachel nearly snorted a second time. At the moment, she didn't particularly feel like a lady. She went first just the same, somehow managing to climb the stairs at a dignified pace, in spite of the knowledge that she was wearing a very short, tight skirt and that Mitch was lagging a deliberate three paces behind. She would have yelled back, ''How's the view?'' except she was afraid he'd tell her.

Mrs. Hanson was in the kitchen, rinsing out her teacup when they walked in.

''You don't have to do that,'' Rachel admonished. ''It's enough that you stayed with Bonnie so I could have an evening out.''

The older woman finished drying the cup. ''Force of habit,'' she said, returning the dish towel to its rack. ''In my day I did dishes for eight every night, with no dishwasher, either. One little old cup isn't any trouble at all.''

She asked about their evening and afterward gave a quick rundown of the games she and Bonnie had played and the stories they'd read. She had tucked Bonnie in at eight and hadn't heard a peep from her since.

"I'm the one who should be thanking you for an evening out," she told Rachel. "Bonnie is such a sweet little girl."

"Thank you. I think so, too," Rachel replied, studying the other woman's expression and demeanor for any hint that something she'd seen or heard here had aroused her suspicion about Bonnie. There was nothing, and Rachel released a silent sigh of relief.

She thanked Mitch for dinner and he left with Mrs. Hanson, his goodbye to her so properly casual no one would suspect that just minutes ago they had been going wild in each other's arms. Only after they were gone did Rachel have time to consider the erotic prediction he'd made downstairs, about their first time together being fast and furious.

He was wrong, she thought with more regret than she would ever acknowledge to him. Their first time wouldn't be fast or furious. It wouldn't be, period.

She locked the door and turned out the light over the sink. For them there wouldn't be... couldn't be a first time. Events of the past few years had forced her to learn to be secretive and—when it was necessary—even duplicitous. But there was no way she could learn to go to bed with a man—a man she could easily care about—and lie to him the whole time. That's what it would be if she let herself become involved with Mitch... one lie after another, one long, cruel lie.

She didn't want that, for either of them. And that's why not only wouldn't there be a first time for them... there couldn't even be a next time.

Mitch sat at the rudder and swung his gaze across the horizon. The day was perfect, warm and sunny with just enough wind, and there was no prettier sound in the world than the blend of lapping surf and his daughters' laughter. It felt strange to be so content.

He had forgotten what the sight of the sea spread out before him could be like, tranquil and restless at the same time. It was one of the main reasons he'd bought a sailboat in the first place. He hadn't even known how to sail at the time. Hell, he hadn't even known fore from aft. Where he'd come from, there were no yacht clubs, no tennis courts, no polo matches. You played hoop at the playground and you ran penny-ante scams when you needed a stake and you hoped you didn't get caught at it.

The first time he set foot on a sailboat was when an opposing attorney had invited him to go sailing after they'd wrapped up a particularly grueling case. He'd accepted because it had seemed the right thing—the advantageous thing—to do. That was the first time he'd seen the sea from this vantage point, an endless expanse of shimmering blue glass, and he'd been enthralled. Out here, alone, anything seemed possible.

Possibilities, that's what the sea represented to him. Back when he'd bought the boat, the only possibilities he'd cared about were work related. He used to come out here all by himself and chart the course of his professional life. Of course, at the time, he thought ruefully, he'd been convinced he had everything else in his life aced. Live and learn.

Somehow, down in the Keys, the sea had never looked as clear to him or as filled with possibilities. He'd sat there day after day, staring at it, trying not to look back and being unable to look ahead. That had all changed now. He was once again seeing possibilities in the ever-shifting currents, and at the moment, every one he saw looked an awful lot like Rachel.

He grinned as he recalled the night before, darting a glance over his shoulder as if Nicole and Becky, busy playing on the deck a few yards away, could read his mind. It was a good thing they couldn't, he thought. His memories of last night were strictly private, and absolutely amazing. The whole night had been pretty amazing. Most amazing of all was Rachel, the way she had felt against him, the way she had heated and melted in his arms, the way she had made him feel. Alive. Really alive and hungry for something besides his own miserable solitude.

He wanted to make love to her, to be sure, but he wanted much more than that. He wanted to talk to her and listen to her talk and get to know everything about her. He suddenly understood what Angie had been trying to tell him the other night, about the closeness she and Bannon shared, and which they never had. He'd never even known it was missing in his marriage, never believed such intimacy was possible. He believed it now, however, and he believed that just maybe, he had a shot at it with Rachel.

Possibilities.

He and the girls had set out at ten that morning and even though the sun wasn't as strong as it was during the summer, by two o'clock he figured they'd had enough. He didn't want to bring them home from their very first father-daughter excursion with sunburns. They docked in town and grabbed lunch at a fast-food place with a playground before he drove them home.

He'd purposely left his beeper ashore that morning, something he would never have even considered doing as recently as a few days ago, and he wasn't at all surprised to see the red light on his answering machine flashing when he walked into the house. There were a dozen messages divided between Darlene and Ollie, all with the same general drift: he was to call Ollie as soon as he emerged from whatever hellhole had swallowed him off the face of the earth. Eloquent guy, his sidekick.

"Where the hell have you been?" Ollie demanded as soon as he heard it was Mitch on the line. "Never mind, I don't have time to hear it. I've got news for you."

Ollie's tone was as effective as a cold shower, washing off the effects of the day spent daydreaming in the sun. "About DelCosta?"

"No, about your mysterious mommy."

Mitch frowned. "Who?"

"Curtis, Rachel J., that's who. You asked me to run a make on her, remember?"

"And you did. Came up empty, you told me."

"So I did, at least on the preliminary. But you know what you taught me, that when you know you've got the right guy, there's no such thing as a dead end, that the piece you're looking for is always there somewhere, you just have to look harder and harder until you find it."

"Are you telling me you've found something on Rachel?"

"I started by going back to square one," Ollie replied, obviously too caught up in his dissertation on strategy to answer Mitch's question directly. "I went back over every word in the police report, every transcript of every interview, every—"

"You get a gold star, Ollie," Mitch interrupted, his stomach knotting tighter and tighter with each passing second. "Now will you just tell me what the hell you found out?"

"I found out that Rachel Jennifer Curtis's social security number was just issued a year and a half ago. Struck me as a little odd for a twenty-nine-year-old woman to wait all that time to apply for something you need to get a job or file tax returns or—"

"I get the picture," he snapped, stomach churning now. His hand holding the receiver was sweating, the other curled into a tight fist.

"You know what this means, don't you, Mitch?"

"I know what it means." He swallowed hard, trying and failing to clear the bitter taste from his mouth. "It means she's not who she said she is."

"Right. I checked, and who she says she is, Rachel Curtis, died in a car accident in Bloomington, Indiana, in 1968. At the ripe old age of five."

Mitch didn't really need to hear any more. It was a classic identity switch. People looking to lose their old identity, for whatever reason, traveled to a new town, scanned the local newspaper records for the death notice of someone of their sex, who would have been around their current age had they lived. They then paid five bucks to city hall for a copy of that individual's birth certificate and used it to apply for a driver's license and social security number and like magic, they became that other person. In this case, one Rachel Jennifer Curtis.

"And you were the one who first smelled something wrong there, pal." Ollie was crowing on the other end of the line. "You had her pegged from day one."

"Yeah, I sure did."

"And now you've got her."

"Right, now I've got her. The question is," he said, rubbing the heel of his hand against his eye sockets, "who the hell is she?"

"Why don't I send a police car out there to pick her up and bring her—"

"No," Mitch ordered without really knowing why. Ollie was right. Bringing her in for questioning was the fastest way to find out what they wanted to know. But at the moment he wasn't interested in the fastest way. He was interested in pulling himself together and arming himself with as much ammunition and protection as he could before he had to face her.

"Is the lab downtown still open?" he asked Ollie, glancing at his watch.

"I think so. If not, there'll be someone on call. What do you have in mind."

"Running some prints."

Ollie sounded impressed. "You got her prints?"

"Yeah. They're on a cup at my office. I'll swing by there and pick it up and be in the city as soon as I can."

He dropped the receiver into the cradle and grabbed his keys. His thoughts weren't pretty as he headed for the car. The last time he had DelCosta on the ropes he'd lost him by letting his personal life get in the way, and he'd just come damn close to doing it again.

Nice going, Dalton. It takes a real screwup to make the same mistake twice.

Chapter Nine

The ringing of the telephone pulled Rachel from the mystery she was reading. She glanced at her watch, surprised to see that it was only seven o'clock. That meant she'd been reading for a mere twenty minutes. Time was crawling today. All day she'd had the feeling she was simply filling empty hours. And the reason the hours felt so empty, she realized with dismay, was that Mitch wasn't there to share them. Not at all a good sign.

She reached for the phone, picking it up on the fourth ring.

"Hello, Rachel," said a deep, familiar voice in response to her hello.

She felt a jolt of excitement. "Hello, Mitch, I didn't expect to hear from you today."

"Really? Why not?"

"I thought you'd be busy," she explained, puzzled by the odd flatness of his tone. "I remember you said that you were taking the day off to take your daughters sailing."

"I did," he said shortly. "But when we got back I checked in with the office and found something waiting that just couldn't be put off."

"I see. No rest for the weary, hmm?"

"Something like that. Look, Rachel, I need to see you. Can I come over?"

"Now?"

"Yes. It's not that late."

"No, I know it's not, but I'm not sure it's such a good idea for us to see each again so soon." She took a deep breath, summoning her prepared spiel. "The fact is, after last night, I'm not sure it's a good idea for us to see each other again, period."

She wasn't sure, but he seemed to make a sound somewhere between a grunt and a laugh before replying.

"The reason I want to see you has nothing to do with last night, Rachel. It's business."

"Business?" She went cold all the way to her fingertips. "What sort of business?"

"The Hanson case."

"But, I thought . . ."

"You thought what?" he prompted when she hesitated.

Rachel attempted a laugh. "I thought I was no longer a suspect, counselor."

He didn't laugh in response. "You know us prosecutor types," he said. "Until the final gavel, everyone is suspect. I have a few mug shots I'd like to show you."

"Mitch, I've told you over and over I didn't see anything that day."

"No, but maybe you'll recognize one of these men from seeing them around town . . . or somewhere."

"I suppose I could take a look," she conceded uneasily, "if you think it will help."

"I wouldn't ask if I didn't."

"Okay, then, come on over."

He arrived about thirty minutes later. Rachel was torn between excitement at the prospect of seeing him and a gnawing premonition that she had unleashed something she might not be able to control. She'd been right in her decision not to see Mitch again, and tonight of all nights she should have stuck to it. The apartment was silent as she waited, dividing her time between pacing nervously and checking her reflection in the bathroom mirror. Not that it mattered how she looked, she chided herself, even as she changed into her favorite sweater, an oversize fisherman knit, and brushed some blush on her cheeks. Primping simply gave her something to do besides pace. And worry.

She smiled as she let him in, icily aware that Mitch made no effort to return it. He was dressed in jeans and a navy crewneck sweater and she was struck by a disorienting urge to fall into his arms. Perhaps the only reason she resisted was that in spite of his casual attire, his manner was all business. Rachel wasn't sure if that was more of a relief or a disappointment. Okay, so a small part of her had been hoping that his mug shot story was just a way around her announcement that she didn't think they should see each other. Clearly that was not the case.

His gaze skirted the kitchen and the hallway leading to the bedrooms.

"Has Bonnie gone to bed already?" he asked, turning to her.

"No. She's not here."

His eyes narrowed. "Where is she?"

Rachel folded her arms across her chest, flashing a perplexed frown at his sharpness. "She's spending the night at Sheila's."

At last he smiled, if you could call the tight slant of his lips a smile. Rachel almost preferred his scowl.

"That's quite an about-face, isn't it?"

"What do you mean?"

"I mean a few days ago, you went crazy at the thought of letting the kid out of your sight and now she's staying out all night."

"Sleeping at a friend's house is hardly the same as staying out all night."

"She's still not here."

"No, she's not . . . and the fact is I'm not wild about the idea."

"Then why did you let her go?"

"Not that I owe you an explanation, but I let her go because her class is going on a field trip first thing in the morning and Sheila's mother is one of the chaperons. It made sense for Bonnie to stay there and be driven to school early with Sheila." She shrugged, but her green eyes still flashed defensively. "Besides, after Sheila was allowed to spend the night here, it was hard to refuse their invitation."

"I see."

"I'm so relieved that you do," she drawled sarcastically. "I believe you said you had something to show me?"

He nodded. "Mug shots."

He took a step toward her and Rachel stiffened and moved away. His lips curled. "Relax, I'm just going to turn on the light so you can see better."

"I'll do it," she snapped, reaching for the light switch. Personally she preferred the soft glow from the light over the sink to the stark white fluorescent light that now filled the kitchen, reminding her of the interrogation scenes in old gangster movies.

"Have a seat," he directed.

Shooting him another sardonic look, Rachel slipped into one of the chairs at the kitchen table. "I know this is going to be a waste of time."

"Don't be so sure. You might recognize one of the men in these photos."

"But if you know who killed Mr. Hanson and you've already arrested his accomplice, what's the point?"

"Just covering all the bases," he said, his dark gaze holding hers.

"Is it my imagination," she asked, head tipped to one side as she gazed up at him consideringly, "or are you a little tense tonight?"

He pinned her with his gaze. "It's your imagination." Opening the manila envelope in his hand, he removed a stack of photos. Rachel was surprised to see that they were grainy, like images transmitted by fax machine. He placed the pile on the table in front of her.

"Just take your time," he instructed. "Look at one photo at a time and tell me if you've ever seen the man before. Around town, at the Y, the beach... anywhere."

She stared at the first photo and shook her head. "Nope."

She went through the next three as quickly as she dared. Although she knew there was absolutely no way she could help him and become further involved, she didn't want to be accused of not making an effort. As she flipped over each photo, she shook her head, and then suddenly she turned to the next shot and it wasn't another stranger staring up at her, but her brother-in-law, Randy Parnell, and the explosion of panic inside her sucked all the air from her lungs.

She jerked her head up to look at Mitch and the intense, smug way he was watching her told her this was no mistake and no coincidence.

"You bastard," she cried, shoving the photos away from her, sending Randy's smirking face floating to the floor. "You set me up."

"Wrong. You set yourself up, Rachel." He grabbed her arm as she lurched to her feet, knocking over her chair in the process. "Where do you think you're going?"

"To open the door. I want you out of here."

"Too bad. Because what you want is no longer a consideration. That's the problem with being a fugitive."

"I am not a fugitive," she snapped, still struggling to free herself.

"The hell you aren't." The look in his eyes was one of cold fury. "That's exactly what you are, lady. You're wanted in Florida on charges of kidnapping, conspiracy to kidnap and a half-dozen other incidental offenses . . . shall I run them all down for you?"

Rachel went still, defeated. There was no way she could win a physical contest with him, and no way she could talk herself out of this since he obviously knew everything.

He relaxed his grip without letting her go, but the tension emanating from him assured her that if she even thought of bolting he'd have her slammed against the wall before she moved an inch. Rachel felt more like crying than she ever had before in her life.

"Every damn thing you told me was a lie," he said, an accusing sneer hardening his handsome face.

"Not everything," she protested wearily.

He snorted. "Oh, no? Well, let's see . . . your name is a lie, that's one thing. You don't come from Indiana and you were never married to a Naval officer who died in a car accident, or to anyone else, for that matter, and last but not least, you, the woman I was stupid enough to think was one of the greatest mothers of all time, who I was stupid enough to let give me advice about my own kids, you aren't any kind of mother at all . . . right?" When she simply stared at the floor in silence he shook her hard. "Isn't that right . . . Rene?"

Rene. It had been so long since anyone had called her by that name, her real name, that it no longer felt real or even familiar. Somewhere along the way, she had ceased to be Rene Lacroix and had become Rachel Curtis. Just as she had stopped pretending to be Bonnie's mother and had become a mother to her, with all of a mother's instincts and worries and love. Ironically it wasn't until this moment, when it was all about to come to a terrible end, that she really understood the significance of that.

Even now, thoughts of Bonnie and what was going to happen to her overrode everything else she was feeling and thinking. And suddenly all the tears of grief and fear and loneliness that she had managed to suppress since that awful moment when she first learned that Donna was dead came seeping forth.

"Can it," Mitch growled. "If you think you can cry your way out of this, you're crazy."

Rachel lifted her shoulder to wipe her eyes on her sleeve as best she could with him holding her wrists. Damn him. Her eyes flashed angrily as she snapped her head up to meet his gaze.

"I have no intention of trying to cry my way out of anything," she retorted. "I'd say the next move is yours."

Except for a flicker of surprise in his dark eyes, his expression didn't change. He stared at her stonily.

"Why?" he asked at last. "Why the hell would you take a little girl—a baby, for heaven's sake—away from her own father? I mean, were you sick? Grief-stricken? Frustrated because you didn't have a husband and family of your own? What? What the hell would make you do it?"

She shook her head, her faint smile bitter as the familiar accusations poured over her, stinging old wounds.

"Yeah, I was sick," she snarled. "Sick and frustrated from trying to get someone to listen to me ... to listen to reason and truth even if it came from someone who didn't grease the right palms and make hefty contributions to all the right campaigns."

"What are you talking about?"

"I'm talking about Randy Parnell ... the man whose picture you came running over here with and used to trap me," she said, her voice rising as she thrust her chin toward the spot where the photo lay faceup on the floor.

"Bonnie's poor, wronged daddy... the bastard who murdered my sister."

"Your sister drowned in her backyard swimming pool," he countered flatly. "Accidental death."

Rachel jerked her hands free. "Accidental bull. It's true that Donna drowned in that pool, but it was no accident, believe me. Randy murdered her."

"Do you have proof of that?"

"Not the kind of proof needed to convince the powers that be in a town that Randy and his family own practically lock, stock and barrel. I'm not even sure what kind of proof would convince them. Based on what I went through down there, I could have had pictures of him holding her head underwater and they probably would have said she was trying to implicate poor old Randy in a suicide attempt."

"If you don't have any proof..."

"I didn't say I don't have any proof. I said I don't have what it would take to convince a sheriff and a judge who don't want to be convinced...who don't want to hear that the son of their golfing buddy is a drunk and a child abuser and a cold-blooded killer." She met his gaze, trembling under the sweet familiarity of it, and against her will felt the anger in her turning to entreaty. "Oh, Mitch, please believe me. I know he did it, I know he murdered my sister."

He dragged his fingers through his hair, never taking his eyes off her as expressions of anger and frustration and reluctance flickered across his face, one after the other. "Tell me what you know," he ordered finally. "Everything."

Rachel took a deep breath, shuddering. This was what she had prayed for all this time, someone willing to listen to her side of the story. Now at last she had it and she didn't know where to start.

Slowly and in slightly jumbled fashion, she began, telling Mitch about Donna, her baby sister, about how she had always been the strong one who looked out for Donna, about how growing up with a stepfather who liked to use his fists, they had both needed someone to look out for them. And she told him about the scars and the determination that kind of abuse created, and about the bonds it forged between victims. She told him about the unbreakable bond between her and Donna, a bond that would cause her to make any sacrifice, break any law...to do what she had done.

Finally she told him about the day Donna had come running to her house with her baby daughter, looking for a place to hide from another man who liked to get drunk and hit women. Her own husband, this time. Tears burned Rachel's eyes and slid down her cheeks as she described her sister's terror, for herself and her baby, and as she recalled for him the physical scars and bruises Donna had been so ashamed to reveal even to her own sister.

She crossed her arms tightly across her chest as she recounted how she had encouraged Donna's decision to leave Randy, and how she had let herself be talked out of going along with her when she returned home to tell him. Her anguish became mixed with guilt and gradually with anger as well, as she told about Donna's parting request that Rachel take care of her baby if anything happened to her and about the frantic early morning phone call from her mother informing her that Donna was dead.

"You ask me if I have proof that she didn't drown accidentally?" she said. "I have the best proof in the world...right here," she said, clasping her right hand over her heart. "I knew Donna better than anyone...I know she had made up her mind that she had to get away from Randy for her baby's sake as well as her own. She wasn't about to be sweet-talked by him this time...she didn't go home that night for some rough sex and skinny-dipping in the backyard, which is how the coroner explained her condition.''

''I know this must have hit you hard,'' Mitch said. ''But face it, Rachel, they were husband and wife. It's feasible that he did manage to sweet-talk her as you say and—''

''No,'' she cut in, shaking her head. ''It's not feasible. For one thing, they never found any sort of robe or cover-up by the pool.''

Mitch's mouth quirked. ''As I said, they were married and—''

''And Donna was still trying to lose the weight she gained when she was pregnant. Even if she had gone skinny-dipping with her husband willingly—which I know in my heart she didn't—she wouldn't have walked out there without a robe... and she wouldn't have taken the chance on someone dropping by—as the Parnells were wont to do—without having a cover-up handy.''

''Maybe she didn't walk out there,'' he suggested impatiently. ''Maybe they were talking out there by the pool and they got...carried away. It happens,'' he said, his eyes going smoky in a way that told her he was recalling the way they had gotten carried away downstairs in the hallway the other night.

Rachel ignored the spark that the memory stirred in her. ''It didn't happen that way,'' she said resolutely. ''If it had, they would have found Donna's clothes by the pool, but they didn't. They never found the clothes she was wearing when she left my house at all. That's because Randy got rid of them.''

''And why did he do that?''

''My theory is that when Donna told him she was leaving, he got crazy mad at her. I think he had to get rid of her clothes afterward,'' she explained in a soft, calm tone, ''because he ripped them and he raped her and then he murdered her.''

She didn't cry as she said it. She didn't even flinch. Only when she finished speaking did her eyes flicker shut briefly and she swallowed hard, the flexing of the muscles in her slender throat the only hint of how desperately she was struggling for control.

For Mitch, it was as effective as being hit with a sledge-hammer. Much more effective than a dramatic display of emotion would have been. This woman had lied to him and misled him from the start, and yet, at that moment, after listening to her talk about herself and her sister, he was knocked out by her strength and her integrity.

He'd walked in here a little while ago armed with facts from the police reports that had come flowing from the fax machine after the fingerprints lifted from the coffee cup had led them to Rachel's true identity. He'd walked in feeling used and angry and sure he knew everything he needed to know about Rachel Curtis and her crimes. He'd walked in knowing that very soon he would be walking out with Rachel in handcuffs.

No longer. Standing there, faced with her quiet blend of resolve and vulnerability, he wasn't sure of much of any-thing. For sure he didn't know if Randy Parnell had killed his wife as Rachel claimed, but he knew that Rachel be-lieved it. She believed it with all her heart and in spite of his well-honed professional instincts and dedication to the truth and nothing but the truth, that put an entirely dif-ferent spin on this whole thing. And left him with one hell of a problem. What was he going to do now?

Blowing out an exasperated breath, he shook his head at her. "Dammit, Rachel, even if this is true..."

"No ifs. It is true."

"All right, it's true. There are ways to handle these things and—"

"And I tried them all. I was a news reporter back then, Mitch, not some hick who didn't know how the system worked. I sat in more waiting rooms than hell can possibly have, waiting to talk to more detectives and attorneys and investigators than I knew existed," she exclaimed, pacing across the kitchen to release some of the restless energy the memory incited. "I filed reports and made phone calls and contacted every government department I thought might have even a tiny bit of influence and I got nowhere...because whatever influence I had, the Parnells always had more."

"So you decided to punish Parnell yourself by kidnapping Bonnie?"

She spun back to face him, her wide eyes hurt and angry. "No, I decided to save Bonnie before the same thing happened to her. Donna had told me he didn't hit Bonnie, but that must have changed once he didn't have Donna around to use as his punching bag."

Mitch had seen enough evidence of child abuse that just the suggestion of it made his stomach wrench and started an angry tic at the side of his jaw. "You're saying he hit Bonnie?"

"Hit, shoved, twisted her arm."

"Did he leave marks?"

She nodded, squeezing her eyes shut against the memory. "Yeah, he left marks...some of them you could even see."

"Why didn't you take her to an emergency room and have them documented so—"

"Because I never had a chance to. He never let me be alone with her," she shouted. "At the end, he never let me near her at all. I wasn't exactly his favorite relative at that point."

"I can see why. The reports indicate you were running around telling anyone who'd listen that he was responsible for his wife's death."

"Because he was," she retorted, the stubborn set of her chin hinting at what Parnell had been up against.

"And accusing him of abusing and neglecting his daughter."

"Because he was."

"None of which is officially established anywhere."

"That doesn't make it any less real." She lifted her chin to look into his eyes. "Maybe you can choose to put laws and rules above everything else in your life, above what you know in your gut and feel in your heart, but I can't."

Her cool accusation hit closer to home than Mitch liked. That's exactly what he had chosen to do. The law and its enforcement were his work, and work was his life. He'd put that ahead of everything else, even his own family. It was the one thing he could count on, the one thing that made him important and successful, the one thing no one could take from him.

It was only when he'd lost sight of that and became entangled in the quagmire of his own emotions that he messed everything up. He'd vowed never to let that happen again. That's why he was so angry right now. From the start Rachel had been challenging the single-minded focus and concentration he needed to do his job. He was angry with her for distracting him and for lying to him, but most of all, he was angry with himself for wanting her just the same. Wanting her with a hunger that clawed at him even now. He was angry with his own weak indecisiveness. He was angry with himself for standing there torn between what he ought to do and what he wanted to do.

The law was the law and Rachel had broken it. His job required him to take her into custody. So why wasn't he doing it?

"Did anyone else ever see Parnell hit Bonnie?" he heard himself ask. "Or see the evidence of abuse?"

She shrugged. "My mother."

"All right, that's something. How about someone outside of your family?"

"No one I can name. No one who would have the nerve to come forward in that town and openly accuse a Parnell of anything."

He rubbed his jaw, feeling the end-of-the-day stubble. *Do it, do it, do it,* prodded the voice of reason. *Call for a police car and get it over with.*

"Tell me about the day you took Bonnie. Did you break into his house to get her?"

"I didn't have to. He'd stayed out the night before and left Kim...that was Bonnie's name then, with neighbors. The Jamisons, an elderly couple who lived right next door."

"They were baby-sitting?"

"I guess you might say that, except Randy neglected to tell them about it ahead of time. They invited Bonnie over for a couple of hours to play with their granddaughter, who was staying with them. That was in the early afternoon. When Randy never came back to get her, they kept her with them overnight. At ten the next morning, Mr. Jamison drove her to my house and told me what had happened. He also told me he suspected it wasn't the first time she'd been left alone for hours. He told me that they sometimes heard Bonnie crying for hours on end and Randy slamming doors and screaming at her to shut up or he'd lock her in the cellar."

"Rachel, this guy was the witness you needed," Mitch said excitedly. "I'll bet he might even have been able to verify the signs of abuse."

"I'm sure he could have," she agreed with a suspiciously resigned air. "He told me he saw Randy shake her one day and when the windows were open he heard what he was certain were hard slaps. The next time he saw Kim...Bonnie, her arm was in a sling."

Mitch scowled. "So why didn't he call the police himself?"

"Because his wife was afraid of the Parnells, and he was afraid that if he got involved in spite of her fear, she would have another heart attack." She leaned back against the counter, her expression rueful. "He made it absolutely clear that he could not get involved, but just the look in his eyes when he told me to please watch out for Bonnie let me know that I had to do something."

"So you just took her and ran?" he countered, his tone heavy with frustration and disbelief. Part of him couldn't fathom anyone doing anything so impulsive and reckless. But another part of him, the part that had come to know Rachel, understood completely. Just as she would commit herself to repairing a lost cause of a dollhouse, she would give up everything she had, everything she was, to save a child who needed her.

"That's right, I just took her and ran. I couldn't let her go back to that house and him...I couldn't put her in danger for even one more minute while I tried to find someone to listen to me...and I couldn't forget my promise to Donna to look out for her as if she was my own baby." Her voice had grown quivery, but now she squared her shoulders and eyed him challengingly. "You have two little girls of your own, Mitch...think about it, what would you do if someone was hurting them?"

Mitch forced himself to work past the surge of violent emotion that just the suggestion unleashed inside him. "I wouldn't have broken the law, I'll tell you that."

"That's very commendable," she retorted. "Now tell me what you would have done...counselor."

"Stop calling me that," he snapped. "I am not a counselor...I'm a prosecutor. It's my job to see that people who break the law are punished for it."

"I see. So that's the bottom line?" she asked, the glimmer of disappointment in her eyes like a knife sliding slowly between his ribs.

"Yeah, that's the bottom line."

"All right then." She held out her hands in the most defiant surrender he'd ever witnessed. "Then go ahead and do your job, Mr. Prosecutor."

Mitch stepped closer, his insides in turmoil, the war between his head and his gut tearing him right up the middle. He reached out and curled his fingers around the back of her neck, jerking her forward until her breasts touched his chest.

Still her eyes gleamed rebelliously. His heart pounded and his blood roared with a need purer and stronger and far more primitive than anything he'd ever learned in law school.

"Damn you," he muttered as he bent his head to her.

He kissed her hard, trying to lose himself in it and nearly succeeding until her hands pushed against his chest. He backed off just enough to meet her gaze.

"Does this mean I'm under arrest?" she asked.

"Not yet," he said, stiffening, his meaning a rough, unmistakable statement of fact. He wanted her; with their bodies pressed together from chest to thigh he could hardly deny that to her, never mind to himself. But he wasn't making any promises, or compromises.

She nodded. "All right. I can live with that."

Chapter Ten

Wrapping her arms around his neck, Rachel drew Mitch closer until his mouth was touching hers. She parted her lips and brushed them against his, first lightly, then harder, her restlessly shifting legs revealing her desire.

Mitch remained stubbornly still.

Rachel was bewildered by his response...or lack of one. It had been a long time since she'd endeavored to arouse a man, if in fact she ever had. Truthfully she'd never understood what the big deal was about sex. She enjoyed men, some much more than others, and she'd enjoyed sex. But it had been something she could take or leave and for the past several years, she had of necessity left it entirely alone.

During that time she'd been troubled by loneliness on all levels, but she had never felt sexual desire as a blinding, racing need at her core. Not until tonight, that is. Not even last night with Mitch had she felt this heavy sense that she needed to be with him more than she needed to breathe. How could he not perceive the fury of what was happening inside her, she wondered. Touching his mouth again with her own, she longed for his lips to open and crush hers, for him to take control as he had just a minute ago.

Instead, as her tongue slid slowly across his lower lip, he released a harsh groan and yanked her head back to stare warily into her eyes.

"Why?" he demanded, his tone rough. "Why are you doing this?"

"Isn't it obvious?"

"Should be, I guess, but I've learned not to take you at face value."

Rachel flushed, knowing she deserved his suspicion and hating it anyway. "You think I'm doing this to bribe you or blackmail you or something? To get you to let me go?"

"If you are, you're wasting your time. You better know that up front."

"I'm not."

"Good. That still doesn't answer my question."

"For God's sake, Mitch, what do you want from me? An expression of undying love?"

"At the moment," he said, his tone dry as he effortlessly quelled her attempt to break free, "I'll settle for knowing why you're so hot for me now when on the phone a while ago you said you didn't even want to see me again."

Oh, what a tangled web, thought Rachel achingly. She could write volumes about how true that old platitude was. She met his wary gaze head-on, determined that whatever happened, there would be no more lies between them.

"I didn't want to see you," she said, "because I was—in your words—hot for you even then. I've felt this way since last night, maybe longer. You have me so mixed up that most of the time I can't think straight. But one thing I knew for sure was that if we were alone together, this would happen. And I knew that making love with you, getting that close to you, could endanger Bonnie, and so I promised myself I wouldn't let it happen."

"And now?"

"And now..." She trembled, swallowing hard. "Now the worst has already happened. You know who Bonnie is and that as far as the law is concerned she doesn't belong here with me. And I understand that you're going to have to turn me in."

Rachel trembled again as she finally put into words the full meaning of the events of the night. The time for running and hiding was over. She was going to have to face the consequences of everything she had done and fight as hard as she could to protect Bonnie in the only way left to her... by telling her story over and over. She wasn't totally unprepared for this development. She had often considered what would happen if they were caught and she prayed that her trial and notoriety might prove to be a silver lining, calling new, unbiased attention to Donna's death and Bonnie's plight.

But that was for later... for tomorrow. Tonight was something else entirely... tonight was a sliver of time stolen from the space between her past and her future, between crime and punishment, she thought ruefully. The past few years had been like a pressure cooker for her and she was smart enough to know that a good number of the years ahead might be spent behind bars. If that was the case, she decided, she wanted to claim this night for herself... and she wanted it to be one to remember.

Tonight there didn't have to be any lies or pretense or holding back. Even though she'd finally been caught, Rachel felt suddenly free.

"I want you, Mitch," she said, her honesty spurred on by the flash of excitement her words sparked in his eyes. "I did what I thought I had to do for Bonnie... and for my sister. Maybe I made a mistake and maybe I saved Bonnie's life. But no matter what the court decides, no matter what happens tomorrow, I want this one night with you."

She rested her hands on his chest, feeling his warmth and the hard pounding of his heart, and she waited through silent seconds that felt like years. As a tremor worked its way through his body, she could feel him resisting her and struggling with his own desires and then finally slipping free of some self-imposed leash.

Joy exploded inside her as his arms tightened across her back, bringing her hard against him.

"I want it, too, Rachel" he confessed in a rasp. "I want you... Oh, God, how I want you."

He ran his hand up and down her spine, sliding lower each time, his caresses growing steadily bolder and more urgent, as if he couldn't press her close enough. Rachel knew the feeling. Leaning against him, she ran her hands over his back, reaching up to curl her fingers into his muscled shoulders, desire pulsing inside her.

Unconsciously she bent one knee, flexing her leg in a yearning caress of his that brought a quick, sharp sound of hunger from Mitch. Threading his fingers through her hair, he once more tipped her head back to stare into her eyes. This time without saying a word. Words had no place here. For tonight, lips and fingertips and soft breathless sounds of pleasure were more eloquent than a book of sonnets.

Slowly his head dipped to her. Rachel instinctively ran her tongue over her lips to moisten them. Mitch grinned, with satisfaction and anticipation, but instead of capturing her lips to continue the hard, driving kiss she'd interrupted a moment ago, he pressed his open mouth to the side of her throat. The contact was wet and warm and thrilling. Rachel arched her neck in response as shivers of arousal skated the length of her back.

The delicate shivers became an explosion of new sensations as Mitch moved higher and plunged his tongue into her ear. Rachel moaned and clung to him as he continued the intimate caress that went from rough to gentle and back again. Her breath was coming in short, fast pants by the time he framed her face with his hands and at last covered her mouth with his in a kiss that was harder and deeper than any that had come before.

Rachel gloried in it, in the heat and the fierceness and the unmistakable urgency that warned her Mitch was as close to losing control as she was. Tonight, that was exactly what she wanted—to lose control . . . to stop thinking and worrying . . . to surrender completely to Mitch and to the long-dormant demands of her own womanhood.

She joined the kiss eagerly, greedily, her tongue caressing his lips and swirling between them to taste him the way he was tasting her, hard and deep, as if he would never get enough. She felt his hands on her breasts, first kneading her through her sweater, learning her shape and weight and the feel of her in his hands. Then suddenly his hands were inside her sweater, sliding higher, his touch sure and aggressive, making her feel the same way. He shoved her bra out of the way, his fingertips moving unerringly to claim the already hardened crests.

Rachel released a broken sigh as his thumb strummed her there, sending pleasure swirling though her.

"I told you this is how it would be for us," he whispered against her hair, still touching her breasts in a way that left her without reason. "Fast and hot," he continued, cupping her in both hands with a rhythmic squeezing motion that had her biting her lip for control.

A muscle worked in his cheek as he turned to look at her through eyes narrowed with passion. "I'll bet you're already wet."

Rachel, who would make no so foolish a bet, unconsciously shifted her legs.

"Are you, Rachel?" he crooned softly. "Are you wet for me? Are you ready?"

Rachel didn't flinch or become flustered by the query. Another time his blunt eroticism might have put her off, but not tonight. Tonight it was exactly what she wanted: honest pleasure with no coyness and no holds barred. Tonight was no time for halfhearted responses. She wanted to feel everything there was to feel. She wanted enough to last her a lifetime if it had to. She let the carnal challenge in his words pour over her. Then she reached for his hand and slowly brought it down to rest at the juncture of her thighs.

A seductive invitation darkened her eyes and Mitch responded by pressing against the denim-covered heat at her core. When Rachel whimpered, shaken by the sharp rush of sensations he caused, he smiled knowingly and reached for her zipper.

This time when he touched her intimately there was no barrier between his fingers and the answer to his question. Inside her jeans and silk panties, Rachel was warm and damp and more than ready for his possession. In a response as natural as breathing, she parted her legs just slightly to accommodate him as his fingers slid deeper.

Gently he guided her backward until her weight was braced against the kitchen counter. Rachel barely knew where she was. She'd never before made love standing up and couldn't imagine herself being comfortable doing it now. But she was, absolutely comfortable both physically and emotionally. The caress of Mitch's fingers on her breast and against the most sensitive, intimate part of her consumed all of her concentration, leaving no room for doubt or discomfort.

He was all she wanted, all she needed, and the feelings he was arousing inside her seemed both a gift and a privilege to be welcomed and savored. Tomorrow she might feel sore where the edge of the countertop dug into her back or feel ashamed at how she had abandoned herself to the moment and to Mitch, but right now all she felt was pleasure and the warm, sweet need to surrender.

Only when the sensations his stroking fingers awakened became sharp and intense in a way she'd never known before did Rachel grow restless, straining against his hand, seeking the magic that was his to bestow.

Her eagerness seemed to inflame his own simmering passion. She felt his heart pounding and heard the texture of his breathing grow rough and choppy. When she gripped his shoulders in mounting urgency, his hand slipped from her breast to the snap at the waist of his jeans.

Rachel heard the metallic rasp of his zipper being lowered and it seemed to her the most erotic sound in the world. A sound full of lusty promise and anticipation.

"Touch me," he murmured and Rachel needed no further urging to lower her hands and reach for him, marveling at the smooth heat awaiting her, thrilled by the way he jerked in response to the sliding caress of her curved fingers.

They were like the ends of a seesaw, with each push on one side prompting a slightly greater response on the other. He stroked her delicate flesh with a callused fingertip and Rachel trembled and captured his arousal in a tugging caress, which made Mitch press harder and deeper in return. On and on until Rachel felt as if she was on fire.

"Please, please," she whispered against his chest and Mitch obliged by grasping her hips and lifting her against him.

With a few quick movements that she knew she could never have managed in her current state, he maneuvered both their jeans out of the way, his intent to take her blatant and electrifying.

Rachel glanced down at the open V of his zipper and caught her breath, awed by the size and strength of his desire. The kitchen light still burned brightly and to her amazement, she was glad. The raw masculine beauty of Mitch's body was one more precious memory of tonight that would be hers to cherish. The contrast of shade and texture as their bodies met and he thrust forward to be welcomed into hers added to her arousal.

As he eased into her, filling her perfectly, Rachel felt a sense of wholeness beyond anything she had ever known. It was both physical and spiritual, something she doubted she could explain even at a far more rational moment, and it grew stronger with each slow, deep stroke. She felt herself racing over thresholds she'd never known existed, moving deeper inside herself and at the same time floating free of all that made her one and alone and becoming half of something much bigger and more powerful.

As the thrusts of his hips quickened, so did the need building inside her. It became sharper and more centered, focused on something she had to strain for, something just out of reach, something she both wanted and feared. To reach it, she realized suddenly, she had to let go of everything else... everything but Mitch.

She felt his hands tighten on her waist. His lips brushed her hair close to her ear.

"Go with it, baby," he urged in a gravelly whisper that was one more caress of her senses. "Just go with it. It's all right."

It's all right. His words were just the balm her spirit needed so desperately. It's all right...she was all right...for just a little while someone else was looking out for her...she wasn't alone. She threw back her head in joyous abandonment, letting go, and letting Mitch's body and her own find their way through the storm.

Release came for both of them at once, as fast and hard as their coming together had been. A blend of soft whimper and broken moan, the quickness of his hands and hammering strength of his passion, and then she was catapulted over a final threshold to someplace she'd never been before, a place without walls or depth, only sensation, explosive and shattering. But for all its violence and fury, the passing left her not broken, but whole, replete, at peace.

Rachel was sure the glorious feeling of peace and satisfaction couldn't last and so she squeezed her eyes shut in an attempt to prolong it as long as possible.

Mitch slowly slid her along his body until her feet once more rested on the kitchen floor. It was hard to ignore the reality of cold vinyl, but Rachel tried desperately.

"Can't bear to look at me, hmm?" Mitch's tone was amused and caressing and just slightly breathless.

Rachel opened her eyes to a smile that reflected what was in her heart, a smile that, under other circumstances, could have warmed her for the rest of her life. It was an effort to remember that, the past few minutes aside, she had little reason to smile.

"I could look at you forever," she said softly. "I just can't help thinking about what we do now."

He rested his hands on her shoulders. Belatedly Rachel saw the darker mood behind his smile and traces of desperation in his eyes.

"The night's not over, Rachel," he reminded her. "You want to know what we do now? Share your bed with me and I'll show you."

If the first time was as Mitch had predicted—fast and furious—the next, and the next, were just the opposite. Slow and easy, a symphony of touch and discovery. It took them forever simply to undress each other, pausing to explore and worship each newly revealed inch of flesh along the way. Rachel lit the candles she kept handy for emergencies and the flickering light played across the hard, strong planes of Mitch's body and cast intriguing shadows on the gentle curves of her own.

Again and again they loved each other, neither saying a word about what would happen when they finally had to emerge from the warm tousled sheets and face the morning.

* * *

Rachel wasn't sure who woke first. Mitch seemed to open his eyes at the same instant she did, reinforcing last night's notion that there was between them a connection that eluded explanation. Even her bond with Donna, as strong and lifelong as it had been, had lacked the mystical intimacy she'd found last night in Mitch's arms.

"Can I ask you a question?" she said to him, knowing she wanted to ask more like a million, indefinitely postponing the inevitable.

Mitch nodded and tucked the sheet around her. Rachel understood the impulse and was grateful. The sunlight filtering through the lace at the window, though not nearly as bright or glaring as the light in the kitchen had been last night, threatened to reveal much more of her soul. Personal pain and vulnerabilities that he probably didn't want to have to confront this morning...that he couldn't afford to let distract him from the job he had vowed to do. In a way, she of all people was able to understand how that felt.

"How did you find out about me?" she asked him.

The slight tensing of his jaw might have eluded anyone but a woman sharing a pillow with him.

"Another lawyer on the Hanson case, Ollie Bennett, noticed that your social security number was issued only eighteen months ago. That was a red flag telling us you weren't who you said you were. From there it was simply a matter of running your prints and finding out they were on file in Florida."

"My prints?" A perplexed frown creased her forehead. "I can imagine that the Florida police must have taken them from my apartment or office after I left, but how did you...?"

"I saved your cup the day we had coffee together," he explained when she trailed off with a suspicious glance his way.

Her small smile was pained. "I see."

"I never hid the fact that I was suspicious of you."

"Yes, you did. The other day in your office," she reminded him. "You said that even if I was hiding something, it was none of your business."

"You're right," he acknowledged, wincing. "I guess I did at that."

"Why?"

"Because at the time I believed it. The preliminary report on you looked fine and I guess I wanted to believe it. Hell, Rachel, even now part of me wishes I didn't know the truth. That I could just put on my pants and walk out of here and spend all day thinking about how soon we could be together again."

"Believe me," she said dryly, "an even bigger part of me wishes the same thing."

He reached out and curled his hand around the back of her neck, his eyes very blue in the morning light and very determined.

"I'm going to help you through this," he said with quiet urgency. "That should go without saying after everything that's happened, especially after last night, but just in case it doesn't, I'm saying it now." He waited for a response that didn't come. "All right, maybe the idea of having me around isn't a big thrill, but you could at least pretend to be grateful for the help. I'm probably a better lawyer than I am a lover."

"Impossible," she said softly. "If you were, there wouldn't be a jaywalker or litterbug left on the streets."

"I'm pretty good at putting people away. Now we'll see how good I am at keeping someone out of jail."

Closing her eyes, Rachel released a heavy sigh. She wasn't doing a good job of holding at bay all the fear and worries she had put on hold overnight. A night's rest seemed to have made them stronger and more persistent.

"You know," she said, "they warned me about the social security number."

"They?"

She nodded, glancing at him. "I had done a story for the station I worked for on the underground network that helps women and children..."

"Stop," he ordered, pressing a finger to her lips. "As much as I want to hear every detail about your life, there are some things I think I shouldn't know...at least for now."

She nodded, understanding that his reasons were professional and that he was looking out for her well-being.

"Anyway," she continued, "I was warned to be careful not to do anything that would invite the kind of scrutiny that would turn up all those suspicious little details in my background, like a brand-new social security number." She released another sigh, this one edged with frustration. "I tried. I guess my luck just ran out that day at Hanson's." She shivered and struggled to sit, bunching her pillow behind her. "God, how callous that sounds. Poor Mr. Hanson was really the unlucky one." She turned to glance at Mitch. "You were right, Bonnie was the little girl in the store that day."

"I know." At her curious look, he added, "Your prints matched the prints on the magazine we found near the scene. No one stole that magazine from your mailbox and tossed it there. It all fit."

"I suppose you'll have to question Bonnie about the murder."

He nodded. "How much did she see?"

"Next to nothing," she told him regretfully. Protecting Bonnie was her first priority, but if Mitch was right about DelCosta, she would also like to see him convicted. "That's the reason I never felt guilty about denying we were there. We would have been putting ourselves at risk for no good reason."

"Let me be the judge of that. Tell me what you saw."

"Personally? Nothing. Bonnie went in all by herself for the first time that day. She's a typical five-year-old and I'm sure she had eyes for nothing but all that candy spread before her. She certainly wouldn't pay attention to two men talking to Mr. Hanson."

"She had to have heard the shots."

"She did, and she remembers seeing Mr. Hanson fall and knock over the telephone. And she remembers the two men fighting over the gun."

"Two men?" he said, excitement in his voice.

Rachel nodded. "That's right. She saw two men, but I'm telling you right now, Mitch, she can't identify either of them. She turned and ran. Somehow she got blood on her dress and when she came through the door, she seemed fixated on that."

"That's why you burned her dress?"

"I didn't know what else to do. I couldn't let you question Bonnie and turn her into some kind of star child witness in a gory murder trial, her picture in papers all over the country."

"Ah, Rachel," he countered, dragging his fingers roughly through his hair, "if you had told me at the start, if you had trusted me, then maybe..."

"Maybe," she said softly when he fell silent, "we wouldn't be here right now. Maybe last night would never have happened. I may be crazy, but I'll settle for this ending."

"It's not an ending," he said, his eyes flashing as he shifted his weight so they were eye to eye. "I meant what I said a minute ago. There has to be a way out of this for you and I'm not going to stop until I find it."

"Are you open to suggestions?" she inquired, only half teasing.

"Depends."

"I know the out-of-town bus schedule by heart."

"I meant there has to be a legal way out of this," he said, his expression an endearing blend of solemn and apologetic. "I can't just let you walk, Rachel, but I can promise you that you won't be facing this alone. This time the people who matter will listen to what you have to say. I'll make them listen."

"If you say so," she said, unable to stop the voice threading through her head, reminding her that Mitch had never squared off against the Parnells. "There is one favor I'd like to ask though. I know it's probably against regulations and all, but..."

"Name it," he interjected.

"I want some time to tell Bonnie what's happened. Alone, in my own way." She leaned forward, grasping his arm a bit desperately as a concerned frown settled on his face. "Mitch, I'm the only mother she remembers.... She's going to be devastated enough as it is when she's taken away and handed over to a man who—" She stopped and brought her thoughts under control. "If I don't even have a chance to talk to her and explain why this is happening it will be so much harder for her."

Rachel held her breath as he thought it over.

"All right," he said just as she was about to give up hope. "On one condition, Rachel. You have to give me your word you won't run."

Rachel turned to look at him in surprise. "My word? That's it? No signing in blood? No guard at the door?"

"That's it. Just your word."

His confidence made her feel foolish for needling him. It also made her feel unworthy.

"Okay," she told him. "You have my word, Mitch, I'm not going anywhere."

She waited until he had left and driven out of sight before calling Sheila's house. Sheila's mother was sorry to hear that a family emergency was going to prevent Bonnie from going on the class trip, but she was more than happy to drive her home on her way to the school.

Rachel thanked her and hung up. Bonnie should be home within a half hour. Gnawing nervously on her bottom lip, she made a mental list of what she had to do and in what order she should do it. First the phone call, she decided, in case she had to call back or wait to get the information she needed.

From her wallet she took out a business card she'd picked up locally. On the back, written in the code she and Donna had invented as kids to write secret messages to each other, was a phone number. This morning it seemed luck was with her. The woman who answered was able to provide Rachel with the help she needed. Arrangements made, she hung up and hurried to Bonnie's room to begin packing.

If anyone had asked, Mitch couldn't have told them why he had defied everything he'd learned from others and experience, not to mention his own common sense, and agreed to leave Rachel alone to break the news to Bonnie. No one did ask, however. Probably because no one had a chance to, he thought as he ran a towel over his damp chest.

Returning home to shower and change, he'd ignored the blinking light on his answering machine and resolved to do the same with any incoming messages. Ollie had a vague idea that his interest in Rachel had edged beyond professional limits, though Mitch doubted Ollie could even imagine how very unprofessional it had turned last night.

The point was that Ollie would give him some breathing room on this one, at least another two hours' worth, which was what he had promised Rachel. At nine-thirty he would return to pick up her and Bonnie and bring them in. The prospect was about as appealing as having a root canal done. No matter how confident he had tried to appear for Rachel's sake, assuring her he would help her deal with this, he knew how much trouble she was in. A lot.

Kidnapping was a serious offense. If they could manage to find witnesses willing to substantiate Rachel's assertions about her sister's death and her claim that Bonnie was being physically and mentally abused by her father, it might swing things her way. If they couldn't... Mitch didn't want to think about that possibility. He always preferred to focus on the desired result rather than on all the ways a case could go wrong. Usually that meant envisioning a guilty verdict. But not this time. This time he was determined to prove that Rachel was telling the truth and that taking Bonnie from her father had been an act of great love and courage.

With or without witnesses and evidence to back up her claims, he believed every word that Rachel had said. He couldn't have explained that, either, but he did. And it wasn't simply a case of his hormones talking, although they were plenty vocal this morning.

Last night had been more than great sex, the greatest sex he'd ever enjoyed, he thought heatedly. It had been a turning point for him.

The trust he felt for Rachel was all new for him. He'd always believed that truth had to come packaged in facts and points of evidence. She offered little of either, yet the trust he felt for her defied all that he had believed until now. Maybe trust was the wrong word, he decided, maybe a better word was faith. His faith in her, and in what they shared, was strong enough that he was able to leave her alone in spite of the very obvious fact that she had run in the past and could conceivably run again. His faith that she wouldn't run from him, that she would honor her word to him, was based on nothing more than a feeling in his gut.

And, it suddenly occurred to Mitch in the middle of tying his tie, in his heart. He stopped with it half-knotted and faced himself in the mirror. Trust and faith were only part of what he felt for Rachel. And they were both part of love. Another part of it was putting what Rachel wanted and needed above his own wants and needs, and above the drive and ambition that had once been the focus of his entire life. He wanted to help Rachel more than he wanted to hurt Mickey DelCosta, and that amazed him.

He shook his head, realizing that in a minute and a half of looking in the bathroom mirror, he'd just unraveled more about love than he had in the entire course of his marriage and divorce. He loved Rachel...that's why he had felt only fury and no sense of victory last night. That's why making love with her had surpassed any fantasy he could ever conjure up. That's why he had trusted her enough to leave her there alone this morning.

And that's why this was all going to work out for them, he thought with a surge of hope as he quickly tightened the knot and slipped into the jacket of his olive suit. It had to work out. Love conquered all, everyone knew that.

The drive to Rachel's seemed to take forever. Mitch suspected that catching the tail end of the morning rush-hour traffic had less to do with that than the fact that he already missed her. To ease his impatience, he used his car phone to check in with Darlene and gave her a reassuring message to relay to poor Ollie, who was probably climbing the walls wondering what the hell had taken Mitch all night. He grinned, remembering the night before as he replaced the receiver in its cradle.

The night he had taken Rachel to dinner, he'd stashed the car phone in the glove compartment, not wanting to explain why he'd lied the time he asked to use her phone. He didn't even consider hiding it this morning. They'd both twisted the truth for their own ends and to do what they believed was right. Now they were making a fresh start, together, and he didn't want any lies between them...not even over something as minor as a telephone.

Not once during his hurried drive did he stop to consider what he would do if Rachel and Bonnie weren't there when he got there. There might have even been a few plausible explanations he could have pacified himself with, but he didn't have even one of them handy when he knocked on her door and no one answered.

Disbelief ran first cold and then hot through his veins, picking up speed and pressure until it was pounding at every pulse point. He knocked again, waiting barely a second before trying the doorknob. It was open.

Instantly the lawyer in Mitch began flashing warnings about unlawful entry and search warrants. But from the start, where Rachel was concerned, he'd been more man than lawyer. That's probably why he'd screwed up along the way, but he was powerless to stop now as he swung open the door and stepped into the kitchen where just last night he had made Rachel his. Or thought he had.

He called her name and Bonnie's as he hurried down the hall to the bedrooms. He'd seen crime scenes up close too many times and part of him was scared to death of what he might find. Another part of him already knew what he would find and was scared of something else entirely. A glance into Rachel's room revealed the bed still in sexy disarray as they had left it. Something in Mitch recoiled at the sight.

He swung around to glance into Bonnie's room instead. On the table against the wall was the dollhouse he'd built for her, looking as deserted as the apartment did with the furniture and little people nowhere in sight. Ridiculously, the empty dollhouse was nearly as disturbing to him as Rachel's rumpled bed. Bonnie's bed was undisturbed, but across the room the closet door was open, and the closet was empty.

"Damn," Mitch muttered, disbelief finally giving way to anger and a need to act. This wasn't the first time he'd walked into an empty house and he knew that the ache in his chest now was nothing compared to what he would feel later, when he was alone with too much time to think. The best he could hope for was to put off later for as long as possible.

He didn't wait until he got back to the car, opting to use the phone in the kitchen instead. He deliberately turned his back on the kitchen counter and the taunting memories it roused as he punched in Ollie's number. He felt like an idiot as he briefly explained that he had let Rachel get away.

Ollie must have judged from his tone that this was no time to ask for details. He stayed one step ahead of Mitch's orders, which was why Mitch had phoned him directly rather than attempting to explain to Darlene how to issue an all-points bulletin for Rachel Curtis.

Chapter Eleven

Rachel sat close beside Bonnie in the back seat of the taxi, holding her hand tightly and trying to think of some sane way to explain to the little girl the insane thing that was about to happen. For the second time in her young life, Bonnie was about to lose a mother.

But this time it wouldn't be forever, Rachel promised herself. She had made up her mind. She was going to face the charges that had been hanging over her head—hanging over both their heads—for far too long, and she was going to win. If she didn't believe that, she wouldn't have the courage to stop running. In her heart she knew that Mitch was part of the reason for her newfound courage, and he was also a big part of the reason for what she was about to do.

The more she came to know Mitch, the more she understood why the Hanson case was so important to him. It went beyond professional pride; it went to the core of him as a man, and as a father. It was a score he needed to set-

tle in order to close the door on the mistakes of the past
and get on with his life. If she could help him do that, she
wanted to. If in the process, she was forced to own up to
what might prove to be mistakes of her own, she was willing to take that risk.

Mitch needed a witness and he was going to get one, but
it wouldn't be Bonnie. She recalled seeing two shadowy
figures when she glanced inside the store that day and she
had clearly heard two sets of footsteps running out the
back. If Mitch needed verification that Leo Belanger
hadn't acted alone, she could provide it.

Night after night lately, she'd lain awake in her bed
wishing there was some way she could help Mitch and still
protect Bonnie. This morning, after Mitch's unselfish offer to do whatever it took to help her, it had finally occurred to her that through this latest twist of fate she was
able to do exactly that. It was fitting, she mused. After all,
she and Mitch had been brought together by an accident
of fate.

Like stars colliding in the night they had been jolted out
of their solitary orbits and forced together. She wasn't
much of a scientist, but she had a hunch that when stars
collided out in space, they both shattered or burned each
other up or something equally destructive. She supposed
that could have happened to her and Mitch as well, but it
wasn't going to. She wasn't going to let it. Randy Parnell
had already destroyed one life too many.

The taxi turned onto the campus of a suburban branch
of the state college, with Rachel still searching for words
to make Bonnie understand why she had to be sent off to
live with strangers. Kind strangers with generous hearts
and deep compassion for women and children in their
predicament, but strangers just the same. True, if all went
as Rachel hoped and prayed, it would only be for a little
while, but how did you define "little while" to a five-year-
old? She finally resigned herself to the fact that there were

no words to make Bonnie truly understand something that she wasn't sure she understood herself.

The fact remained that it was happening, and maybe her sudden loss for words was for the best. It meant that Bonnie hadn't had too much time to anticipate what was ahead for her. At least this way she'd enjoyed the rare treat of riding in a taxi, accepting it as a second-best substitute for her class trip with the same good-natured ease with which she accepted most things. Rachel prayed that same spirit would see her through the weeks and months ahead.

Leaning forward, she asked the driver if he knew where the cafeteria was located. That's where she was supposed to meet the woman the network was sending to pick up Bonnie.

"No," he replied, "but I can ask."

He got directions to the cafeteria from a passing student and dropped them off in front of a long, low building built of sand-colored brick. Rachel paid him, adding a tip. For once she wasn't worried about having enough money for groceries or rent. She almost wished she was. Starting today, she had much bigger things to worry her.

Inside the cafeteria, she bought two sodas from a vending machine and settled Bonnie at a corner table to wait as instructed. A quick glance around didn't turn up a middle-aged blonde wearing a white raincoat, so she made use of the time to finally break the news to Bonnie.

"Bonnie," she began, doing her best to sound confident and upbeat, as if this was a great adventure and not something that was already tearing her apart with doubt and misgivings. "Do you remember the day your old dollhouse fell and broke?"

Bonnie nodded with her straw clamped tightly between her lips.

"Do you remember how you felt?"

"Sad," Bonnie replied. "Very, very sad because it was all broke in a million pieces."

"At least a million," Rachel agreed, a flicker of a genuine smile finding its way to her lips. "You felt sad because you loved the dollhouse very much and you were afraid you were never going to be able to play with it again, right?"

"Right." She took another sip, her small legs swinging back and forth beneath her chair in a display of her ever-bubbling energy.

"And do you remember what I said that day to try to make you feel better?"

Bonnie scrunched up her face in thought. "You said for me not to cry 'cause you would fix it."

"That's right, and later, when I tried to fix it and found out how hard a job it was going to be, I told you that if I tried as hard as I could and couldn't put it back together, that somehow, some way, I would make sure you got another dollhouse to replace it, right?"

"Right, and you did. Mr. Dalton made me the most beautiful dollhouse in the world."

"Yes, he did. And even though you felt sad after the old dollhouse broke, you were happy all over again when you got the new one."

"Happier than with the old one, too, 'cause this one is bigger and the windows can really open."

"I know. It's a wonderful dollhouse," Rachel agreed, her heart filling with tenderness for the man responsible and for poor Bonnie, who, for at least a little while, would be losing her precious dollhouse along with everything else. She had taken time to pack the furniture and tiny people so Bonnie could improvise, but it was still a poor substitute and the unfairness of it made her feel like screaming. Instead she forced a bigger smile and reached out to stroke the satiny skin of the back of Bonnie's small hand.

"Bonnie, the reason I'm reminding you of how you felt back then is because today is going to be a sad day, too... for both of us, but that means that there will be happy days ahead for us, too.''

The straw slipped from between her lips as her dark brows curled downward in a worried frown. "Is my new dollhouse going to break, too?'' she cried.

"No, no, sweetie, your new dollhouse is safe and sound back at home. But I'm afraid you won't be able to play with it for a while because you're going to be spending some time away from home.''

Rachel saw her frown grow perplexed as she tried to decide whether this was good news or bad.

"But where will we go?'' she asked.

"Do you remember before we moved to Plymouth, how we stayed in lots of different people's houses?''

"Sort of. I remember Jenny's house.''

Jenny was a little girl who had befriended Bonnie at one of their stops along the way. Rachel didn't bother to explain that the house where they'd met didn't belong to Jenny and her mother any more than it did them, that they, too, were temporarily homeless, running from a bad situation that had become lethal.

"Well, that's what you'll be doing now. A very nice lady will be coming here to meet us and she's going to take you someplace where you'll be safe and sound.''

"Just like my dollhouse.''

Tears bit at the back of Rachel's eyelids. "That's right, Bonnie love, just like your dollhouse.''

"Then why can't we stay at home and be safe?''

"Oh... lots of silly grown-up reasons. The important thing for you to remember is that it's only for a while. You have to promise me you'll say that to yourself every day, every morning when you wake up. Say to yourself that every new day is one day closer to getting back home... back to your dollhouse.''

Rachel wished vehemently that she'd been able to stuff the entire dollhouse into the bag so that Bonnie could take it with her wherever she was going. Now she made a vow that whatever happened, she would see to it that it was taken care of so that when Bonnie came home it would be there waiting for her.

"I will, Mommy," Bonnie promised, her smile reappearing. "I'll say it every single day. And if I don't, you can remind me, okay? Will we sleep in one big bed again or two little skinny ones like at Jenny's house?"

Rachel swallowed the lump in her throat. Of course Bonnie would assume that she was going with her, that they were in this together. That's how it had been for as long as she could remember and Rachel had stopped short of saying the words that would make it clear to her that this time was different. The words she had to find the courage to say now, she realized as she caught sight of a woman in a white raincoat standing by the entrance.

"Bonnie, I'm afraid I won't be there to remind you, sweetie. You see, while you're away, I have things I have to take care of, and the sooner I take care of them, the sooner we'll be back together again."

"You mean you won't come with me?" she asked, eyes widening.

Rachel shook her head. "I can't, baby...not this time."

"But...I don't want to go away all by myself." Tears filled her eyes and spilled onto the table in large splotches. "I don't want to go, Mommy."

"I don't want you to go, either, Bonnie," she said, her heart splitting apart as she reached to gather Bonnie against her. She felt so tiny that for a second Rachel changed her mind about doing this. The urge to protect Bonnie at any cost rose in her as fiercely as it had the day she left Florida and again the day Mr. Hanson was shot. All she could think of was taking Bonnie and getting out of there.

A hand on her shoulder intervened just as she started to rise.

"Rachel?" asked a smooth friendly voice.

Rachel looked up at a face that matched the voice perfectly. This had to be the woman she'd been waiting for. She smiled at Rachel understandingly and the lines that crinkled at the edges of her eyes and sides of her mouth assured Rachel that smiling was something she did easily and often. For some reason, that thought stopped the chain of despair that had been taking control of her from growing any longer.

She sensed immediately that this woman who had gotten up early and come out in the rain to rescue a stranger in need was, like everyone Rachel had met through the underground network, a kind and caring person. The kind of person who could be trusted to look after Bonnie while she couldn't. Perhaps she was grasping at straws to make such a hasty judgment, but what choice did she have?

"Yes, I'm Rachel," she said to the woman.

"And this must be Bonnie," the woman said, smiling at the child clinging to Rachel for dear life.

Bonnie tightened her hold on Rachel and stared at the woman with fear and confusion.

"I'm Betty," she said. "And I was wondering if by any chance Bonnie liked puppies. Do you, Bonnie?"

Bonnie nodded cautiously. Rachel understood that any talk of dogs was just too tempting to resist for a little girl who loved anything with fur and four legs.

"Why, that's wonderful," Betty exclaimed with an enthusiasm that was contagious even for someone in the emotional depths Rachel was mired in. "Because I just happen to have a bunch of new pups at my house and they're just so lonesome and hoping for someone to play with. Do you think you'd like to come and stay at my house for a little while, Bonnie, and keep those puppies company?"

Bonnie's lower lip quivered as she darted a glance from Rachel to Betty. God, how she wanted to see those puppies...Rachel could see it in her eyes. But she was also smart enough to know that going with this stranger meant leaving her mother behind.

"I know," Betty said gently. "It's hard to try new things, but that's all I'm asking. Give me—and the puppies," she added, her eyes sparkling with humor, "a try. Okay, Bonnie?"

Although still racked with regret, Rachel felt better than she had thought possible as she gently untangled Bonnie and got to her feet. "Betty is right, sweetie. Just give it a try... I'll be checking on you all the time, I promise."

"You'll come see me?"

"Just as soon as I can," Rachel promised, her voice catching as she bent to hug Bonnie a final time. "And I'll call whenever I can to make sure you're all right."

Still smiling, Betty caught her eye as she stood. "You understand that direct contact is—"

Rachel cut her off with a quick nod. "I know. I've been in the program before, but we...."

Betty touched her arm. "I understand, dear."

"This is just so damn hard," Rachel muttered, pressing her lips together in a struggle for control.

Betty nodded. "Hard and painful and unfair as hell...just like the situation that forced you into this in the first place. I can't change any of that for you, but I can promise you that for as long as you need me, I'll look after this little one here as if she was my very own."

"Thank you. God, I don't know how to thank you."

"No thanks necessary...but can I give you some advice?"

Rachel nodded, fighting tears as Bonnie, listening, wrapped her tiny arms around her hips, her cheek pressed to Rachel's tummy.

"Kiss her goodbye and leave and don't look back," advised Betty. "I've been through this a time or two myself. Dawdling doesn't make it any easier."

"I know," Rachel murmured. "I know."

Reaching down to hug Bonnie, she whispered to her how much she loved her and made one hurried promise after another about how soon they would be together again and how everything was going to be all right...better than all right, better than ever. She meant to keep every one of those promises.

Then she quickly turned and walked away, the roar of pain inside her head making it impossible to tell if Bonnie really called after her or if she just imagined it. She only knew that Betty's advice didn't tell the whole story. Dawdling might not make it any easier, but neither did this.

Once outside the building, Rachel started to run with no idea of where she was going. She only knew that she didn't want Bonnie to come out and see her sitting there crying and have to go through the agony of parting all over again. Off campus she finally came to a phone booth and calmed down enough to remember that getting Bonnie to safety had been only the first part of her plan.

She fished the correct change from her purse and slid it into the coin slot, intending to phone for a taxi to take her to Mitch's office. Turning herself in was step two. And probably the last step she would make on her own, she thought bleakly. After that, it would be out of her hands. And probably out of Mitch's hands as well, a small voice goaded. After all, he had no jurisdiction or influence in Florida. Despite his adamancy about helping her, would he really be able to?

Rachel had no way of knowing. She only knew that she had gone it alone for years now, trusting no one and refusing to accept help, much less ask for it, and she wasn't much better off than she had been the day she decided to run away with Bonnie. Who was she kidding? she thought, resting her forehead against the receiver gripped in her hand. She was far worse off today. She was damn near down to her last dollar, wanted by the police in at least two states and without Bonnie. The only thing that had changed for the better was that she was no longer alone.

The time had come when she had to ask for help, she had to trust someone, and Mitch was the only one possible... the only one she dared to trust. Now all she had to do was convince him of that. After the stunt she'd just pulled, it might not be the easiest task she'd face today.

With that in mind, Rachel changed her mind about phoning for a taxi. She first needed to speak with Mitch somewhere where they could be alone, not in his office with heaven knows how many people alert to who she was and what she was doing there. It occurred to her that it might not even be safe to take a taxi. Surely by now Mitch had discovered she was gone and had the police looking for her. She knew that train and bus stations and taxi drivers were often the first sources the police checked. The thought of being arrested and tossed into a cell and having to do her explaining to Mitch through bars or one of those glass panels in a prison visiting room made her frantic.

Rummaging in her purse, she found the business card he'd given her the first time he questioned her and punched in the number of his office. She recognized the voice of Darlene, the floating secretary, instantly.

"Hello," Rachel said, "I'd like to speak with Mr. Dalton, please."

"May I ask who's calling?"

She hesitated. The truth or a ruse? The truth, she decided quickly. From now on, nothing but the truth. "This is Rachel Curtis."

She half expected the woman to start shouting, "It's her, it's her, America's most wanted." She didn't, however.

"I'm sorry," she said, "Mr. Dalton isn't in just now."

Rachel was in no mood to be charitable. "Then why did you ask who was calling if he's not even there to take the call?"

"It's policy," she replied without pause.

Of course, Rachel thought. Policy. She'd bet Darlene would never find herself in a phone booth in a strange city with next to no money and fifty odd years of prison time staring her in the face.

"Fine," she said tersely. "Does policy permit you to tell me where he can be reached?"

"At home most likely."

"Can you give me his home number?"

"I'm sorry. Policy..."

"Right, right." Rachel thought for a moment. "Can you tell me when he is expected to be in the office?"

"No."

"For heaven's sake, is this any way to run a government? Whatever happened to full disclosure? My taxes help pay this man's salary and I can't be told his office hours?"

"I meant," said the unflappable secretary, "that I can't tell you when Mr. Dalton is expected in because he's not expected in."

"Not for the whole day?" she asked, growing worried.

"Not forever." Rachel wasn't sure if the other woman had shifted to a whisper because she was about to break policy or if she was just naturally dramatic. "Mr. Dalton is no longer with the Massachusetts Attorney General's office."

"Since when?"

"Since this morning. Actually...oops...can you please hold while I..."

"No, that's all right," Rachel replied distractedly. "I know what I needed to know."

As she hung up, she realized what a stupid statement that last one was. She didn't know anything, at least not anything that made sense. When he woke up this morning Mitch had still been a prosecutor; now, a few hours later, his secretary was saying he no longer worked for the Attorney General's office? She suspected Darlene wasn't the most reliable source and could possibly have been mistaken, but somehow Rachel didn't think so. Saying your boss no longer worked there wasn't a mistake even someone like Darlene was likely to make.

So why would he quit? Or did he? Could Mitch have been fired? Because of her? Damn, she should have held on and pried all the details from Darlene. She might have phoned back but for the impatient rapping on the phone booth glass. Reluctantly she surrendered the booth to the scowling man waiting outside. She had no idea how long he'd been waiting there and, she realized as she moved a short distance away and tried to think, no idea what she was going to do now.

Common sense told her that Mitch hadn't lost his job simply because he'd left her alone this morning and she'd taken off. Reading between the lines whenever he spoke about his work, she understood that Mitch's track record had made him something of a local legend and that his boss had desperately wanted him to return to his job at the A.G.'s office. He wasn't likely to fire him over a comparatively small error in judgment. After all, she was hardly Charles Manson.

No, she decided, if Mitch was through as a prosecutor, it was his own doing. But why, she fretted, why would he walk away from a job that meant so much to him, especially in the middle of a case he considered a personal crusade and when he had just turned up the witness he needed so desperately to win that case? She felt an intuitive shiver creep along her spine. And then he had immediately let that same witness slip through his fingers because he was thinking with his heart instead of his head.

It all made such perfect sense that Rachel felt sick to her stomach. Of course that's how all of this must appear to Mitch, as if he'd once again screwed up and blown the chance to nail Mickey DelCosta. When he returned to find her gone, he must have felt like he'd stepped into a nightmare of déjà vu.

It must seem to him that once again, just like the last time, the woman he trusted to be there for him had deserted him, and just like last time his emotional involvement with that woman had interfered with his work in a way for which he would blame himself. And just like last time, she thought, her mouth going dry, his instinct would probably be to check out and get away from everything and everyone so that he couldn't screw up again.

And Rachel knew exactly how he would manage that. The *My Way*, she thought. If Mitch was hurting, and she knew in her heart that he was, his boat was the only place he would want to be. He'd told her so himself.

Maybe he was there already. As far as she knew, the boat was docked behind his house. For all the good that did her. If Darlene wouldn't give her Mitch's phone number, there's no way she would give her his home address. Rachel knew that he lived on the coast somewhere east of Plymouth. In the town of Barnstable, she recalled. She concentrated, racking her brain to remember the name he had mentioned when talking about the specific area where his house was located. Something Heights. Windward. Wayward. Bellwind, she thought suddenly. That was it, Bellwind Heights.

As soon as the phone was available she called for a taxi and asked the driver to take her to Bellwind Heights in Barnstable and to hurry. The rush was because she was impatient to see Mitch and find out what was going on. She was certain he would still be there. He had to be. No one left town that fast, she told herself, and then nearly groaned out loud, recalling a time or two when she had left places even faster. But this was different. Mitch wasn't running for his life, simply from it. Surely she would be in time to stop him.

The driver turned in his seat and gave a long hard look at her dressed in the jeans and sweater she'd thrown on that morning. She imagined her hair was a mess from running and she hadn't had time for makeup. Not exactly a case of putting her best foot forward.

"Bellwind Heights, hmm?" he drawled, his curiosity plain. "You work out there, do you?"

"No," she countered, irritated. "Now are you going to drive me there or not?"

"Depends."

"On what?"

"On whether or not you got forty bucks on you to pay the fare for going all that way."

"The ride will cost forty dollars?"

He nodded. "Up-front. You can't be too careful these days."

"That's outrageous. It didn't cost me half that to come here from Plymouth."

"Well, Bellwind Heights ain't Plymouth. Look at the map...it's that far again from where we're at. Plus there's a surcharge for going out of my territory."

"Then don't bother," Rachel snapped, getting out and slamming the door. "I'll take a bus."

He chuckled. "Good luck."

His chuckle proved portentous. Rachel soon discovered that while the shortest distance between two points might be a straight line, when you traveled by public transportation, such a journey just wasn't possible. She had to transfer and detour and wait at every stopping point along the way. As the hours passed and her nerves pulled tauter each time a police cruiser passed, Rachel gritted her teeth and reminded herself that since she didn't have forty dollars, she didn't have any choice.

In the end, she had to walk the last few miles. No bus routes ran through Bellwind Heights, she was told, and the closer she got to that area, the more she understood why.

Bellwind Heights wasn't a public transportation kind of place. It had been Rachel's hope that she would find someone around to ask which of the widely spaced homes belonged to Mitch, but unfortunately it also wasn't the sort of neighborhood where the neighbors were out washing their cars in the driveway or mowing their own lawns. Bellwind Heights was an enclave of wealth and privilege where others were paid to handle the more mundane tasks of life.

Over dinner, Mitch had mentioned that he played the futures market for fun and profit and she could see for herself that he must be as successful at that as he was at practicing law. No state worker short of the governor earned a salary large enough to pay the mortgage on one of these beauties.

Rachel couldn't help thinking also of what Mitch had told her about his wife leaving him for a man with much less money. For some reason, it gave her a feeling of satisfaction to look around and know that for a woman to leave one of these houses, her life in it would have to be very empty indeed. It was further evidence that there were no smoldering embers between Mitch and his first wife. With all the trouble she was in and all the things she had to worry about, it was an absolutely idiotic reason to smile as she trudged along, but Rachel smiled just the same. She smiled with satisfaction, and anticipation.

As she rounded a corner bordered by a tall hedge, she saw the first evidence of human life in Bellwind Heights. An elderly woman wearing a rain hat was pruning the shrubbery by the end of a long curving driveway. It was obvious to Rachel that this was no hired gardener. If the woman lived here, she probably knew Mitch.

Rachel hurried to the end of the driveway and called to her. "Excuse me, ma'am."

The older woman turned, lifting her chin to gaze at Rachel from beneath the wide brim of her hat. Evidently de-

ciding she didn't present a threat, she took a step closer and
tipped her head as if she had trouble hearing.

"What can I do for you?" she asked.

"I'm hoping you can help me find one of your neighbors... Mitch Dalton. Do you know which house is his?"

"I might," the woman replied. "Are you a friend of
Mitch's or something?"

"Good question." Rachel wasn't aware she'd muttered
it aloud until she heard the woman's throaty chuckle.

"So which is it?" she demanded.

Rachel smiled ruefully. "A little of both, I guess. I think
I'm his friend and if 'something' means more than a
friend, I guess I hope to be that, too."

The older woman chuckled again. "Good answer. You
know something, I like you." She pointed at a house in the
distance. "That's Mitch's place right there, the big white
house. You tell him Ruth Crandall said hello."

"I will, Ms. Crandall, and thank you."

"Don't thank me. Just being neighborly. If you want my
opinion, Mitch Dalton's a man who needs a good
friend..." Her eyes crinkled. "Or something." As she
turned back to her pruning, she added, "Might want to
run a comb through your hair while you're at it."

Rachel walked away with a wry smile. She doubted that
combing her hair was going to do much good at this
point... either to impress Mitch or distract him. None-
theless, as she started up the front walk to his house, she
pulled her brush from her purse and ran it through her hair
as Ms. Crandall suggested.

Her pace quickened in spite of her tired legs. This was
where she had been struggling to get all day. She didn't
spare a thought about what she was going to do if Mitch
wasn't there or if he was no longer willing to help her. She
was running on adrenaline, along with a type of energy
that had been missing from her life for far too long.

In the past few years she had been driven by anger and frustration and desperation, as well as a searing fear of what would happen to Bonnie if she didn't act. Now she was being propelled forward by something else entirely…hope. Hope rooted in trust and love. The two went hand in hand, she realized now. Maybe that was why, until now, she hadn't been able to trust anyone else to help her. With Donna gone and her mother aging, there had been no one else in the world whom she loved, and whom she believed loved her in return, enough for her to trust them with her life. Now she had found just such a person. Mitch.

She wasn't sure how it was possible to fall in love so deeply and so quickly under such trying circumstances, only that it had happened for her. Maybe it had happened because of the difficult situation they were trapped in together. She and Mitch hadn't had time for flirtation or coy games. They had been tested by the kind of fire that leaves you bare to the soul and somehow they had found in each other what was missing in themselves.

At least she had found it. She couldn't isolate the exact moment when she had fallen in love with Mitch or even when she had first realized she was in love. For her, the process of falling in love had been more like the incoming tide that she could hear in the distance than the explosion it was sometimes portrayed as in books. With each fresh surge, Mitch had claimed another small piece of her, until her whole life felt his impact, until she was his.

And as for Mitch? Rachel took a deep breath as she reached to ring his front doorbell. She wasn't sure exactly what Mitch might be feeling toward her at that moment.

When no one answered on the first ring, something inside her panicked. Still she stood there and rang it three more times before hurrying around the huge house and trying the back door as well. Another time Rachel knew she would have been awed by the beauty of Mitch's home, with its rolling lawn and careful landscaping, which even in autumn was lush and colorful...if a bit neglected. In fact, the place had the sad look of a house that desperately needed love and attention to make it what it should be. A little like its owner, she mused, her heart swelling with the desire to be the one to give Mitch all the love and attention he deserved.

Again no one answered when she rang. Rachel would have resorted to banging on the solid wood door or even trying the knob and walking in, if not for the ominous-looking security panels beside each entrance. She'd gotten all this way without being apprehended; the last thing she wanted was to set off the alarm and have the police show up now.

Growing steadily more desperate, she turned and started down toward the water and the wooden dock extending out about forty feet from the shore. She didn't have to go quite that far to see that there was no boat tied there. Beneath an overcast sky, the dock was deserted. Rachel stopped in her tracks and gazed at the desolate sight, her heart caving in under the pressure of her disappointment.

It was hard to believe that Mitch could have quit his job, packed his things and sailed out of her life so quickly. But at the moment, she wasn't up to fashioning a more palatable explanation.

She had been so sure he would be here, so certain that her courage in deciding to do the honest thing would be rewarded, that her defeat now was nearly overwhelming. She sank to the grass where she was, heedless that it was still wet from the rain that had fallen earlier in the day. The cool dampness quickly soaked through her jeans and the bottom hem of the fisherman knit sweater she had hurriedly pulled on again this morning. How she looked had been the least of her worries, then and now.

She bent her knees and rested her forehead on the bridge of her arms, feeling like a gambler who had just wagered everything on a single roll of the dice and lost. She was cold and tired and as alone as she had ever been. It would be dark in a few hours. She couldn't return to her apartment and she had no money to go anywhere else. And without Mitch to support her, the prospect of turning herself in to face the charges against her seemed a thousand times more frightening than it had that morning.

She hunched her shoulders, huddling against the cold. The same question she had asked Mitch last night rose in her again. Except this time she had only herself to ask and it reverberated through her in a mocking echo for which she had no answer.... What was she going to do now? What on earth was she going to do now?

When Mitch first came over the small crest at the edge of the back lawn, he was sure he was as crazy as any man who had ever wandered around the desert for too long and chased after pools of water that just weren't there. This had to be a figment of his imagination, he told himself as he stopped and gazed at a spot about halfway between where he was standing and the house.

Rachel was gone. She had run from him the second his back was turned and he couldn't conceive of her coming back on her own. He'd spent the day hunting for her, checking the bus and train stations between here and Boston, driving to Logan Airport and using his title to gain access to the passenger list for every flight out. Or rather, he'd used his former title, he amended, feeling not a trace of remorse over his resignation.

Over and over again as he searched, he had envisioned Rachel and Bonnie climbing aboard a train or bus or being stashed in the back seat of some stranger's car as they were once more absorbed into what he knew was a highly secure and well-organized underground network designed to help women and children escape from abusive situations.

And over and over again he had found nothing. He'd returned home to check his messages—and to brood, he thought derisively. He always did his best brooding down by the water. There had been no possibilities glimmering on the ocean for him tonight, only regrets.

The result of all that useless searching and brooding was that he was distraught enough to hallucinate. He had to be. Why else would he swear that Rachel was sitting there dead ahead on his back lawn? The mirage—that's what it had to be—was bent over, wearing the same clothes she'd been wearing last night, her hair gleaming like a beacon in an otherwise dark and dreary landscape.

As mirages went, he greatly preferred this one to a puddle of water...or for that matter, even a pot of gold at the end of some rainbow. He'd hoped that Rachel was his pot of gold...the real thing this time, rather than all the glossy illusions he'd spent too long chasing.

There was only one problem with this mirage of his and Mitch's chest muscles clenched as it occurred to him what that problem was. A mirage couldn't cry.

Chapter Twelve

The soft, muffled sound of Rachel's sobs held him motionless for a moment. Finally, propelled by an explosive need to know if this was, as he feared, too good to be true, Mitch started toward her.

"Rachel?" he said as he drew closer, whispering, ridiculously afraid that too harsh a sound or sudden a move might make her disappear into the fog creeping steadily from over the ocean at his back.

She lifted her head at the sound of his voice, her startled expression slowly giving way to one of amazement and such happiness that Mitch knew he would remember it forever.

"Mitch?" she said, struggling to plant her feet on the wet, slippery grass, then crying his name aloud, not a question this time, but a cry of joy as she came bounding toward him.

Mitch had his arms open wide as she threw herself against him. They held each other as if they were afraid to let go. Again and again he ran his hands over her back, needing to make sure that she was real and not a figment of his imagination, that she was really there, that she was in his arms again. The way Rachel's fingers curled into the fabric of his shirt told him she needed the same reassurance.

Finally he moved his hands to her face, framing it with them as he tipped it up, staring at her for a long time before he kissed her, gently, a kiss to soothe and heal and begin to tell her all the things he'd spent the whole day cursing himself for not having said last night.

"I love you," he said suddenly and completely out of character. Here he was dispensing with all the preliminary arguments and cutting to the heart of the matter. "I love you, Rachel."

She was crying again he noticed as she peered up at him. Or maybe she hadn't stopped crying. This time, however, she was crying and smiling at the same time and a small piece of the ten-ton weight on his heart started to chip away.

"I can't..." She stopped and sniffled. "I thought you... oh, Mitch, I love you, too. I love you... I love you..." She touched his face and throat and smoothed the hair from his forehead. "I love you so much."

His mouth sloped into a smile. "Bet I love you more."

"Impossible," she argued, laughing and sniffling at once. "I thought you were gone."

"Gone where?" he asked, rubbing her shoulders.

"Away... to Florida or wherever it is you go when you're mad at the world."

"The only place I've gone today is crazy... looking for you."

A bewildered frown creased her forehead. "But they told me you had quit your job."

"Who told you?"

"Your office... your infamous floating secretary."

"Darlene," he said, nodding understandingly. "She was wrong to tell you, but right on the facts. I did quit."

"Actually she just said you didn't work there anymore. I couldn't imagine them firing you, so I assumed you had quit."

"So I could run away and lick my wounds again?"

She shook her head. "I didn't think of it that way."

"You had every reason to. I did it once before."

"I was afraid that you would think this was like what happened before," she admitted.

"No, this time is different. Loving you makes everything different."

"Then why did you quit?" She gave him a regretful look. "I hope they didn't blame you for agreeing to give me some time alone."

"They didn't."

"Good."

"Probably because no one knows."

"What?" Her eyes were wide and astonished. "But how..."

"Well, actually Ollie knows. He's the guy who first noticed the date on your social security number."

"Oh," she said, her tone like ice.

Mitch laughed and hugged her. "Ollie's a good guy... and a good friend. When I called him back this morning and asked him to pull strings to put a hold on the APB I had put out for you and give me forty-eight hours to find you myself, he agreed. No questions asked."

"An APB?" she asked. "You put out an APB on me? As if I was some sort of criminal?"

"Fugitive. And you are," he reminded her gently.

"I suppose that's why you had to quit your job. So you could associate with known fugitives."

He laughed at her tart tone. At the moment, he felt good enough to laugh at just about anything short of the prospect of losing Rachel again.

"You're close," he replied. "Very, very close. I quit because I knew it would never work for me to try to straddle the fence between doing my job as a prosecutor and doing whatever the hell it takes to keep you out of jail."

Her deep sigh brought her chest closer to his. Mitch wished she would sigh again.

"I was so afraid you would have changed your mind about helping me," she murmured.

"Never," he said, his lips in her hair as she rested her cheek on his chest. "Don't ever think that again."

"I can't believe you quit your job because of me... to help me."

"Why not? You quit yours to help Bonnie."

"That's different."

"How?"

"Bonnie was in trouble."

"So are you."

"But she's only a child... she needed me."

"You need me."

She didn't even attempt to deny it and knowing what a giant step that was for them, Mitch's heart soared.

"Still," she persisted, "Bonnie is family and I love her."

"I love you, and just as soon as this whole thing is straightened out, one way or the other, I want to make you family. I want to marry you, Rachel. I want to take care of you. I want to prove to you, and to myself, that I can let someone close enough to make a marriage work." He looped his arms around her neck. "I've learned a lot the hard way. You should at least give me a chance to put it to good use."

"I would, Mitch," she said, but there was an undercurrent of resistance in her voice that alarmed him. "If things were different, I'd say yes to you in a second. But I can't make any promises until I know what's going to happen to me, and to Bonnie. I certainly can't say I'll marry you... how did you put it? One way or the other."

"Sure you can, but we don't have to talk about that right now. In fact," he said, holding her close and rubbing his hands up and down her arms in an effort to warm her up, "it's too cold to talk about anything out here. Come on in and I'll make you some hot coffee."

"I thought you couldn't make coffee," she said.

He shrugged, grinning unabashedly. "I'll improvise."

Inside, he offered her a warm wool blanket to wrap around her shoulders and did a far better job making coffee than he'd led her to believe he would. They sat in his den and Mitch added a log to the fire he'd built before settling into the seat beside her. As soon as she'd warmed up a bit, Rachel wanted to hear more about his sudden decision to leave the A.G.'s office.

"Did you actually quit," she asked, "or is this more like another leave of absence?"

Mitch chuckled. "I think they're hoping that's all it is, but I know it's for good this time. I want to make a fresh start, Rachel."

"What about your dream of being elected Attorney General?"

"I found a better dream. What I want now is to do work that I enjoy and that will earn enough to pay the bills and leave me as much time as possible for what really matters most to me...you...and my kids. I thank God I realized that now, before I wasted any more of my life."

"That's a pretty dramatic shifting of gears," Rachel observed, warming her hands on her coffee mug.

"It ought to be. I learned from a pro." When she shot him a quizzical look, he grinned and said, "You."

"Come on, Mitch, I'm hardly a role model. I didn't even want to quit my job...I had no choice. Even our reasons for quitting are very different."

"Maybe not." He put his cup aside and leaned forward to take hers away as well so he could hold her hands in his. "You quit because you had to in order to do what needed to be done to help Bonnie. Like I told you outside, I quit to help you. That's my number-one objective right now and I'll do whatever it takes. But I still have honor... I wouldn't have felt right abusing my office in the process or, on the other side, withholding information about criminal activity I might become privy to in the course of planning your defense.''

''You mean like about the underground network that helped us?''

Mitch nodded. ''That's right. Anything you tell me from now on is privileged information. You don't have to worry about incriminating the people who helped you.''

Her eyes glistened. ''I can't believe you're doing this for me... turning your whole life upside down.''

''I can't believe that you, of all people, think it's so amazing. Like I said, I'm not doing anything you didn't do first. You threw caution to the wind and followed your heart to save Bonnie. This morning, when I finally thought everything through and made the decision to leave my job, I did the same thing. I threw caution to the wind for you... for us.''

She shrugged apologetically. ''You may live to regret it. My future is a big question mark right now and I can't make you any promises of a happy ending.''

''Well, that's where we differ, because I can. I do promise you a happy ending, Rachel,'' he said, squeezing her hand. ''All you have to do is trust me.''

''I do trust you... I really do, Mitch. If I didn't, I wouldn't be here.'' She smiled sheepishly. ''I'd probably be on a bus to some town I never heard of, looking forward to spending the night with people I never met.''

His thumbs caressed the soft spots on the insides of her wrists. ''That must have been tough for you, being on the move for so long, depending on others for everything.''

"It was tough...not just on me, but on Bonnie, too. Just the thought of having to resort to it again makes me cringe."

"What made you change your mind?"

Her brow furrowed. "About what?"

"About running back to the underground...about running away. What made you decide to come back here and try it my way after all?"

"Oh, Mitch, you don't understand. I was never running from you...after last night, how could I? I should have explained everything the minute I got here, but you just seemed so happy to see me, I got sidetracked."

"I don't get it. Explain what?"

"Why I left before you got back this morning."

"I think it was pretty obvious. I was coming back to take you in and you didn't want to go. So you took off."

"No, that's not it at all...although I knew that's what you would think and I hated having to hurt you that way even for a little while."

"Then why did you leave?"

Rachel, who thought he would have guessed her plan by now, was caught by surprise. "Why...to take care of Bonnie, of course."

His eyes narrowed and suddenly she felt as much a suspect as she had that first day he questioned her.

"What do you mean 'to take care of Bonnie'?"

She hesitated, unsettled by his reaction. "I mean to protect her, to keep her safe, to make sure some judge doesn't send her back to live with a man who is perfectly capable of killing her the same way he killed her mother." As she spoke, she withdrew her hands from his grasp, deeming the slight rise in her voice totally justified.

"Let me get this straight, you mean you've hidden her somewhere?"

"I mean I've been in touch with the same people who helped us before and they're taking care of Bonnie until I'm able to again."

"You're hiding her," he concluded in a hollow tone of disbelief. "You're goddamn hiding her all over again."

"You make it sound like it's some sort of big surprise to you."

"It is," he said loudly.

"Mitch, surely you must have wondered where Bonnie was when I showed up here alone."

He stood, shaking his head as if trying to clear it. A growing sense of dread gnawed at Rachel as she watched him pace restlessly, his hands shoved into the pockets of his dark pleated-front trousers. His suit jacket was missing and his shirt was wrinkled, the sleeves rolled haphazardly. She had never seen him look so rumpled, or weary. Clearly his day had been as exhausting and trying as her own and now, without meaning to, she had delivered another blow.

"I guess I jumped to a lot of wrong conclusions," he said finally. "When I got to your place this morning, I assumed you had taken Bonnie and run away again. At first I was furious...and hurt. Hurt that you hadn't trusted me. The first thing I did was call Ollie and order the APB on you."

Rachel nodded and said, "I want you to know that, in spite of my reaction outside, I really do understand why you had to do that."

"It was my job."

She nodded again.

"But," he went on, "the more I thought about it, the more I realized that for the first time in my life, something was more important to me than the job." He held her gaze. "You. I knew even before then that I was in love with you, but at that moment I realized that I loved you enough to do anything I had to do, give up anything I had, in order to hold on to you. Including my job and all the old vendettas that go with it.''

''So you decided to quit...and call off the APB?''

''Not quite that fast. At first I fully intended to have you hauled back and locked up until I could talk some sense into you. I was still feeling betrayed. I couldn't understand why you couldn't understand how much I wanted to help you...why you couldn't just trust me to do what was best for you and for Bonnie. I mean, I'm a lawyer, for Pete's sake, and a damn good one if I do say so myself.''

''Mitch, I told you...''

''I know,'' he said, silencing her protest. ''You do trust me...to help you, at least. You just don't trust me to look out for Bonnie.''

''Mitch, please...''

''No,'' he said, overriding her once more. ''The fact that you're here without her means that that's the bottom line, Rachel, and I'm just going to have to come to terms with it. Don't worry,'' he said, his weary smile tearing at her heart, ''I figure I'm still better off than I was this morning. At least you're here with me.''

''Mitch, please,'' she implored, standing to go to him, ''you have to understand my feelings. Bonnie is my responsibility. As far as I'm concerned, her life is literally in my hands.''

''I know that's how you feel.''

''I have to put her safety ahead of everything else... ahead of myself...ahead of us.''

''I know that, too,'' he told her. ''I figured it all out this morning.''

''Then you know why I had to take her away.''

He nodded. ''And I understood...or thought I did. It really blew me away to realize that I already know you better than I've ever known anyone in my whole life. Ever,'' he repeated, holding her gaze. ''I know what makes you tick, and I know that the thing you're more afraid of than anything else is failing Bonnie.''

"You're right.''

"Once I realized that, it was easy for me to decide to call off the APB and asked Ollie to give me a chance to find you myself. Because once it penetrated my thick skull that you were doing what you thought you had to do, what you thought best for Bonnie, I didn't feel betrayed anymore.''

"You didn't?'' she asked, not quite understanding why, if that was so, he seemed so dismayed a few moments ago.

"No. I felt even more in love with you than I did before, and I felt very lucky that I had found a woman who could love that way, without reason or limits, who would go to the wall for someone she loved. And I wanted you to love me the same way.''

She reached for him, relieved when he didn't move away, but let her wrap her arms around him. "Mitch, I do...I can love you that way. I just need time.''

"I know...and you've got it. In the meantime, I plan to love you all the way...without limits. When I saw you there on the lawn, I just thought...'' He stopped and shrugged.

Rachel tightened her hold on him, her chest tight with emotion. "You thought that I had changed my mind somehow. That I had brought Bonnie back with me to face the music.''

He nodded, his smile sadly sheepish. "Yeah. I thought the fact that you were here meant that you'd come to the same conclusion I had, that if we go to the wall together, we can do anything.''

She hung her head. "I'm so sorry, Mitch. I want to tell you it's like that...part of me—most of me—even believes it. But the small part of me that's afraid won't let me put Bonnie in jeopardy.''

"You don't get it," he countered. "My feelings about this aside, from a legal standpoint you and Bonnie are both in more jeopardy this way."

"How?"

"Because in cases like this the goodwill of the court is essential . . . and you're not going to win any judge's heart with this stunt."

"But I'm the one who's wanted, and I'm turning myself in. That has to count for something."

"You see it as turning yourself in. A judge might see it as an ultimatum . . . a case of your saying that if things go your way, you'll produce the kid. Otherwise . . ."

His voice trailed off, letting Rachel fill in the unflattering blanks.

"All I want is to protect her. I have no way of knowing . . ."

"No, you don't," he agreed before she could finish. "You have no way of knowing how this will play out in court. I made some calls this morning, called in some favors I was owed with some colleagues locally who also have connections in Florida. I'm trying to find out what your brother-in-law has been up to in the past few years."

Excitement lit Rachel's expression. "Do you really think he might have done something else? Something that could help prove I was right about him all along?"

"That's what I'm hoping. I know this much, guys with his track record don't usually turn into saints overnight. But my point is, that no matter what we turn up beforehand, you're going to walk into that courtroom without any guarantees. The best you can do is to have faith . . . faith in yourself, faith that you're in the right and that justice will prevail, and faith in whoever's there fighting for you."

"That's what you really mean, isn't it? That I have to have faith in you?"

"If I'm the one you decide to let defend you . . . and I hope to God you do. But if it's going to work, it can't be halfway, Rachel. No hedging your bets. Not in court...and not with us, either."

"It sounds like you're the one who's issuing ultimatums now."

He immediately shook his head. "Not at all. I've made my decision. I've hedged my bets in the past and I've learned that love doesn't work when you go at it halfway. I'm with you all the way. The rest is up to you."

She lifted her hands to grip her head as if that might hold it together when all the thoughts spinning inside threatened to split it apart. "I do have faith in you, Mitch...for myself. But it's different with Bonnie. I promised Donna..."

"You promised Donna to take care of her...and you have, the way you thought best at the time. But things have changed, Rachel. We both know you can't run and hide forever." He pulled her against him, enfolding her in his strong arms. "You don't have to go it alone ever again, Rachel."

"I don't know if I can do it, Mitch. I don't know if I can just turn Bonnie over to them."

"To me," he corrected. "And you can do it. You can if you trust me all the way...the way I trust you." He moved his hands over her back in a comforting caress, letting her think in silence for a few moments.

"You know," he said softly, "I heard a song the other day in the car, a country song on a station I never listen to. If you believe in omens, this was one, because the words stuck in my head, and this morning, when I was thinking about us and was furious with you for taking off, they came back to me."

"What song was it?"

"I don't know the title, but it was a play on that old chant kids use when they're showing off. Look, mom, no hands."

She nodded, smiling slightly against the steel pillow of his chest. "Bonnie's not quite at that stage yet, but I remember yelling it to my mother."

"Well, that was what this song was about, only the line was 'Look, heart, no hands.' It was about loving someone with no strings and no nets, with only your lover there to catch you when you fall." He hugged her tightly. "If I fall, you're the one I want there to catch me, and I know you would. This time, let me catch you, Rachel. I'm here . . . and I can do it."

"You make it sound so simple," she said fretfully.

"It is simple," Mitch countered, his deep tone offering the same reassurance as his embrace. "Just let go . . . I'm here."

Rachel held him tighter. "I'm not sure I can."

"You can. I saw you . . . last night in your kitchen."

Rachel lifted her head to meet his gaze, her green eyes shy and smoky at the memory he evoked.

"I saw you fighting for control," he told her, "wanting it and afraid of it all at the same time. And in the end you let go of everything else inside you and went for it all the way . . . and the world didn't end, did it?"

"This is different," she protested.

"Not very. You trusted me then and you can do it again . . . you just need practice," he said, bending his head and finding her mouth with his own.

Chapter Thirteen

Kissing Rachel had a way of making him lose track of time... and space. He was barely aware of moving from the den to the bedroom, but he must have, driven by instinct alone, because suddenly he was standing by his bed with Rachel cradled in his arms and his body on fire for her.

Carefully Mitch dropped her onto the bed and followed her down, rolling with her across the king-size mattress in a sexy tussle for mastery that only fanned their already smoldering desires. He succeeded in pinning her first, with her arms stretched over her head, and holding her there long enough to work off her sweater and unclasp her bra. As he lowered his head to capture one temptingly aroused tip with his mouth, she rolled aside, her throaty chuckle both victorious and provocative.

Seizing control of their love play, she returned the favor, unbuttoning his shirt amidst lingering caresses of his arms and chest before finally peeling it off and tossing it aside. Mitch stretched out, tacitly inviting her to continue.

He was more than content to let Rachel have her way with him for the moment. He knew that in the end she would surrender, they both would, to the tumultuous rush of pleasure that would claim them body and soul, ultimately overcoming whatever they were alone and making them one in every possible sense.

The room was dark, with only the faint glow of moonlight through the windows illuminating the dark blue drapes and spread. In a fit of resentment after Angie had left, he'd thrown out everything in the room they had shared that reminded him of her in particular and women in general, and had hired a decorator to redo it in somber masculine shades.

He no longer felt resentful or somber, but he was glad the room was all new for this night with Rachel, and all the nights he was determined would follow this one.

It took a ridiculously long time for them to finish undressing each other, but speed was hardly their purpose. Desire was. Arousing it with excruciating attention to detail, prolonging it with the sweet ministrations of hands and tongues, driving each other to the outer limits of pleasure, then slowing down, backing off, turning gentle, only to take each other to the edge again . . . and again.

When Mitch sensed that Rachel was as close to exploding in his arms as she could be, he ran his hands over her breasts and tummy in a slow lavish massage, which ended with his hands hooked at the back of her knees. He gently lifted her legs so they rested on his shoulders. As he did, he watched her face and the excitement and trepidation that flickered in her passion-dark eyes.

Then, trembling with the force of his love for her, he raked his gaze downward as he murmured words of praise and adoration, telling her all the ways that she was beautiful and precious to him. He accompanied his words with

the fevered touch of his lips, paying homage to the firm
swell of her breasts, the curve of her waist and the entic-
ing valley where hip met thigh.

His sensual invocation ended with his lips at the heart of
her womanhood, hovering, savoring the anticipation of
this supreme intimacy until the need for her surpassed
whatever tatters of self-control he had left. With his tongue
he feathered an intricate pattern of sensations on her delicate flesh, flicking, stabbing, discovering how to make her
tremble and melt.

Her fingers moved through his hair, her touch growing
steadily more erratic and desperate, her soft moans becoming fractured and urgent in a way that made Mitch feel
at once powerfully masculine and an absolute supplicant
to her womanhood. Her climax left him awed, with the
beauty of her body, the strength and heat and gentle af-
termath of her passion, the way she clung to him throughout.

The feel and scent and taste of her had been sending
shock waves through his own body and now they shot out
of Mitch's control. The fierce need she created in him
drove him up to claim her. He groaned as her heat and
softness pulled him deeper and deeper. He wanted to stay
there and feel that way forever. He wasn't nearly that lucky
or that disciplined.

Thrusting deeply rushed him toward his own explosion,
until pleasure was a fire bolt in his veins and with a hoarse,
exultant cry he collapsed on top of her, lost with her in a
dark world of quivering aftershocks that gradually faded,
leading them to contentment . . . and sleep.

Mitch wasn't sure how long he'd slept, only that after
the day he'd had it wasn't nearly long enough. He probably would have stayed asleep for hours more if not for
some inner sense that he was alone in his bed. Even before
he opened his eyes or stretched out his arm, he was at-

tuned to the empty space where Rachel belonged. Barely awake, he found his pants and went in search of her.

He found her outside, sitting on the back steps wearing the heavy terry robe he kept hung on the back of the bathroom door and the blanket he'd given her earlier. She smiled at him as he lowered himself to the step beside her.

"What are you doing out here?"

"I couldn't sleep."

"Aren't you cold?"

She shook her head. "The cool air helps clear my head. It's been so long since I've been someplace where I felt free to come outside and sit at night. I've missed it."

"So," he said, wrapping his arm around her shoulders, "what has all this night air got you thinking?"

"Same old thing, I'm afraid. I keep trying to see into the future and figure out what's going to happen tomorrow and afterward. But all I've come up with is one answer and lots of questions."

"Well, since good lawyers always start with the facts, why don't you tell me the answer you've come up with and then I'll try to tackle the questions."

He felt the deep breath that lifted her shoulders and he tightened his hold on her reassuringly.

"It has to do with Bonnie," she explained, "and with what I'm going to do about her. I've decided that first thing in the morning I'm going to call and tell them I want to pick her up as soon as possible."

"I probably ought to say I hope I didn't twist your arm in this, but the fact is I don't. You're doing the right thing, Rachel, and you have my word that I won't let anything happen to her." He took her chin in his hand and turned her face toward him. "I swear to God, if I have to kidnap her myself to keep Parnell from getting his hands on her, I will."

"I believe you probably would," Rachel said, her smile, as unsteady as it was, a welcome sight. "That's why I decided to do it."

Mitch wanted to hold her. He wanted to gather her in his arms and carry her back inside and make love to her all over again. What held him back was his understanding that her mood was too pensive for that. Rachel needed something else from him now, just as she would need different things at different times during the hard days ahead, and he planned to deliver on it all. Right now she needed someone to listen and to help her come to terms with the fear she must be feeling about the future . . . for both Bonnie and herself.

"Now, how about those questions?" he asked when she seemed to turn back in on herself, staring out over the ocean as if hypnotized by whatever was going on inside her head.

She shot him a grateful smile, her hand slipping from under the blanket to find his where it hung over her shoulder. "Actually all my questions can be wrapped up in one big knockout blow...what's going to happen to me, Mitch?" she asked, a catch in her voice that made him want to move mountains for her. "I mean after I bring Bonnie back and turn myself in. We'll be returned to Florida, right?"

"There'll be an extradition hearing first, but yes, at some point you'll be returned to Florida to face the charges there."

He felt her shudder.

"And then?" she asked. "I mean, I know you have no way of knowing for sure, but what do you think the odds are of my being found innocent or acquitted or whatever the best is that I can hope for."

"It's funny you should ask that," Mitch replied, his tone intentionally even and relaxed in spite of his own rioting concern for her. "I've been doing a lot of thinking about that since yesterday. I've tried to do the same thing I do for every case I take on . . . create a best- and a worst-case scenario." He flashed her his cockiest grin. "I like to be prepared."

"I see. Well, counselor," she said, "I assume I'm allowed to call you that now?"

"I sort of like what you called me a while ago . . . in the bedroom," he added when she shot him a quizzical look.

Her blush was visible even in the darkness, prompting him to accompany his grin with a satisfied chuckle.

"But as long as we're discussing business," he went on, "'counselor' will do just fine. Now, what were you saying?"

"I think I've forgotten."

"I was telling you about my theory of best- and worst-case scenarios," he prompted.

"That's right. I suppose I should save the best for last, but I could use some good news about now, so tell me the best-case scenario first."

"Sure. This was the easy part. The best-case scenario has the D.A. in Florida dropping all charges against you and finding that there's sufficient new evidence to reopen the investigation into your sister's death and eventually bring charges against Parnell."

"Wow," Rachel said when he finished. "You don't dream halfway, do you?"

"Where you're concerned, I don't intend to do anything halfway."

"Could all that really happen?"

"Sure it could. If we can turn up new evidence strong enough to implicate Parnell and justify what you did to protect Bonnie and if we can somehow, somewhere, find a witness to support your testimony and if we get a judge who's willing to listen with an open mind."

"That's an awful lot of if's."

"Are you kidding? I've come out swinging with much less to go on."

"Are you saying there's really a chance that all that could come true?"

"An excellent chance," he lied without compunction.

Rachel was going to need a surge of strength and confidence to get her through the next few days and he was determined to provide it. The truth was that he didn't yet know enough about this whole mess to make an educated appraisal of her chances for anything. There would be time enough as matters unfolded to give her an honest appraisal of what they faced. By then, she would have become used to the idea that whatever it was, they would face it—and survive it—together.

"Excellent," she said softly. "Even if that's a wild exaggeration, I thank you for it. Now—" she squared her shoulders "—I'm ready to hear the rest. What's the worst-case scenario you came up with?"

Mitch turned to meet her gaze and if he'd had a glimmer of doubt that he could really do what he promised—give her a happy ending to all this—he lost it right then and there.

"There isn't one," he said. "For the first time in my career, I can't even imagine losing. That's because I'm not going to."

"You're teasing?" she said, her hope that he wasn't apparent from her tone.

"I've never been more serious," Mitch assured her. "If you trust me to take care of you, and Bonnie, I promise you that we're going to go down there and prove to them that far from being a criminal, you're a heroine. And once that's settled, we're going to get married and we're going to get custody of Bonnie and then we're going to come back here—or anywhere you want to live—and we're going to hope like crazy that I can find another job."

Rachel laughed and leaned against him.

"And when I do," he continued, "we're going to live happily ever after. What do you say to that?"

"What can I say?" Rachel replied, turning to him with her arms open wide. "Look, heart, no hands."

Epilogue

The Following September...

Mitch's house looked much the same as it had the first time Rachel had seen it a year ago. Most of the changes that had taken place since fell under the heading of maintenance. Still, the effect was dramatic. Far from appearing forlorn and neglected as it once had, the house looked fresh and new.

Then again, Rachel thought with an easy smile, maybe it was simply that the entire world looked bright and shiny and new to her these days. And that whenever she looked at this place now, she saw not simply a beautiful house, but a real home. Her home.

With Mitch's approval she was overseeing the upkeep of the house and yard. She had plenty of time for it...at least for another few months, she thought, instinctively laying her hand on her tummy, where only yesterday she had felt the first fluttering movements of the baby she was carrying. A warm feeling of pride filled her as she paused for a moment on her way inside and gazed around her. The lawn and shrubs were freshly trimmed, red geraniums bloomed in the window boxes and new blue-and-white-striped awnings that matched the umbrella and chair cushions on the deck shaded the windows and kept the house a cool haven on hot summer days.

As she stepped into the kitchen to put the finishing touches on the birthday cake she had baked in honor of Nicole's eighth birthday, the sound of laughter followed her. Mitch and the girls—Nicole, Becky and Bonnie—were flying kites in the backyard. The weather was warm and windy, making this a perfect day for it, and a perfect day for a barbecue and birthday party, a perfect day to spend with family and good friends, a perfect day to be alive. And free.

Nicole's birthday was actually tomorrow, but they were celebrating today because she was spending the weekend with them and tomorrow she and Becky would be back home with her mother and stepfather. Mitch's daughters visited often. The two girls and Bonnie had hit it off from the first time they met, and watching the three of them together brought back to Rachel memories of herself and Donna around their age. She was glad that Bonnie finally had "sisters" with whom to share the special moments and rituals of childhood.

As she had gone through the house, making the small changes any woman did when she moved into a new place, she had purposely left Nicole's and Becky's old rooms exactly as they were, wanting them to always feel that they weren't merely guests, but that they belonged there. Because they did.

In a very real sense, her marriage to Mitch was a union of their separate lives and of all the people they loved. And Rachel wouldn't have it any other way. Seeing Mitch with his daughters and with Bonnie made her love him and want him even more. Who'd have ever guessed that she, of all people, would be a sucker for the tall, dark, handsome daddy type?

"But you never had any time for just the two of you to be alone," some guests at their wedding had remarked sympathetically. Except for a few days stolen for a Caribbean honeymoon, that was true, but neither Mitch nor she minded.

They weren't starry-eyed newlyweds who needed time to make adjustments to each other and to the demands of married life. They had each been through some of the hardest and most wrenching experiences life had to offer, and they had survived. Thanks in part to each other, but also because they shared a sense of honor and responsibility. They each knew that in the other they had found someone who had what it took to get through tough times...someone they could count on.

What they had been through made them what they were and enabled them to bring to each other in marriage a depth of trust and commitment that more than compensated for any sacrifices. In fact, Rachel couldn't imagine the two of them being as happy as they were if not for having Bonnie and Nicole and Becky in their lives, and being able to plan and look forward to the new baby due in the spring.

Her brow furrowed in concentration as she carefully filled with pink frosting the decorating tube she had purchased just for this occasion and prepared to make her maiden voyage into what the instruction booklet described as "The Fascinating and Fun-filled World of Cake Decorating." The booklet included directions for making roses and once she figured out how much pressure she needed to apply to the plunger to keep the frosting flowing smoothly, it wasn't as hard as she anticipated to make the layers of petals that vaguely resembled a rose.

As she got the hang of it and began creating a border of roses around the cake, her thoughts meandered where they often did, to daydreams about Mitch and how lucky she was to have him in her life. She'd even come to be thankful for the stubbornness that had caused him to dog her so persistently back when all she'd wanted was to be left alone. If he hadn't been so stubborn, she might still be running for her life, instead of being here, sharing it with a man she adored and who had come to mean everything to her.

Mitch filled all the empty corners of her life. He was a rough and gentle lover, the first man to ever stir the deepest currents of her sensuality. He was also the world's best father, with a coffee mug emblazoned with that slogan to prove it. He was her best friend...not to mention her own personal psychic. Who else but a psychic—or a man who was crazy in love—could have predicted with such flawless accuracy how things would turn out for them?

That night when they had sat on the back step and Mitch had explained to her his version of the best she could hope for, Rachel had wanted to believe his hopeful scenario so much that it hurt. She hadn't quite been able to, however, and she had a sneaky suspicion that Mitch never quite believed it, either, although then and since he refused to admit it.

Rachel paused to rinse out the tube and refill it with green frosting so she could add stems and leaves to the roses, recalling as she did those tense days last year when Mitch had accompanied her and Bonnie back to Florida to face everything they had been running away from.

As it turned out, Mitch's contacts in Florida proved to be very influential, including the state attorney general himself. Part of Rachel despised a system in which who you knew mattered more than the truth, the same system Randy Parnell and his family had used so effectively against her. But another, more practical part of her was

glad that if strings were going to be pulled, that this time
hers were longer than theirs.

Not that there had been anything unscrupulous about
the final outcome. Mitch's influence helped to get the right
people to listen, but once they did, it became increasingly
evident that she was telling the truth. For starters, Mitch's
prediction that Randy hadn't turned into a saint since
murdering Donna was right on target. Mitch was able to
turn up two complaints filed against him and summarily
buried by local authorities, complaints by women he'd
dated who claimed he had gotten drunk and assaulted
them—in one woman's case by holding her head underwater in her hot tub. Hearing about the evidence of Randy's continued abuse of those weaker than he was had
filled Rachel with both hope and fury.

The existence of the complaints was enough to cause an
impartial judge to postpone returning Bonnie to Randy's
custody. The weeks Bonnie was forced to spend in state
care were agony for both her and Rachel, but the forced
separation proved to have a silver lining. The newspaper
photo of their anguished parting at the courthouse brought
help from an unexpected source.

The day after the photo ran, Mitch was contacted by a
Mr. Jamison, who asked to see him right away. Jamison
was the elderly neighbor who had brought Bonnie to Rachel that long-ago morning and whose confirmation of
Rachel's worst fears about how Randy was abusing Bonnie had made Rachel decide that she had to get her away
from her father at any price.

Mr. Jamison explained to Mitch that his wife had passed
away in the time since and that he was now more than
willing to tell everything he knew, about how Randy had
abused and neglected his daughter, and also about what he
had seen and heard the night that Donna drowned...about
the argument, the slaps and screams, and about the shadowy struggle he'd glimpsed through the hedge, which had

been followed by a loud splash and then an awful silence he hadn't fully understood until the following day when the rescue squad arrived hours too late to save Donna.

Unconsciously Rachel's grip on the decorating tube tightened, turning the stem she was working on into a tree trunk. She grimaced, wondering if she would ever get over this rage she felt whenever she thought about Donna and the senseless waste of her life. In the end, Randy's high-priced lawyers had advised him that the evidence against him was overwhelming and persuaded him to plead guilty to a charge of manslaughter.

Knowing that he was behind bars and that he would stay there for a good number of years to come helped. Hearing the judge award permanent custody of Bonnie to her and Mitch had helped. But it wasn't enough to atone for the loss of her only sister. Nothing short of swapping his life for Donna's would be enough, she thought sadly.

She finished putting the final leaf on the final pink rose and stood back to admire her work.

"Not bad," she muttered.

Not perfect, by any means, but not bad at all for a woman who never in her wildest dreams thought she would be blissfully content to spend a gorgeous afternoon baking cakes and flying kites. She was turning out to be pretty good at a whole lot of things she hadn't given a thought to back in the days when her only dream was to be a major network correspondent. Someday, she hoped to work in broadcasting again, but for now, like Mitch, she'd found a better dream.

She put the cake at the far end of the kitchen counter where it had the least chance of getting bumped or crushed between now and the time for dessert. Then, piling paper cups and a pitcher of lemonade on a tray, she headed back outside, lowering the tray to the patio table just as Ollie Bennett came around the corner of the house.

He had a watermelon under one arm and was swinging a bottle of champagne with the other. By his side was Darlene, Mitch's infamous floating secretary from the days before he left the prosecutor's office and opened his own law office here in Barnstable. Mitch loved being his own boss...mostly because his office was close enough for him to come home for lunch occasionally and because he was able to earn even more than he used to in fewer hours, leaving him plenty of time for Rachel and the girls and the pro bono work he enjoyed.

Ollie and Darlene had met at their wedding and Rachel didn't think she'd ever get used to them as a couple. Mitch, who had become some sort of latent champion of romance in any guise, just smiled whenever she mentioned them.

"Hi, Rachel," Ollie said.

Rachel smiled easily as she returned his greeting. For Bonnie's sake, she had decided to continue using the new names, which had become so much a part of them during their long months on the run.

"We're not late, are we?" Ollie asked.

"Right on time," she replied. "I was just about to tell Mitch to light the grill. Hello, Darlene."

"Hi, Rachel. Can I do anything to help?"

"Maybe later. Maybe you can chop vegetables for the salad?"

"I sure can learn."

Rachel, who wouldn't bet on that, refrained from comment.

"Have you and Mitch listened to the news at all this afternoon?" Ollie asked her.

Rachel shook her head. "We've been out here all afternoon."

He rolled his eyes behind his horn-rimmed glasses. "That explains why you never returned my calls."

"You called?"

"Half a dozen times. I left messages."

Rachel shrugged apologetically. "Sorry, Ollie. What's so important?"

"The jury came back . . . just after noon."

Rachel felt her heart stop, then start pounding. "So soon? Mitch thought . . ."

"We all thought they'd be out longer," Ollie told her when she trailed off. "Even when the judge asked them to deliberate through the weekend, I never figured we'd get the call to hear the verdict this soon."

"Just tell me what it is," she urged, although the lightness of Ollie's mood seemed to suggest the news had to be good.

Even though Mitch was no longer a prosecutor and so not officially involved, they had all been involved in the case against Mickey DelCosta—she and Bonnie as witnesses and Mitch in spirit—and it had taken a lot out of all of them. The case had gone to the jury yesterday and, like Ollie, they had been certain the deliberations would last into next week. They had decided to put it out of their minds as best they could and enjoy the weekend, for Bonnie's sake if nothing else. Now Ollie was standing there telling her it was finally over.

"What was the verdict, Ollie?" she asked again, more urgently.

"Guilty," he replied with a jack-o'-lantern grin. "Guilty on all counts. Sentencing is next month and with old Throw-away-the-key Guilmette doing the honors, I'd say our boy DelCosta better pack himself a very large suitcase."

Darlene giggled. Rachel laughed aloud, then she reached out and hugged them, first Ollie, then Darlene. She would have hugged anyone within fifty feet, she was so happy.

"We have to tell Mitch," she said, turning to wave at him across the yard, where he was helping the girls reel in their kites.

It seemed to take forever until they started moving toward the house. The girls moved faster than Mitch, who was lugging all the kites and rewinding the balls of string as he walked. The three girls said hello to their guests and had disappeared inside to play before Mitch even reached the deck.

He greeted Darlene and Ollie, instinctively moving to stand close beside Rachel, his arm looped over her shoulders in a casually proprietary hug that warmed her more than the sun overhead did.

"What can I get you to drink?" he asked them.

"All we need are glasses," Ollie replied, holding aloft the champagne.

Mitch whistled through his teeth. "Champagne? Are we celebrating something?"

His quizzical glance took in all three of their smiling faces.

"We sure are," Ollie told him. "I thought you'd like to drink a toast to the prospect of our pal Mickey DelCosta growing old inside Walpole."

For a second Mitch looked puzzled, then the reference to Walpole State Prison hit home. "Are you serious? The jury's back?"

Ollie nodded, still grinning. "A few hours ago. I tried calling but you were out here doing your family bonding thing."

Mitch was beyond being teased or harassed. His ecstatic expression told Rachel he'd already guessed the outcome, but clearly he had to hear it just the same.

"So are you all just going to stand there grinning like idiots or is someone going to tell me the verdict?"

"Guilty," the three of them said at once.

"On all counts," Ollie added.

Mitch instantly turned to Rachel, and she knew in her heart that forever, in good times and bad, he would always turn to her, that they would always be there for each other. The sense of aloneness she'd lived with for so long was truly gone.

"Congratulations, counselor," she said, sliding her arms beneath his as he pulled her into a rollicking hug.

"I'm not the one who deserves the congratulations," he said pointedly, glancing at Ollie over her shoulder, "but coming from the star witness, I'll take them just the same."

"Bonnie was really the star," she insisted.

"Both of you were," Mitch insisted. "I'm a lucky man."

His kiss worked the same magic it always did, making her forget everything and everyone else around them until Ollie cleared his throat loudly.

"Hey, you two, are you sure this barbecue is going to be suitable for kids to attend?"

Laughing, Mitch reluctantly released her and extended his hand to shake Ollie's. "Congratulations, Ollie. You did it."

"I feel I should point out that I couldn't have done it without your help... all the way through."

Mitch shrugged off his thanks. "I wanted him convicted as badly as you did. More, even."

"Impossible."

"We'll argue about it while we get the glasses," Mitch said, leading Ollie into the house.

"Don't forget a corkscrew," Rachel called after them.

"I hate corkscrews," Darlene announced, slipping into the chair across the table from Rachel. "You know, that awful sucking sound they make when they pull the cork from the bottle."

"Mmm, me too," agreed Rachel, feeling benevolent.

"So, how've you been feeling? I mean, you know, being pregnant and all."

"Fine," she replied. "A little tired."

"I guess you have a right to that, what with carrying those extra pounds around."

Rachel, who would prefer not to think about the extra pounds, remained silent.

"But at least," Darlene continued, straightening the bodice of her perky little halter top, "you don't have all those usual first-time mother worries."

"How do you figure that?" countered Rachel, who'd erienced her share of first-time mother worries since finding out she was pregnant.

"Why, because it's not like this is your first baby or anything, not really. I mean just take a look at Bonnie and you shouldn't have a worry in the world about what kind of mother you are."

As if on cue, Bonnie came running out of the house at the mention of her name. Rachel did look at her, so precious, so very much a part of herself that she fully understood how adoptive mothers could say that their children had grown not under their hearts, but in them.

In a very real way, Bonnie was every bit as much her child as the one she carried now. She'd always felt that way deep inside, but it had taken Darlene's insight to remind her in a way that chased away any fears she might have about impending motherhood. Maybe, she thought, smiling at her across the table, she had been wrong about Darlene.

"It could take Mitch a while to find the corkscrew," she said, reaching for the pitcher. "How about some lemonade while we wait?"

"Sure," said Darlene. "I'll hold the cups."

The banging of the screen door announced that she had judged Mitch's knowledge of the kitchen too harshly. He approached the table with the corkscrew in one hand and what looked like the front door of Bonnie's dollhouse in the other. Though having a real home and family of her own seemed to have lessened Bonnie's obsession with the dollhouse, it was still one of her favorite toys.

"I have a minor crisis to take care of," he explained, showing her the broken door. "Hold the toast for me."

"Becky broke it off," Nicole revealed.

"But Daddy can fix it, can't you, Daddy?" Bonnie asked.

"Sure I can," Mitch said, shooting Rachel a hopeful look.

"See?" Bonnie crowed. "I told you. He can fix anything."

Nicole folded her arms with true eight-year-old disgust. "Nobody can fix everything."

Bonnie thought for a second. "Well, he can fix everything I break."

How right both girls were, Rachel thought, as Mitch herded them back inside for the repair procedure. No one could fix everything, but Mitch could fix all the important stuff...broken dollhouses and broken lives. What more could a woman ask?

* * * * *

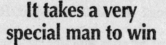

Take 4 bestselling love stories FREE

Plus get a FREE surprise gift!

SPRING

fancy

'94

They're sexy, single...
and about to get snagged!

Passion is in full bloom as love catches
the fancy of three brash bachelors. You won't
want to miss these stories by three of
Silhouette's hottest authors:

CAIT LONDON
DIXIE BROWNING
PEPPER ADAMS

Spring fever is in the air this March—
and there's no avoiding it!

Only from

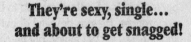

where passion lives.

SF94

It's our 1000th
Silhouette Romance
and we're celebrating!

Join us for a special collection of love stories by the authors you've loved for years, and new favorites you've just discovered.

**It's a celebration just for you,
with wonderful books by
Diana Palmer, Suzanne Carey,
Tracy Sinclair, Marie Ferrarella,
Debbie Macomber, Laurie Paige,
Annette Broadrick, Elizabeth August
and MORE!**

Silhouette Romance...vibrant, fun and emotionally rich! Take another look at us!

As part of the celebration, readers can receive a FREE gift AND enter our exciting sweepstakes to win a grand prize of $1000! Look for more details in all March Silhouette series titles.

**You'll fall in love all over again
with Silhouette Romance!**

As seen on TV!
Free Gift Offer

With a Free Gift proof-of-purchase from any Silhouette® book,
you can receive a beautiful cubic zirconia pendant.

This gorgeous marquise-shaped stone is a genuine cubic
zirconia—accented by an 18" gold tone necklace.

(Approximate retail value $19.95)

Send for yours today...
compliments of ▼ *Silhouette*®
™

To receive your free gift, a cubic zirconia pendant, send us one original proof-of-purchase, photocopies not accepted, from the back of any Silhouette Romance™, Silhouette Desire®, Silhouette Special Edition®, Silhouette Intimate Moments® or Silhouette Shadows™ title for January, February or March 1994 at your favorite retail outlet, together with the Free Gift Certificate, plus a check or money order for $2.50 (do not send cash) to cover postage and handling, payable to Silhouette Free Gift Offer. We will send you the specified gift. Allow 6 to 8 weeks for delivery. Offer good until March 31st, 1994 or while quantities last. Offer valid in the U.S. and Canada only.

Free Gift Certificate

Name: _____

Address: _____

City: _____ State/Province: _____ Zip/Postal Code: _____

Mail this certificate, one proof-of-purchase and a check or money order for postage and handling to: SILHOUETTE FREE GIFT OFFER 1994. In the U.S.: 3010 Walden Avenue, P.O. Box 9057, Buffalo NY 14269-9057. In Canada: P.O. Box 622, Fort Erie, Ontario L2Z 5X3

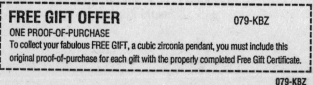

FREE GIFT OFFER 079-KBZ

ONE PROOF-OF-PURCHASE

To collect your fabulous FREE GIFT, a cubic zirconia pendant, you must include this original proof-of-purchase for each gift with the properly completed Free Gift Certificate.

079-KBZ